Lilian's Story

Kate Grenville was born in Sydney and holds degrees from the Universities of Sydney and of Colorado. *Lilian's Story* won the *Australian*/Vogel Literary Award in 1984 and has recently been filmed. Grenville has also written *Dark Places*, a companion novel to *Lilian's Story*, *Bearded Ladies*, *Dreamhouse*, *Joan Makes History*, and two best-selling books about writing.

Lilian's Story

Kate Grenville

ALLEN & UNWIN

Original edition published in Australia, 1985, by
Unwin Paperbacks.
Revised paperback edition published in Australia, 1991 (7 impressions).
Hardback edition published in Australia, 1995.
New paperback edition published in Australia, 1996.
This paperback edition (2nd ed, imp 7, new cover) published in
Australia, 1997 by
Allen & Unwin
9 Atchison Street
St Leonards NSW 2065
Australia
Phone: (61 2) 9901 4088
Fax: (61 2) 9906 2218
E-mail: frontdesk@allen-unwin.com.au
URL: http://www.allen-unwin.com.au

National Library of Australia
Cataloguing-in-Publication entry:

Grenville, Kate, 1950– .
   Lilian's story.
   Rev. Ed.
   ISBN 1 86448 284 2.
   I. Title.
A823.3

Printed by Australian Print Group, Maryborough, Victoria

10 9 8

CONTENTS

1

A GIRL

*I*t was a wild night in the year of Federation that the birth took place. Horses kicked down their stables. Pigs flew, figs grew thorns. The infant mewled and stared and the doctor assured the mother that a caul was a lucky sign. A *girl?* the father exclaimed, outside in the waiting room, tiled as if for horrible emergencies. This was a contingency he was not prepared for, but he rallied within a day and announced: *Lilian. She will be called Lilian Una.*

Later, the mother lay on her white bed at home, her palms turned up, staring at the moulding of the ceiling with the expression of surprise she wore for the next twenty years. *You didn't tell me it would hurt,* she whispered to her friends as they patted the crocheted bedjacket, and she was already beginning to suffer her long overlapping series of indispositions. The friends picked up the baby from its crib beside the bed and placed it in the mother's arms. *A lovely picture,* they agreed, and left.

Sunlight slanted between the curtains so that a band lay across the bed like something alive. The carpet

3

flamed where the sun fell over it, and on the ceiling the reflection of the waves of the bay outside flickered on and on like a conversation. Eucalypt leaves rubbed against each other and a kookaburra pealed in hysteria somewhere. The baby slipped further down off the breast, but the mother lay smiling and staring at the ceiling, listening to the bird, until the baby fell to the floor. When Alma came in, reddened from dusting the banister, she saw Lilian's tiny fingernails scraping weakly over the patterns of the carpet, and her wet mouth opening and closing on air.

If it was mine, Alma thought, and picked the baby up. She said to Cook, later, *If it was mine I would take better care*, but Cook was having a mood and plunged her ladle into broth without speaking. Lilian cried and was fed, cried and was changed, and so many nappies kept everyone busy.

Four years are enough to change every pore of one's skin, but were not enough for Lilian's father, that man of moustaches and excessive ear wax, to produce a son. He was beginning to feel that even another daughter might go some way to proving something. His wife began to dread the slippery shine of the peach nightdress over her skin. Behind his shoulder she watched the shadows coming towards her across the ceiling, and in the room below, Lilian lay across her bed with a pair of white bloomers on her head, mumbling through dreams like dull lessons. *Feelingly*, she said, and sat up.

In the room above, a wax-like bead of sweat fell cooling from her father's forehead. *Don't move*, he told her mother, and convulsed. *Don't move*, he said again, and clapped waxed paper between her legs. *Keep it in.*

Mother's Story

Mother was a woman of pale colours: lilacs and lavenders and the grey of galahs. She cut roses in the mornings and laid them in the flat basket I was allowed to carry. *Alma will take care of it*, she soothed when I dropped a vase that shattered into astonished pieces around my feet. *Alma!* she called, and rang the little brass bell. *Alma is a maid*, she explained when I asked. *And I am a lady. You will be a lady one day, but now you are a little girl.* Her eyes became curved when she smiled, and close up she smelled of flowers. *Your father is a gentleman, and is writing a book.*

In the parlour there was a photograph of her standing erect and winsome, smiling, one hand on the saddle of a stuffed donkey, a waterfall frozen behind her, in a dress made of chips of light. *That was when I was younger*, she explained and apologised when visitors picked up the frame and commented on the halo effect the photographer had achieved around the hand resting on the donkey. *And sillier.* I watched Mother titter. She had little to say about the wedding photograph next to it, full of people looking anxious for the camera, in which the train of her lace dress had succeeded in drawing her feet into its coils. *He courted me*, she said, *and we married in St. Andrew's*. Father's story was almost the same. *I found your mother charming*, he said crisply, *so I courted her. We were married in the rain.*

Father's Story

Albion was a man of moustaches and of shiny boots that squeaked when he walked. His boots on the stairs filled the house, his hand with the powerful black hairs gripped the banister hard enough to make it tremble. *Lilian, do not bang your feet like that*, Mother exclaimed. *What do you think you are doing?* I tried explaining, *I am being Father, Mother*, but she did not hear, only said, *A lady glides, Lilian.*

When I asked him, Father said, *Your mother is a wife and mother. And a lady. And I am a gentleman.* He hoisted me up onto his shoulder and from such a height the floor shone in a strange way and the ceiling made me dizzy. *And you are a young lady whose bedtime it is.*

Some mornings Father went to an office and returned in the evening with a newspaper under his arm. At the office he *kept the business afloat*, and came home smelling of the ferry. *Someone has to keep the business from going under*, he said when I asked him about that office. *So that you will have something to come into.* I thought, and asked, *Will we live in a boat?* I was looking forward to the sound of waves against a hull at night, but Father sighed and slapped the paper against his thigh. *Anything is possible, Lilian*, he said, and went up to the study.

Yes, Lilian, he agreed when I badgered him. *I am writing a book, but first I am gathering my material.* Father's book kept him out of sight in his study, but I could hear newspapers being read and shears slicing through paper when I tiptoed close to listen.

In the chilly dining room in the depths of the house, sounds echoed in startling ways from the cedar chiffonier with the decanters, from the sideboard with the thick carved legs, from the floor that Alma, on hands and knees, polished, panting, until she could make out a murky threatening shape that she knew must be her face. The legs of mutton stiffened in their fat, potatoes shrivelled as they cooked, and Alma's breathing was loud as she tiptoed from Mother to Father to me with the mint sauce. Mother ate slowly, chewing thirty-two times as someone had recommended, refusing mint sauce. Father's knife sliced vigorously across his meat and his voice ricocheted off the walls.

I waited until he had forked such quantities of meat into his mouth that he had fallen silent, chewing hard, staring at the salt-cellar, before I spoke. *Will your book have pictures, Father?* I asked, and Mother shook her head warningly at me from the end of the table. But Father laughed a thin laugh: *Ha! Ha!* and Mother pressed her fingertips into a headache. *No, Lilian, no pictures will be necessary. Norah, leave the room if you are suffering.*

I was slow for my age, bad at hints, and perhaps shouted in my excitement, *But, Father, what is your book about? Is it about pirates or burglars? Or adventures in balloons?* I had not finished, had hardly begun my list of all the things a book might be about, when Father began to shout back at me, *No, no, no, no, no!* until I was silent, showing egg in my open mouth, and Mother with a hand over her face had pushed her plate away. *Swallow that egg,* Father commanded, *and do not be dreadful, Lilian.*

Alma stood at the sideboard and her breathing was loud. She looked hard at the bowl in her hand as Father glanced around the room and I swallowed egg. *Alma, how many times must I tell you not to dust?* Father asked suddenly, as if he wanted an answer, and waited for one as Alma stood with her bowl of peas in butter and looked congested. *How many times?* If I had been able to count so far, I would have tried to give him the answer he was waiting for. *Alma, do not dust,* he said at last, when the silence had wrinkled around us all, and went back to his mutton, and Mother had to say, *Not in the study, that is, Alma,* and Alma nodded over her puckered peas.

The Treasures of Albion

That study of Father's was a silent and dusty place. Sun leaned in between the curtains and travelled slowly across the piles of newspapers on the floor. Dust hung in a nervous way in the beam of sun and there was not enough air, so that I panted and saw the dust motes dance. Stairs creaked outside although I knew Father could not be home, something rattled somewhere, a branch scraped along stone, and I knew I should hurry out and not come here again. But the pile of newspapers on the floor was a good height to climb and sit on, swinging my legs, and I hummed into the silence in a brave way.

It was a while before I had hummed enough to go over to the desk and look at the papers there, clippings from the newspaper pinned together in heaps. I picked them up and read with a slow finger underlining each word: "Rising Eggs a Menace," one said, and the next, "Brick Man Fondles Nephew." I looked at the handwritten notes, too, that spoke with Father's voice: *Norway has seventy thousand miles of coast and a population of ten million*, and *This year I have smiled seven hundred and four times*. In the end, I could not keep up my humming in the face of these facts and was frightened at the way the silence roared in my ears when I stopped. I could not remember just how the clippings had been arranged on the desk, whether *Dew falls faster in summer* had been on top or not, and when in my fear I knocked against the pile of newspapers and sent so many old headlines sprawling, I could not arrange the pile just as it had been.

Someone sneaky has been in my study, Father said at dinner that night. *Someone sly. And has interfered with my research*. I had to say to myself, *I am sneaky*, and felt hot with shame. I could think of no excuses, but refused more pudding in penance. *But since you are so interested, Lilian, I will tell you*. Father's research was so many facts that Alma had cleared away every plate and fork, and Cook could be heard distantly above the sounds of washing up, and Father was still going. There were the lengths of rivers and frontiers, the populations of cities, why bats were blind, the distance all the eggs in the world would go if laid end to end. I watched the jabbing finger and counted as he ticked off so many facts on his fingers that I thought he might have to start on his toes. *The fact of the matter is this*, he said. *In point of actual fact, the facts are these*. I regretted having been sly. *Take for a moment the following fact*, he demanded, and lifted a finger into the air as if testing for a breeze. *Consider this fact*.

There could be nothing secretive about so many facts. My fingers read the smooth starched patterns of the tablecloth, I sucked at a grape seed caught in a tooth, watched a morsel of something dangle in Father's moustache, lost count of facts, and Mother nodded and nodded and squinted at another headache approaching her across the room.

In my room later, I put the bloomers on my head and played nurse or cook or milkman and talked to my patients or saucepans or cows. *The fact is this*, I whispered sternly, but could not think of any facts. *I want you to consider the following facts*. At last it occurred to me that I could invent my facts, but even with the authoritative white bloomers on my head, I knew I lacked Father's talent.

I was a child of unpromising lank hair and small eyes. In photographs I was caught looking sideways, looking sly, in fact, and unhappy at standing in frills while a man shouted, *Don't move*. In those photographs my hands were too large for me, as if I was trying on someone else's. But Father photographed well. His moustache came out nicely, the knob of his cane gleamed, his boots were planted on the rug in a masterful way. His moustache was the model of moustaches for me, thick and drooping, giving his face a look of manly melancholy. I saw other moustaches on other fathers, but they looked like nothing more important than hair. Above his moustache, Father's eyes were sleepy in the photographs and his hair lay slicked down against his skull so that the flatness of his head was apparent. In my early paintings, I drew his head as a square brown box on his shoulders, and drew the facts coming out of his mouth. *What are those lines, Lilian?* Miss Vine asked at school. *Has he been speared, dear?* and I would have to try to explain, *Those are Father's facts, Miss Vine.*

There Is Everyone Else to Consider

Mother believed in conversation. *A lost art, Lilian, you must sit and learn.* She sat in the parlour on breezy afternoons when everything in the garden shook and swung in the wind from the bay, and poured tea, and I sat but did not learn. Ladies arrived and removed their gloves, smoothing them on their knees, and withdrew long pins from their hats as they watched Alma breathe too loudly. Mother did not have headaches on the days the ladies visited. She laughed and talked quickly as if there was not enough time for everything but she would like to try to fit it all in, just the same.

Lilian, how old are you now, dear? a lady with a big black bust asked me. *And are you enjoying school?* I thought she should know how old I was, since she asked my age each time she came, but perhaps she was absent-minded. She had a silver watch pinned to her heart, where she could not forget it. *I am going on five,* I said for the sake of a change, although I was only just four, *and school is good.* School was naps on mats in the blowfly afternoons, and cutting out coloured paper. It was painting in a smock and learning about King Arthur. *I have only been at school a little while,* I admitted. *But Mother taught me to read.* I was proud of that, and pleased when the lady with the black bust made her mouth an O and gave a surprised sound, and several other ladies looked. *She is already reading,* the lady with the black bust said, and all the ladies smiled without showing their teeth.

I wanted to astonish them further and brought out of my pinafore pocket the pebble with a vein in it like rainbow cake. *What I found*, I explained. *I had to get wet for it*. In fact, I had had to wade into the bay up to my thighs, and then a wave had taken me by surprise and drenched me. Now that it was dry, the pebble was boring and I could see that the ladies were about to lose interest, so I popped it into my mouth and then held it out, shining like a jewel in my palm. *Look, it is very valuable*, I crowed. The lady with the bust did not make an O again, but smiled without showing her teeth and said, *Norah, what a little tomboy you have*, and the other ladies nodded, and they began to comment on May's hat, and the pebble dried.

I asked Mother later, *What is a tomboy?* but she was fatigued by so many ladies and said, *I will explain later, Lilian, but now I will rest*, and lay back on her couch.

Among the Sisters of Albion

There were those ladies who visited, and there was Aunt Kitty who lived in a house with blood-red stained glass beside the front door. Mother and I walked to her house on the next bay and listened to the bell jangle inside when Mother pressed the brass button. *Why, my dears!* Aunt Kitty cried out at us as if amazed, *come along, come along*, and hurried us down the hall to the parlour. There was a tinkling and a continual tiny chiming around her from so many necklaces and shivering earrings, so that I had to tell her, *You are like a chandelier, Aunt Kitty*, and she laughed on a high note. *Try how it feels*, she shouted, and began to drape me with her necklaces, but I was shy. Her hair at the back was slithering out of its combs, but her face was pink, her eyes shone, and everything made her laugh and hurry. *Come on, quickly now*, she said, and hurried

Mother onto the couch, hurried a doll into my hands, hurried to fetch barley water and biscuits.

I am a happy widow, Aunt Kitty said, and whenever I asked she told me how Uncle Forbes had passed away in thirty seconds of anguish, clutching the shirt over his chest so that it came away in a long shred. *It was quick*, Aunt Kitty finished by saying, *and he was a serene corpse*. She poured more barley water and said comfortably, *It was a long time ago*. I watched her swallow a mouthful of barley water and say, *And now I am a happy widow, and a philosopher*.

Mother sat on the couch and laughed at the kapok that puffed from a rip when she moved. Aunt Kitty shook her jewellery at her. *It will come to all of us*, she said, *and I will try not to mind*. Mother laughed again and laid her glove over the rip in the couch. Her laugh in Aunt Kitty's house was louder and longer than her laugh at home, and it was easier to imagine her with the stuffed donkey when she sat with her glove over the rip in Aunt Kitty's couch. Here it was easier to imagine her being sillier. When Aunt Kitty exclaimed from nowhere, *I'd like to eat my past*, Mother nodded and smiled and waited for more. *Just spread it on thin bread and butter and pop it in my mouth*. They laughed till they spluttered, but I was restless, the doll Aunt Kitty had given me was stiff and boring, I did not like barley water. *Then go and play with a pup*, Aunt Kitty cried, gesturing at the back verandah, *and let us ladies be important*.

Kitty is my cross to bear, I heard Father saying downstairs at times. I hung further over the banister but could not hear if Mother answered. A teacup fell against a saucer and I imagined Father dabbing his moustache with his napkin and lining up the spoon in the saucer. *She is my trial*, he sighed. *And error*, he added, and laughed his jerky laugh. Blood rushed to my head from hanging so far over the banister and the stairs came up at me in an odd way, but although I wanted to hear more, no more was said.

Listening Japanese Ladies

Sounds carried well in this house, from room to room and up the stairs. *The fact of the matter is that doors are a waste of time*, Father maintained, so sound was free to slide from one room to the next. Father's research was an exception to the fact about doors. *My research will blow about*, he explained, and the door of the study was always closed. But whispers carried down the stairs from Mother's and Father's bedroom upstairs, past the curved banister and over the stair carpet that was worn to brown on the treads. Laughs and the tinkle of cups floated up from the parlour when the ladies visited, and Cook could be heard shouting at spinach when Alma opened the door that led down to the kitchen. On the verandah upstairs I could hear every rustle of Mother's silk as she took her constitutional on the flagstones of the terrace, pausing every few yards to look at a sea-gull dive for a fish, or watch a bit of flotsam that was trying to escape from the beach. In every room, on every verandah, the lapping of the bay at our beach could be heard and, however often Alma swept, there was always sand gritty underfoot in the hallway. In the dining room, the Japanese ladies on their scrolls above the sideboard looked askance at our mutton, and the sound of the waves ebbed and flowed with Father's voice, fading when he spoke, surging up to fill silences. In my bedroom underneath Mother's I could hear most things. *Oh, Albion*, Mother complained from her room at night. *Oh, Albion*, and was stopped in the middle of saying, *No*.

Birth, the Slippery Adventure

My brother was a small triumph. He lay in state, everything around him brand-new and pale blue. Father spent a week in the study before he could decide on a name for his son. I made one or two suggestions, but although Mother arched her eyebrows and nodded, Father seemed not to hear. When I caught him alone, staring at an ant on the verandah, he said with loud bogus enthusiasm. *Oh, good idea. I'll make a note.* He went so far as to scribble something in his little notebook, but it did not look like *Ivanhoe* or *Gideon*, but more like *I will not ape snails*. In the end, *John Thomas* was disappointing.

On the lawn I was enormous, bending over my brother's crib, the shadow of my head covering his whole body. One foot had freed itself from its wrapping and waved at the sun, and at the gulls floating overhead, watching. Salt was thick in the air, the tide was coming in strongly against our beach, and every branch tugged up and down, waving back at that pale foot. Above us the palm tree was a dutiful umbrella, but I could imagine how my brother's tiny face would congest if it was peppered from above by those berries. He would cry and everyone would come running. Veins of his skull were fragile as he blinked and made small frantic movements of his fists like someone inventing boxing, but we both knew he could not get away. When it grasped the finger I poked at him, his hand felt like the tentacles of a sea anemone, but his grip was strong. This pale blue bundle would soon be strong enough to do more than grip fingers. *You're fat*, I whispered in despair, and his fist clenched weakly, striking nothing, a thread of blue caught in a nail. *Fat.* From his open mouth a rapid dribble ran down his chin like an explorer. *Fatty fat.* When he yawned I could see his tongue as pink as salmon and the strong swallowing muscles of his throat, and knew that nothing could be done. I had to remind myself that I would always be four years older than my brother.

Mother saw us from the verandah and ran across the lawn towards us crookedly, like someone in an egg-and-spoon race, panting over me while a hand hid the freckled skin at the top of her dress. *Your brother, Lilian*, she gasped, and we watched the words evaporate between us. *I know, Mother*. I was all ugly whine. *Sisters love their brothers, Lilian*, Mother said. *A brother is a very precious thing*. She brushed away a fly and glanced up into the palm tree. *Is he safe here?*

Upstairs a shutter banged once like a command and Father's head appeared at the window of his study. He gestured and called at us and Mother picked the baby up, put him down, opened his smock, closed it, pulled at his blankets, saying, *that's right, that's good, that's better, yes, yes, yes*. Father appeared on the verandah and strode towards us until he stood erect beside the crib. His son popped a loud wet bubble and looked startled, gesturing up at Father in an exclaiming way. Father thrust his chest out and clenched his buttocks, setting an example, but the baby scratched peevishly at the sky. *Needs changing*, Mother apologised, and Father unbent to permit his son to grasp a proffered pinkie. Mother smiled at the baby, at Father, at me. No one smiled back. *If he needs changing, Norah, he must be changed*, Father said, and stared down a gull trying to strut on the grass. Mother bundled the baby up and was calling for Alma even before she reached the verandah.

A berry fell into the empty crib, onto the shawl crocheted by Aunt Kitty, and Father was beginning to turn away towards the house. *Father*, I yelled, running to a patch of sun and attempting to stand on my head. *Father, look!* I shrieked when he did not, and ran to the low branch of the jacaranda, where I tried and failed to hang by my legs. *It was this*, I shouted and tore at the impeding pinafore. *Other times I can do it.*

15

Father smiled and waved in a general way but by the time I had tucked the pinafore in and tried again, succeeding this time, hanging red-faced while the lawn swung to and fro, he had gone into the house, and I had to go behind a bush and be sick from swinging too fast for no one. *Bravo*, I heard Alma call out from the kitchen door, and she clapped, but although I knew she meant well, her applause was hollow.

Modesty

My brother's first word was *astrakhan*. The lady with the large black bust, who was also the lady with the astrakhan muff, exclaimed, *Norah! He said astrakhan!* and all the ladies laughed. John stamped into the lady's lap and showed his gums to the room. *It is his very first word*, Mother cried, *perhaps it means he will be a traveller*. The lady of the bust caught at John's hand, which was plucking at her silver watch, and held it as she said importantly, *It means he is bright, Norah*. All the ladies nodded at each other and said, *Brains*. But in spite of coaching, and coaxing and mouthing *astrakhan* at him, John did not repeat his triumph, and when the ladies lost interest in the way his mouth puckered and pouted at them and I was allowed to hold him, he began to cry and smell of a full nappy.

Later I asked Mother, *What was my first word?* and she thought it was *Mama* or perhaps *Daddy*. When she saw how this disappointed me she said, *It is not important, Lilian, it does not mean anything*. Father became all chest, though, when she told him. *Astrakhan*, he repeated. *Astrakhan, eh?* and tickled John's stomach until Mother warned him he would make his son bring up his puree of plum. It was enough to make me risk Father's study again, and when I had watched him leave for the ferry and the office, I lay on the floor there with the big dictionary, sneezing and learning words.

Crenellations, I tried on the lady with the bust. *Peripatetic*. The ladies looked at me and said, *Pardon, dear?* and I tried again. *Osmosis*, I said, and *ventricular*, but there were a few minutes of tea-sipping in silence until one of them thought to ask, *Will you recite for us, Lilian?* and I had never refused to recite. I stood with my feet at an angle, the way Miss Vine taught, and readied myself for appropriate gestures. The ladies all watched and smiled, listening closely. I loved to watch them watching, and I projected my voice so that everyone in the room would be able to hear. *Never mumble, children*, Miss Vine had told us. *Great poetry must be spoken out proudly.* They all applauded when I finished, and although I did not hear them comment on my brains, I knew that I had never forgotten my lines, and always remembered the appropriate gestures. *Lilian, when they ask you, you should refuse once or twice*, Mother had said. *It is called modesty.* But when it came to the moment each time, I could not bear to run the risk. *They will ask you more than once*, Mother had assured, but I was never sure enough.

Albion in Love

Mother's ankles were thick these days. She liked her feet to be in mustard or up on a cushion, and her smile was becoming vague. Her room was darkened, the baby lying in the crib in the corner and Mother forever putting a finger to her lips. She sighed and fluttered now among headache powders and tisanes. *I am unwell, Albion*, I heard her tell Father from her prostration on the couch. *Too unwell. Later, please, Albion.* In her curtained room the brocade of the chaise longue gleamed secretively. Her room smelled of moth-balls and perfume and the smell of her fur when the wardrobe was open, and it was a room of whispers now. *Lilian, less vigour if you please*, she sighed when I ran into her darkened room too quickly, to share a leaf or shell with her. *Think of my head, Lilian*, she said, or, *A lady does not hurtle, Lilian dear.*

The Fruits of the Sly

I was under the sideboard at the end of an empty afternoon when Father and Mother came into the room and Father said, *Kitty is constantly pickled.* I heard Mother sigh twice. There was a long silence in which I began to suck at a splinter in my hand, but silently. The place under the sideboard smelled of silver polish and varnish, and was hung with cobwebs and dust, and was an interesting place to sit and pretend to be invisible. *Pickled constantly*, Father said. I knew that Aunt Kitty did not live in a barrel, but in a small house with blood-red stained glass beside the front door, but pickled things came in barrels, and I was willing to believe that there was a barrel in Aunt Kitty's house for her to climb into after we had gone.

The silence went on so long that I would have thought I was alone in the room, under the sideboard with only the chair legs and cobwebs for company, but I could see one of Father's glossy boots standing on a piece of floorboard. The leather of the boot seethed and wrinkled as if Father was clenching his feet like fists. *Is blood thicker than water?* he finally burst out in a way that made the room ring. *Is it, Norah?* Mother said nothing, although I could have told him that the blood that came out of cuts when I trod on oyster shells was thicker than the sea water that stung, and that it floated through the rock pools in a sluggish way. Norah might have been shrugging, or staring at Father, or at her feet in the slippers embroidered by Aunt Kitty that I could see across the room. Aunt Kitty had made the slippers' roses green and the leaves purple. *Unusual*, Mother had said, and Aunt Kitty had cried out in a soprano, *My word it is!* and laughed.

Father's boots suddenly came towards me across the polished floor. He stood against the sideboard while underneath I stopped sucking my splinter, stopped doing anything at all, tried even to stop breathing, and stared at his boots, side by side inches from my hand. Above my head, something was making groanings and wet moanings and cries thick with tears, and the boots were shifting hopelessly on the floor. A shiny drop fell down onto one polished toe, liquid that paused before sliding in a lingering way down the leather. *Why must she shame me? Why does she hate me?* Mother's slippers approached silently across the floor towards the boots and placed themselves toe to toe against them. *Why? Why?* Father cried out in a honking tearful way. *Why?*

In so many old cobwebs and such a smell of varnish it was hard to stifle a sneeze. It surprised me how big their faces looked, red with bending down, when they discovered me there at their feet. *You are spying*, Father shouted. *You are secretive and sly. You are horrible.* I shook my head and began to cry with the shouting and the size of those faces looking in at me. I would have liked to stay under the sideboard, where I could see the rough wood that did not show, that no one had bothered to polish. But Father pulled at my arm and Mother prodded me with a finger, saying, *Gently, Albion, she did not mean*. There were no traces of tears on Father's face now.

Father took hold of my wrist and led me upstairs to the study, opened the door violently with one hand but continuing to grip my wrist. *There*, he pointed, and I stood among the piles of newspapers, watched a rose of the carpet being squashed under my foot. I had not noticed Mother's old belt when I had been sneaky here before, but it was coiled on the desk now like something dormant. *Your ankles?* Father said on a rising inflection like a question, and I looked at them. *Your ankles*, he repeated, and picked up the belt. Finally I understood and bent over. Holding my socks, I could feel blood rush to my face and my cheeks hanging, and could see Father's calves upside down, the tops of his trousers brushing against his boots. One boot was at a neat angle to the other and a little behind, like someone demonstrating a fine point of cricket. He brought the belt down on my pinafore with a muffled sound. *No bloody good*, he said crossly, and pushed the pinafore up, pulled my bloomers down. When the belt came down again it cracked against skin. The top of his boot creased at each stroke as his weight came forward, and a deep wrinkle appeared in the leather. *It is only skin*, I told myself and heard a yelping from somewhere that made me want to laugh. Mother spoke from the doorway, but Father was in his stride now and did not stop to answer her. I was laughing to feel the belt singe my skin.

Leviathan

I ate in private as well as in public, and Alma was on my side. *Here, lovey*, she said, and slipped a piece of cake or a handful of date slices into my hand. *Alma*, I would whine at the kitchen door, and she would come from the pantry at last with a handful of raisins or four cold pikelets. *Alma, I'm hungry*, I would pester her while she tried to polish the silver, and I would be silenced by a cold potato from last night, or a piece of pie. I crawled under the plumbago and did not let a single crumb escape for the ants there on the dry ground. *Mother*, I said, and knew how to make my voice nasty. *Mother*. Mother sighed from under her cold compress. *In the box, Lilian dear*, she said, *but quietly*, and for the sake of quiet continued to keep the box filled.

Chocolates were my favourites, the ones with soft centres that ran down my chin when I bit into them, the ones with hard centres that had to be sucked and chewed, or the ones with nuts that could be crunched. But cold potato would do, and even bread and dripping filled my mouth satisfyingly. I could feel the muscles of my face working to chew through the crust and swallow, but then it was time to want more.

I cannot keep up with you, Lilian, Mother said and tried to slide her fingers behind my waistband. *It is not three months since Haddon let this out.* Haddon, that rouged woman with lipfuls of pins, was pleased as she exclaimed over her tape measure. *A full two inches, Mrs Singer*, she said, and made Mother look. *Look, Mrs Singer, she'll have to have a new one.*

Now I was fat. *I am a fat girl*, I whispered in bed, and did not mind being left behind in the playground when everyone ran to get the good place under the best tree, or to escape from Rick, who had threatened to kiss the first girl he caught, and had to kiss me, so that I smelled his private ant smell and saw a patch of freckles close to my eyes. I was the one called on to jump up and down if anyone needed a stick snapped. I could hold two or three other girls shrilling in the air on the other end of the see-saw. I had grown big and could knock people down if I took a run at them, and block doorways, and there was too much flesh now for Father.

The brass knob of Father's study had become familiar to me. It became warm in my hand as I stood holding it for as long as possible. It was like keeping an egg warm, *Well, come in, Lilian*, Father said. *Do not add dawdling to your crimes*. It would have pleased me to think that he was joking, but he was not. *In, Lilian, for God's sake*, he said, and I would at last have to let go of the doorknob and shuffle forward to stand in front of the desk, where a square of carpet had been cleared of newspapers. I carried the feel of the knob in the palm of my clenched hand and promised that I would soon return and hold it again on the way out, even though I knew that on the way out I would forget. *Over*, Father said. He had had to stop commanding *Your ankles* because I was no longer in a position to reach them. *Over*, Father ordered. *Down and over*, and I pulled down my bloomers, held up my skirt, and bent over the desk. *It is just skin*, I whispered to myself every time. *And there is too much flesh for him now*. The sound of Mother's old belt had become very resonant against so much flesh.

A Tougher Nut

John had a way with sand-castles I never had. He frowned and did not hear when I yelled at him, his eyes on the horizon and a hand deep in the secret heart of his heap of sand. His smile was maddening, but I had to fall silent, too, and watch for the finger that would curl like a caterpillar out of the side of the sand-castle. *Right through*, John whispered and patted the sand smooth. *See?* And when I lay with a cheek on the sand to make sure, I could see his eye, and a patch of skin, through his tunnel. *It will be washed away*, I tried to discourage him. *It is pointless*. But he squinted into the sun at me, showing wet teeth, waiting for a better reason. *It is sissy*, I hissed, but he was still too young to mind. I had never thought of flags, drawbridges, windows, people on parapets, but John had them all. The gum leaf turned loosely in its socket on the highest point of the castle. *Like a real flag*, John said, and squinted again in pride.

From where I climbed up the rough cliff of the headland, the waves looked flat and leisurely. *If I fell, I would break my back*, I told the air. *What I am doing is very dangerous*. Below, I could see John's blue play-suit crawling with the yellow bucket between the sea and the castle, endlessly filling the moat. *It is silly*, I yelled, and felt the words scatter into the breeze. *It will never be finished*. From this height it seemed I could have crushed my brother with one strong leap. But Father, who strolled out from under the umbrella to check on his son, and whose red bathing-suit had faded to the same shade as his burned skin so that for a moment I thought he was naked: Father would be a tougher nut to crack.

Three Types of Crustacean

What is a fact, Lil? John wanted to know. *It is all the things Father knows*, I said, and wished I had a better answer, but tried John with a few facts of my own. *I can see germs*, I told him. *Only sisters can see germs*. He wanted to know: *What is a germ, Lil?* and went on blinking until I pinched him.

Over the mutton we heard all about the length of the Amazon and the number of hairs on the average head. Our meals were bushels of facts and John nodded when he saw Mother nod. I did not nod, but ate under the cover of so many facts. But Father was no fool. *Alma, give Lilian no more*, Father said, and Alma's spoon stopped so suddenly on the way to my plate with another spoonful of trifle that a daub of cream flew onto the chest of my pinafore. Father leaned over to stop me catching it on my finger and licking, but was too late. *No more, Alma*, he said and stared at me, but I knew there was too much flesh for Father now, trifle or no trifle.

It is a fact, Father said, and his voice bounced off the walls and made the Japanese ladies sneer, *it is a fact that Eskimos never eat ice cream. And here is another fact: in France, the French, the French eat* snails and have invented implements for extracting them from their shells. Here is a fact: the French eat four million and several thousand snails each year. Father's voice did not rise into the shadows of the ceiling but chose to rebound from wall to wall, looking for a window and not finding one. The sound of the bay bided its time and waited until he had finished speaking before filling the space again. Snails, Father went on after swallowing the last of his trifle, snails have an average life span of seventy-two days, barring accidents. This is a scientific fact.

Across the table from me, John ate and ate. He did not eat trifle, however, or cold pikelets under the plumbago, or potatoes from last night. Across the table he refused meat, Cook's soggy cabbage, anything silent. He had grown dangerously thin before Father had agreed to his demands, but now while we all became greasy from mutton, John crunched his way through entire bunches of celery, heads of lettuce, raw green beans, apples that sprayed juice, anything loud. John! Father would exclaim, I cannot hear myself think! and John would stop chewing, staring at the tablecloth with a mouthful of carrot until Father began to speak again or left the room.

Blind Ambition

John was pale and frog-like in his glasses. It is a sign of brains, Father told everyone. He promises to be bright, and of course his sister is bright, it is in the family. I was proud to hear Father say I was bright, and decided then and there to learn the works of Shakespeare by heart, or perhaps the Bible. John stared through his glasses and poked them further up his nose. They seemed too big for his peaked face, with the rabbit-coloured hair that fell over his forehead and hid the top of the frames. They have to be kept clean, John told me under our plumbago. I chewed the heel of the loaf, which was the best Alma could do for me, and had to treat John with respect. When I looked through his glasses, my eyes felt as if they were trying to turn themselves inside out, and John laughed so hard at the sight of me that he had to beat the ground with his fist and point. *Your face is too big for them*, he said. *You have a big face.* He tweaked them off my face and breathed deeply on them before polishing them with the special cloth. *They get dirty*, he explained, and finally put them on, but took them off again immediately and polished some more. *Is it fun?* I asked, and John thought, then nodded. *When I take them off I cannot see*, he said, and put them on, took them off, to demonstrate. *I am as blind as a bat without them.* He had heard them talking about him. I had heard them, too, Father and Mother discussing us, and had craned over the banister until the blood pounded in my temples, and heard Father say, *And she is as fat as a sausage*, and laugh. John and I had nodded at each other in the dark and went to bed happy, hearing Father's laugh drift up from the parlour and Mother laughing with him.

Quite the little professor, the ladies exclaimed, and John blushed and steamed up his glasses so that he had to take them off and clean them. *Quite the intellectual*, the lady of the astrakhan muff maintained, but it was I who recited passages of Shakespeare, pausing at the end of every line as Miss Vine taught, and hurrying through the parts that made no sense. *Bravo*, the ladies cried, and Mother said, *Thank you, Lilian, and more tea, May?*

In his room, John sat for hours staring at Mother's picture catalogues and folding the lobes of his ears inwards. *What are you doing?* I asked, but had to shake him before he would hear. *Mother says you are to have fresh air*, I lied, but John would not leave the catalogues. *It is the feet and hands I like*, he said and tried to explain, but I needed someone to be an explorer with. In the end, when he agreed to come with me as far as the old swing, I was willing to accept that. *Real feet*, I said and pulled off the boots that were always too tight. *Real feet, not just pictures*, but John sat on the swing, not swinging, and shook his head. His silences were a trial to me. *What are your ambitions?* I asked, and hoped he would ask me mine. I had many ambitions and would have listed some of the less private ones. I would not have told him about my ambition to have the long oval eyes of the Japanese ladies above the sideboard, and knew that would never be possible. Life was tragic as I stared at my face in the mirror and knew that long oval eyes were forever beyond me.

John did not ask me my ambitions, however, or undertake one of his long silences, but answered suddenly. *I will be a deaf man*, he said, and fingered his gums where the new teeth would come. *I will be completely deaf*. He took off his glasses and held them tightly. I was also silenced and rubbed two stones together in envy. *How will you get deaf?* I wondered at last. *I am praying for it*, he said. *One morning I will wake up deaf*.

Correspondence

Where a row of snowdrops indicated a border that implied a path, I was a beauty in velvet with a hat like a cake. It had been necessary to use Chinese burns and pinches on John to get him to leave the hands and feet. *Don't wanna, Lil*, he whined, but as Marco Polo or Captain Cook it was important for me to have an expedition to lead. *We'll get into strife*, he warned and whined, but I remained four years older than he would ever be. *Only three and a bit*, he claimed after he had learned about months, but in any case I was much bigger than John and would stop at nothing. *Father will give you a hiding*, John said, and lagged behind as I led the way into Miss Gash's jungle. *I would not want to be you.*

Along that path towards the swing, John pretended not to know me, but pointed out how Mother's velvet was brushing the ground. *She will tell Father*, he said, and breathed on his glasses. *And Father will give you a hiding*. Now that he was seven, he knew how things worked.

Snails crunched under my sandal while John sat on the cracked seat of the swing and I pushed further into the wilderness. Mother's velvet impeded my progress through the grove of bamboo, and I could no longer hear the creaking ropes of the swing. The knuckles of the bamboo seemed about to erupt out of the cool green skin and the leaves shivered against each other in a foreign way. It was easy to imagine snakes coiled in here, and I made haste. When I crept up the stone stairs on all fours I felt John down below watching my velvet back. It seemed a long way down when I looked back, and John on the motionless swing looked like an invention.

Ahead of me, Miss Gash's house sat waiting behind its trees like a face behind hair. Shutters were clenched over some windows in the shadow of the verandah and hung askew from others. A curtain frightened me by puffing out from an open window and sucking back suddenly.

My run across the lawn was watched in shock by every window, and the verandah drew back horrified as I ran under it behind a screen of lattice. There were rakes there, clogged with old grass, and piles of wooden crates that leaked straw. It smelled of the decay of everything and the cats that had squatted every-where. In the crates among straw I could see heavy slabs of tiles with pictures on them, and mouse drop-pings, but I was not afraid of pictures or mice.

I was as brave as Richard the Lionhearted until there were slow footsteps above my head and I wished I was a mouse, and crouched in my velvet behind a crate. Through the lattice I watched Miss Gash, in a dress covered with a pattern of postage stamps, walk out over her lawn to a banana tree. She slapped its trunk and ripped a leaf or two, shading her eyes from the glare as she looked up into the tree. The big green hat hid her face but she walked as cautiously as anyone old. When she looked back at the house, at the lattice where I crouched among mouse dirt, I glared back and made myself invisible. She walked back to the house as slowly as if modelling the dress, the rip down the back showing skin, and the hat that did not hide a neck like a tortoise. Her steps sounded overhead on the verandah and faded into the house. When I heard her begin to sing, I took one of the tiles from the nearest crate. It seemed part of a larger picture, there was half a thumb and a quarter of a very pink peach. Then I ran back across the lawn. Rick would be impressed. He would at last believe that Lil Singer was worth something.

John sat, swinging slowly and folding his earlobes into his ears. His face tried to ignore me, even when I shook him hard and told him I had seen a boa constrictor and had a souvenir. He would not touch the tile, but stared at my face as if at my corpse. *Why do you want to go there?* he complained. I told him, *I am Marco Polo*, in what I thought might be the right accent. *And I have brought back treasure.*

You are not Marco Polo or anyone, he said. *You are just a girl*. He pointed at Mother's velvet. *You have torn it*, he said, and the long rip could not be denied. *It cannot be mended*, he said. *Mother will cry*. He was not a cruel boy, but was stating facts. *Father will kill you*. He was shouting now, and began to fold an earlobe until I slapped his hand away. *She is just some old witch and you are not Marco Polo*. A fly hovered, fascinated by his nostril. He brushed it away, caught his glasses just in time as they unfolded from his face, began to cry in a jerky way. *Rick says you're loony. I got a loony sister*. I wanted to curl up among the paspalum and wait until everyone ran out of words. If I had thought that the knobs growing on nasturtiums could be eaten, I would have run away into the weeds and lived there for ever.

Wishing Well Enough

It was easy to see that boys had all the fun, even though timorous John behind glass had little fun. I was the biggest girl, as well as the roughest. In the school band I was the only girl who had ever played the drums. While Ursula pinged at her triangle and pale Anne smoothly blew into her recorder, I stood flanked by Rick and Kevin and imagined myself in red, leading Napoleon.

I screeched and shouted the loudest in the playground, and sometimes Rick looked. I hung upside down in trees and practised for hours so that Rick would come across me juggling three oranges, or standing on my hands. Upside down between my quivering wrists in the moment before I fell, I saw his sharp teeth as he sang out, *Look at Lil Singer's bloomers!* I handled all the small dead things I found in the bush and kept the fish I caught for longer than they could stand, in case Rick came by and saw me in triumph with corpses. Alma washed and scolded, Mother sighed and scolded, John became queasy at the long threads of guts, but Rick was never impressed. At night I rescued him from burning buildings. It was a joy to feel my hair burn off in one crisp frizz. Among waves pounding the shore only I saw the pale weakening hand about to go under for the last time. When everyone else had fainted dead away I alone lanced the puncture marks on his ankle and sucked out the venom.

John admired, too. *You're too little*, I jeered. *You can't be a mate of his.* John did not argue, but I had no answers when he said, *You're just a girl.* Rick had given John a black eye once by accident, and John had treasured it. I had come across him loving it in the mirror, and *the time Rick gave me the black eye* had become a measure of the months.

What had Rick ever given me? He had not quite given, but I had a piece of stick he had whittled on a wet day, when lunchtime in the tin shed went on too long and the rain would not stop. George, whose toes and fingers were webbed like a duck's, had collided with Rick's shoulder, spilling his slice of pie, and Rick had dropped his bit of whittled stick and was ready to hit, but saw it was only George, who wet his pants when alarmed. Miss Vine had clattered the big brass bell then and I sat all afternoon holding Rick's stick in the pocket of my pinafore. Under the girls' tree in the playground next day I was the centre of attention, and even pale indifferent Anne, and Ursula who pretended she thought it was dirty, crowded closer to see what Rick had given fat Lil.

With the cricket bat over a shoulder, Rick was my idea of heroism. I could not be a hero myself except in my mind, but I knew what to admire. In the long holidays in summer, when weeks and weeks all looked the same, there were not enough boys for the cricket team. John was allowed to stand out in the middle of the paddock, shading his eyes with the hand that should have been catching the ball, and I watched, feeling ants crawl over my legs, as Rick in white ran up and down the pitch and swung the bat high into the air when everyone screamed, *A century!* At last, in the sticky last days of January, when the choko vine in the tennis court at Miss Gash's was spilling all its pimpled fruit into the lap of the umpire's chair, Kevin was too sick to hide it from anyone. *Kev's gone and got sick*, Rick shouted in his disgust. *We're a man short.* John stood very straight, doing his best to be two men, and tossed the ball carefully from one hand to the other. *Or a man too many*, it occurred to Rick. Majestic in his flannels, he walked towards John. But by the time he was ready to say, *We don't need you now, Johnny*, I was there, panting, trying not to pant, breathless at possibility. *Me*, I gasped, and was already tucking my pinafore into my bloomers. *Use me, go on, Rick!* Even deafness would not have saved John from this mortification. *Aw, Lil*, he whined. *Aw, shuddup, Lil.* I did not hold it against him that he spoke to me like this in public. We both knew it was I who had stolen the tile with the thumb and watched Miss Gash in her postage stamps.

I waited for the chance to dazzle Rick with my tile and courage, but stood watching his deciding face and felt that this was not the right time. We watched Rick fingering the bottom of his bat where it was stained green, watching his fingers as if we could see through the skin to golden bone. *All right, Lil. Let's give you a try-out.* My bloomers were full of pinafore, my cheeks purple with blood.

I ran after every ball, leaped up and fell back even for those that sailed far over my head, and at the end of the day Rick said, *Tomorrow then, Lil, but not if Kev's better.*

John was proud. *You were not bad, Lil*, he said. The hem of my pinafore was pleated around my knees from so many hot hours in my bloomers, and a shoe buckle had not been able to take the strain of a sudden spring at a fly ball. *Rick thought I was great*, I boasted. *He didn't!* John shouted, and punched me on the arm. *He didn't think you were great.* I had let him hold the whittled stick from time to time, but I never let him forget it was mine. *He didn't think you were great.* Reckless at the thought of what Alma would say of

31

the green stain on my pinafore where I had slid after a low one, I said, *You said I was not bad*, and John threw a stone at a cat and hit a letter box. *Not bad for a girl*, I meant.

Men of Destiny

In the end, Ursula was the best I could do. *We are a gang*, I told her. *You are my gang, like Rick has a gang*. Ursula sucked the end of her plait where the brown hair was pale and brittle. *Girls don't have gangs*, she said and squeezed a drop of spittle from the plait. *You can't have a gang*.

Ursula's white collar lay neatly on the grey pinafore. Where mine buckled on one side or looped around under itself, Ursula's lay like a small tame animal round her neck. Ursula was a tidy smiler and did not show too much tooth. She could go on smiling tidily for as long as it took the photographer to arrange us, the tallest at the back and the prettiest in the middle, and disappear under his black cloth. She smiled tirelessly out of photograph after photograph.

In those photographs, someone is always caught blurrily waving away a fly, and I am the one looking cross. We had to pack together, shoulder behind shoulder, and smelled each other's hair in the sun. No one wanted to be next to shy Gwen, whose hair was always in her eyes and who glanced away at the moment the shutter clicked so that she was caught for ever as a shy blur. Pale Anne in the strong sunlight of those class photographs was an angel, the same white as the sunlight. *You're an old witch with white hair*, we taunted her, and Ursula tossed her brown plait. *Witchy, witchy*. Knowing that soon she would be a tall pale beauty, sought after by good prospects, Anne stared back at the fat girl who led the taunts and said nothing, just shaded her face from the sun until we lost interest.

It was Ursula who was chosen to give the bouquet to Lady Goodwin when she visited the school. The band blared dozens of notes at once, Mr Pinnock carefully fitted a chair under Lady Goodwin's big taffeta bottom, and Ursula curtsied. My palms were sweating. She was my friend, and if it had been me I would have tripped on my curtsy and dropped the flowers. But Ursula, who had been excused history to practise the curtsy, could be relied on. Lady Goodwin smiled down at us, and although I tried to catch her eye, her glance slid away from the fat girl in the front row whose plait was coming undone. Miss Vine was flushed, but patriotism kept her smiling. While we all stood stiffly and sang "God Save the King", Lady Goodwin did not sing, but stood very straight and stared into the distance, perhaps at the Union Jack nailed to the back wall. The anthem might have been sung in her particular honour, as she was the nearest thing to royalty we had with us that day. *She said, "Thank you,"* Ursula reported to us all later. *She said, "Thank you very much". And smiled.* I was proud that she was my friend. My friend had curtsied to something close to royalty.

Ursula loved Rosecroft's slice of the harbour, and the old boat with the heavy oars we could hardly hold, and she loved Alma's pumpkin scones. Her own neat house, with its clipped privet and bricks the colour of lamb's fry, was not called anything but 7 Allambie Crescent. *But what's its name?* I asked, and she answered as if it was a matter for pride, *It's got no name. My dad says, who needs a name for a house?*

In my own mind, as I forced reluctant Ursula up another rise in the headland—*We are Sir Walter Raleigh and his men*, I said, *looking for Spaniards*—I was as much a hero as Rick. I ate the raw fish that was the initiation, gagging on the cold slippery taste, but when Ursula put her hands in her pockets and gave me an ultimatum: *If I'm going to be your gang I'm not eating any horrible fish*, I had to think again. *You will collect fifty of these shells*, I pronounced, and she was happy to search the beaches on our headland for her pile of gold shells. She swam tidily off the public beach, where Rick bombed the water and I showed him the soles of my feet, standing on my hands under water, and she glanced for approval at the adults on their towels and rugs. *Not too rough, dear*, someone would call out as I straddled Ursula and held her under. *Not too rough*. Ursula often went home crying, but always came back for the boat, and those scones.

Portrait in Brown

I was never anything but plain. *John got the looks*, Father said. *And who got the brains?* He was a disappointed man. *It is the cross I have to bear*, he said when he was unhappy, and looked at his children. *Children are terrible crosses*. But I had also heard him telling Mother, *My ideas are a terrible burden. I carry a weight of ideas that must be set down*. But however many slices of newspaper were cut out, however many headlines riffled through, there was never the squeak of a nib over paper when I crept up to listen. *I am lying fallow*, Father shouted when I asked over the leg of lamb. *Fallow, Lilian, you will never understand*. Mother shook her head without meaning *Yes* or *No*, and left the table before Alma brought the pudding.

John got the looks, Father said, but I could not see that John's pale face and thin hair were *looks*. I myself was brown from so much scrambling among rocks and by the beach. My hands and knees were scarred from oyster cuts, and grazed where a rock had been too slippery or a branch too thin. I was fat and brown, my plait thin—*A rat's tail*, Father said, fingering it and letting it drop—and was a tomboy, they all agreed. *A grubby little tomboy*, the lady with the big bust called me now. *You must learn elegance*, Mother said, *and beauty*, but lay too fatigued on her sofa to say more. She was now a mother of cold compresses, Dr. Benn's Pastilles, camphor on red flannel. *It is my chest*, she might sigh, or, *My head, Lilian, think of my head*, and I would tiptoe away. *You are grime and filth!* Aunt Kitty exclaimed. *Norah, what a ragamuffin!* but still offered me barley water and pups and tweaked at my straggling plait in an amused way.

John, moon-faced in glasses, afraid of loud noises and the way pups made for your nose, seldom smiled, but when he did every lady commented on his dimples. No winsome dimples ever appeared on my cheeks, only another fold of flesh creasing out around my face, and my bony knees were embarrassing to everyone. Even after I was fat, my knees were as uncompromising as rocks under my pinafore.

Flourishing in Foreign Soil

From the domed centre of the plumbago bush we could watch most things and not be seen. *This is our place*, I told John. *It is a secret*, and he nodded and blinked. From here we could watch Peg, who came to wash, poking at the clothes drowning in the copper and crouching red-faced over the fire underneath. We could see Mother slowly *taking a turn around the house*, or if we parted the blue flowers on the other side, we could see the bay lapping at our rocks. The light under our plumbago was green and hot. I had hoped that when it rained the thick canopy of leaves would be a roof, but heavy drops fell through the bush and down our necks. *Told you it wouldn't work*, John said as we ran back to the house. *Nothing venture nothing gain*, I said, all in one word as Miss Vine did. *Only the brave deserve the fair*. It was easy to feel brave saying such things and thinking of men in armour on big horses, or the crossbow men drawn in the book, bombarding a fortress with arrows.

Miss Gash's house behind its jungle was a challenge to anyone with courage. Under the plumbago, the stolen tile was propped up on a rock. When I wet a corner of pinafore with spit and rubbed the tile, it was like a window in church. Even John stared and was silent. *You must not tell anyone*, I said, because I wanted that triumph for myself.

Long to Reign Over Us

Joan of Arc was hurried over in the history book, being against the English, and Boadicea was just a witch in woad. Elizabeth, though, was the *perfect lady*. Miss Vine told us all about the red hair and the pearls and the men going on one knee before her. Judith, whose orange hair and enormous freckles were a nightmare she had to live with, blushed through her transparent skin and for a moment considered the possibility that she might be acceptable. *A regal head of auburn hair*, Miss Vine said, and her glance at Judith dismissed her red frizz. *Did she ever get married?* asked pale Anne, whose thoughts ran to marriage when they ran at all, and Miss Vine was haughty. *No, she did not.* Safe on her own finger was the diamond cluster chosen by Mr Eckstone. *Why didn't she?* Anne persisted, and Miss Vine ended the whole subject when she said, *She was a queen*.

She was on steadier ground with Henry. *A man of enormous vitality and eccentric tastes*, she read from the books. Someone asked, *What are eccentric tastes?* and Miss Vine thought for a while, turning the diamond cluster before she answered, *What kings enjoy*. Rick's voice was unctuous, imitating Anne's when he asked, *Was he married?* and Miss Vine frowned and then smiled. *Oh yes, he married six times*. There was a silence before someone whistled and everyone laughed in relief.

Miss Vine approved of Ursula's neat drawing of A Roman Invading Britain, and her maps of England with a red freckling of Major Towns and Their Products: a tiny not-quite-square lace handkerchief hovering over Nottingham, scissors about to cut Coventry in half. She was pleased to explain just why *the sun never sets on the British Empire* and we did not shrink from the second verse of the Anthem. But she did not wish to *hold up the whole class* for questions such as mine. *What are knavish tricks, Miss Vine?* I asked, or, *When did they invent bathrooms?*

On the boys' side of the room, Rick made a noise like a fart with a piece of the best-grade rubber his father manufactured, but that did not stop me wanting to know everything. *What is universal suffrage, Miss Vine?* I persisted, having seen it in Father's clippings, and she said, *That means everyone can vote, Lilian. Who is grown up, of course*, she added, in case my next question concerned my own voting. That was not my next question, but she added again, *And the insane do not vote, of course.* But I had other questions: *Why is it called suffrage, Miss Vine? Does it hurt?* Miss Vine was exasperated at last. *Lilian, for heaven's sake!* She was sweating lightly under her ashes of violets, for it was a hot day and there were times when the children filled the classroom with their smell of bananas and ink, and there was not enough air for a person to breathe. Miss Vine had been brought up in Kent, and she hated the way birds in Australia laughed at a person from the tops of chimneys, and the way the sun brought the moisture out of a person. She decided it was time for stammering Gwen to read aloud. *Page fifty-three, Gwen, under the picture.* Gwen could not be prevailed on to stand and read, nor would she read sitting down, and continued to shake the silky mouse-brown fringe that hid her face, and make tiny anguished gestures with her fingers until the bell rang for recess.

Poetry was Miss Vine's special pleasure. Her voice became creamy, and the poetry book trembled in her hand as she read "The Death of Arthur". *But what did he die of, exactly?* I had to ask. She waved her lace-edged hankie at me as if at one of those flies that love eyes. *Poetry, children, is for people with souls*, she said, and called on Ursula to recite.

I drew my picture of the Lady of the Lake as a portrait of Miss Gash, but Miss Vine was scathing about the white face and red cheeks, the hat like a green blancmange, the parasol I had added with poetic licence. *I said to use your imagination, Lilian, I did not say to use your sense of humour*, Miss Vine said and jabbed the clasp further into the French roll that clung like a sausage to the back of her head.

Pastoral

A child died of the snake that year. *Absolutely and unequivocally out of bounds*, Mr. Pinnock repeated while our feet grew hot on the bitumen. The sun beat down so that a tiny shivering column of heat hung above each head. The school buildings were flimsy on such days, brittle with heat, the boards warping away from each other, lines of ants making inroads. The fence that separated the patch of bitumen from the overgrown orchard next door, where the grass was knee-high, could not be expected to keep much out, or in. I had not tried to resist the orchard and had one or two encounters there myself, and screamed once, thinking a stick underfoot would turn and strike. They were silent as they slithered away into the grass like black water. Nothing about them was beautiful except their speed through grass. Stumbling and panting, dripping from the nose as I tended to do when agitated, I myself was far from beautiful.

Mr. Pinnock was sweating and gesturing from the top step and had to shout above a derisive kookaburra. Flies could not resist his wet open mouth or his shining domed forehead, but he did not brush them away. *It is a matter of will*, he shouted. *No child is to move. See, children, there is no need to fuss about a few flies*, and we did not move, fascinated by the flies crawling over that shining forehead and the one that was making its way up a cheek into his eye.

We all knew by heart the "Instructions in the Event of Snake-Bite," printed in red on calico and tacked to the classroom wall. Two men with moustaches stared into the distance as one lay on his back, foreshortened dramatically, while the other knelt over his ankle with a tourniquet held tight in one hand and a knife in the other. "Step Three: Suck Out Venom" the caption said, but I did not believe it would be so easy.

Father's Fame

The orange peel I dropped on the ground at lunchtime never made an R. Usually it was a C or an S and it meant I would marry Charles or Samuel. Ursula's orange peel, and Anne's, and Judith's, never made an R either. It seemed we would all marry Charles or Samuel.

Although I would never marry him, Rick asked me questions in the dust. The palm tree in the middle of the schoolyard was polished blunt on its bumps from so many children, and was where Rick liked to question me. The palm threw shade, but far from me, where I stood under the blast of sun. *What's yer father do?* he shouted. Gary beside him picked at a scab on his chin and Kevin stared. Andy brought John over so that we stood together with our backs to the palm. *Writer*, I said, and John repeated, *Writer*. Rick had more questions but we had no more answers. He went away but came back. *My father says, what's yer father write?* and John and I each hoped the other might have an answer. John was silent behind his glasses. *Dirty books, I bet*, Rick said and a fleck of spit flew and landed on my pinafore. In my pockets my hands balled into sweating fists and I was breathing quickly, seeing John out of the corner of my eye take his glasses off and put them in their case in his pocket. Father had warned that he *could not be expected* to pay for another pair. Rick's mouth moved vaguely over more words. The tongue that flickered over his lips was the raspberry colour of a birthmark from the rainbow ball he was sucking. *Dirty books*, he repeated, then less certainly, *Smut. He writes smut*.

After school there was another hot assembly in the yard, watching the flies crawl on Mr. Pinnock's face. *Until the child who did this steps forward*, Mr. Pinnock repeated until even he forgot and slapped at a fly, and *the child who did this* had still not *stepped forward*, and finally when the shadows were long and hopeless across the yard, we were allowed to go.

John and I hurried through back lanes towards Rosecroft, pretending boldness. The stick I ran along the fences made a snarling sound and dogs were ferocious behind gates, but we knew it was no good. When Rick and Kevin appeared in front of us, waiting, and Andy and Gary closed in from behind, the air in the lane became thin. High paling fences were unfriendly on each side, the blank wooden gates did not offer any escape, and the dogs continued to bark. There was a smell of garbage and all those dunnies with the wooden flap soiled from the night man's fingers.

What do ya reckon? Rick shouted, and the gang shouted back, *Yah!* The smell of the dunnies was making John pale and the barking was making my head ring. In this thin smelly sunlight, Rick's eyes were the green of bottle glass, his nose sharp. In his pocket he twanged his father's rubber bands as he spoke, as if accompanying himself on an exhausted lyre. *Yer father's a no-hoper*, he yelled. *And writes dirty books*.

I was a big girl, as rough as the boys and just as angry, and John was a boy of courage, though of little strength, but we were outnumbered and had no faith in victory among such smells of dunnies. Andy tried to swing me by my plait, but I used my bulk and knocked the wind out of him, feeling his ribs bend as I sat on him and yelled into his purple face. Rick grabbed John and twisted his arm behind his back until his face greyed. John's screams were shrill and made Kevin laugh, but we would not agree that Father wrote *smut*. They had me pinned now, three skinny boys smelling like socks, and my bulk heaving under them. *Say he writes dirty books*, Rick yelled, *or I'll break his arm*. Although John squeezed his eyes closed, he could not stop us seeing the wet stain at his crotch. I did not betray Father, and Rick did not break John's arm, but pulled down his pants and laughed at the way he looked, worm-like in the sun.

I did not give in, I reminded John as we came in sight of Rosecroft's fences. *We were not traitors to Father*. It was hard to know if John's face was full of admiration or reproach. We thought about Father and the beating I would get later. *Your father will have to deal with you*, Mother would say, and sigh. Where John's nose had bled, the striped school tie was stained, although his pants would be dry by the time we were home. *I do not care*, he said, but would not say what he did not care about, and practised being deaf until bedtime, and did not want to hear about my beating.

A Proud Boast

I have something historical, I shouted at Rick, *that you do not know about*, and he was stopped by my flushed triumphant face. *There are lots of them, and they are priceless*, I yelled, but Rick stared and then shrugged. *What ya yelling for, fat-face?* he said. *Think I can't hear ya?* I could not prevent myself laughing at the thought of the surprise he would get. *I will make the whole picture*, I shrieked, *and then you will see.* Beside me, John tugged at my arm to make me stop before I said too much. *You will be sorry*, I satisfied myself by taunting, and allowed John to lead me away. *Lilian, do not shout like that*, Miss Vine said, passing on her lunchtime rounds. *You are a young lady, remember, not an animal*, and I saw Rick behind her back mincing in imitation of a lady, but I did not care.

I will take them all, I boasted to John later, *and make the whole picture.* But the whole picture eluded me even after I had collected ten tiles and had some narrow escapes. I had several parts of feet and the whole frightening face of a bearded goat. There was a bunch of grapes and a flesh-coloured thing that I did not recognise no matter which way I held it up.

My narrow escapes alarmed me. I froze against the crate, hearing Miss Gash walk overhead, stop, and sing. Miss Gash's songs had words, but were not about *lilies* or *tranquil meadows*, as Mother's wavering songs were when she was in a good mood. Mother's voice quivered with feeling as she sang, sweetly but tunelessly, of the *gypsy that I loved* or how she *pitched her lonely caravan at night.* Miss Gash's songs were about her own dramas. *I will walk into the garden now*, she sang, and did so, or, *Will I eat a banana?* and I would wonder too.

Banana trees beside the verandah tinkled shredded leaves, and high up, where the leaves joined the stem, fists of green bananas hung. I watched Miss Gash in her postage stamps struggling to bring down one of these bunches with a rake. She was frail, the green hat a nuisance, the rake heavy. When the bananas finally crashed through the leaves she sat on the steps of her verandah and ate one after another. The skins landed near the lattice where I crouched, saliva rushing into my mouth. I sucked a knuckle and heard my stomach growl. *Now I will paint bananas*, Miss Gash sang through hiccups and went into the house, and I snatched the first tile I found in the straw, a boring piece of patterned background, and fled across the lawn. I was losing patience with *the whole picture*, and Rick was starting to point and yell, *What's the famous secret then, fat-face?* and even Ursula was asking, *Lili, what is it really, is it anything at all?*

Running in the Family

Father liked to return home in the evenings to an embroidering wife. From under the plumbago I could see the ferry dock at the wharf and guess which dark figure was Father striding up the hill. There was a patch of the road where trees hid him from sight and I settled deeper into the mauve dusk under the plumbago, beside the hundred empty snail shells I had collected. I sat very still and watched Father stride up the last part of the hill, jabbing his furled umbrella in front of him at each step as if poking someone along, and swing into the gate. Some evenings he strode up the path and rattled at the front door until Alma let him in and took the umbrella. On other evenings he tiptoed across the lawn to the french windows and peered inside at Mother making another stitch in her parrot or rose. He watched for a long time as Mother stitched and yawned and rubbed the camphor into her temples, and at last he tiptoed around to the front door and rattled for Alma as if he had just arrived. *I didn't come down in the last shower*, Father was fond of saying.

Father liked to come home to an embroidering wife but was sometimes early, and was angry then. *Seeing Kitty?* I heard him exclaim. *You expect me to believe that?* and would shout so loudly then that I would not be able to hear the words. Later I would hear him again, *Norah, you must forgive*, and Mother would murmur, and I would hear the clinks as they took a sherry together, and the trumpeting as Father blew his nose.

We had visited Aunt Kitty and her hair had been undone and her cheeks red, as if she had been running for hours in high wind. *Come in, in, in*, she had cried at me and Mother, and gave us a deep curtsy like the one Ursula had made to Lady Goodwin. *Honour my humble.* I had asked, *Where is your barrel, Aunt Kitty?* and she had laughed, showing the muscles in her throat, and called out, *That is my secret, darling!*

Aunt Kitty brought the barley water and a plate of broken biscuits, and dusted the bursting sofa before Mother's bottom touched it. She sat and slurped at her barley water, then said with slyness, *You are my sister-in-law, Norah.* Mother nodded, but this did not stop Aunt Kitty giving a laugh like a shout and going on, *My brother Albion services you.* Mother peered inside the glove she had just taken off and her face contracted as if she saw a spider inside. *Kitty, I am unwell*, she said, and her voice had never sounded punier. *We will have to come again another time.* But Aunt Kitty shouted so that her voice cracked, *He was such a skinny boy, and inept. Is he heavy now?* A silence slipped down from the ceiling and settled over us all.

When a bird gave a tiny panicked squawk and flew in the open window, blundered up to the bunches of fruit on the ceiling, and fluttered in fear, the silence was broken. I laughed to see my aunt, bursting the buttons on her dress, galloping around the room with a prawn net, her red face turned up to the ceiling, gasping. Mother stood on the piano stool and made hopeless shooing gestures while she called out, *No! No! No! No!* over and over. It was finally at my feet that the bird dropped when it dashed itself into a mirror. *Pick, pick*, Aunt Kitty yelled, making scooping gestures, and I picked up the bird, frightened of its warmth in my hands. When I let it go outside the window, the bird dropped and swooped away.

From that day, Mother postponed the visit to Aunt Kitty. *Next week, Lilian*, she said, until I stopped asking.

The fact is, Kitty is the work of the devil, Father called down the table to Mother. *It is a long-established fact that women are the familiars of Satan. John, do not gnaw like that.* I watched Father, who was becoming excited about facts again, and wondered how heavy he was. I had lifted his arm once or twice to make him pay attention, and it had been ponderous, but that could have been Father resisting. I did not think anyone would be able to lift Father.

Fifty-one percent of births are female, Father trumpeted. *That is why there are old maids. But one female child out of four is dead by the age of three. The fact is they lack will.* Mother nodded and nodded at the end of the table and stared at her congealing mutton and John gnawed on a carrot with his eyes shut. *The population of this country will reach ten million in the year 1993. Then there will be five million ten thousand women here.* So many facts were overwhelming Father and he was becoming agitated. *Lilian*, he shouted over the pumpkin. *Are you paying attention to me?* Mother made a noise like a parrot as Father's hand began to hit the tablecloth and the wineglasses danced. *Albion, Albion*, she called, but Father would not stop, the Japanese ladies shook on the wall in the storm of facts, Alma came in with junket and stood shivering against the wall, and finally it was Cook with her red face and mottled arms who ran in heavy-footed and flung water in Father's face while everyone screamed.

Deadlier Than the Male

Miss Vine held her hankie to the face and Mr. Pinnock shone glassily as he poked at the spider in the jar. *You see, children, how aggressive he is. He is attacking the ruler, children, because he thinks it is my finger.* The funnel-web gleamed in a big hairy way. Rearing on its back legs, it struck and struck at the ruler. The class-room had never been so silent as when we waited for the spider to swarm up the ruler onto Mr. Pinnock's hairy hand. We would see him scream, probably. We strained to see the venom shining on the ruler, did not blink for fear of missing something. There was no cure for the bite of a funnel-web, we had been told, but someone would have to try sucking out the venom. Miss Vine's white lace hankie would be of little use to anyone.

The girls' lavatory in the basement had been found to be aswarm with these spiders. *They like damp and cool*, Mr. Pinnock said. *Under the seat especially.* Some boy guffawed.

Other People's Magic

Rick's father was rich from those rubber bands, his mother fatter even than I was, and his birthday cake had two layers, held up by tiny columns like those at the library. There was a conjurer who drew endless streams of ribbon out of his mouth, his sleeve, his ear.

Rick's father knew our father. His cheeks, rubbery themselves, shook when he asked. *And how is your clever father?* His glance at John's hair standing on end, and at my fat forearms, left bare this year by the cardigan with the cherries embroidered on it, was a comment on our clever father. *Still writing his books?* His bulk, which to my nose smelled of perished rubber, massed over us and prevented us from sidling into the room where the chocolate cake was. It was Rick's mother who rescued us at last, and with too many smiles told us that *Mr. Palmer likes to have his little joke.*

Even smiling at the head of the table, or eating another slice of cake, Rick looked sharp. I adored from afar. John and I had not been able to fit at the main table, and along with wordless Gwen, who rocked backwards and forwards on her chair and hummed through her cake, and George with the webbed fingers and toes, John and I sat at a small table so low we could not fit our knees underneath. Rick's mother was attentive with jellies quivering in strange shapes, and sugar sandwiches, but it was obvious that Father's brains and Mother's manners—*A lady's gloves are always buttoned before she leaves the house*—were not enough. John and I ate our way through the tableful of food in silence, our paper hats askew.

The thought of our clever father preyed on me throughout our cake and jelly, throughout the singing and the blowing out of candles. Rick's face was like a surprised angel's as he blew into the golden light. Jelly and cake sat heavily on my stomach. There was something shameful about Father that made me frightened of this noisy room, its tables littered with bright icing. Too much was hidden. When the conjurer began to draw the pale yellow streamers out of his mouth, I was afraid. With a sleeve to my mouth I had to wail, *Don't like magic*, and they took me outside. Later, in the tram with John, I wiped tears and snot onto the embroidered cherries. *The magic made me seasick*, John said, and leaned forward to bring up his cake on the floor between us.

47

Alma shook me until my teeth chattered and my eyeballs rolled. There seemed no particular reason why the shaking should ever stop. *It is me*, she hissed. *Me that has got to do the cleaning up*. The cardigan with the cherries lay in a damp ball on the floor and in the tub John stood crying from where Alma had rubbed him too hard with the flannel. *It is me who has to deal with you and your smells*, Alma said, and threw water at John to rinse the soap off. I crouched in the corner waiting for my turn and wished for once I was smaller. *If I was to have children they would not be like you two*, Alma cried. *Oh my very word no*. The thought made her angrier with the flannel in John's ears, because Rob the milkman had not shown interest after all. But next day Alma pressed me into her smell of soap and sweat and gave me a wooden brooch made of good things to eat. *That'll cheer you up*, Alma said, and watched, smiling with her bad teeth as I fingered the wooden cherries, a slice of bright pink melon, a tiny shiny apple. *Look, Mother, how beautiful*, I called, and ran in to Mother's shaded silence, making her lift the cold cloth from her forehead and blink out. *You should not have done it*, she told Alma, and seemed to mean what she said. She did not wish to touch the gift and her smile was tight. *Did you say thank you nicely to Alma, Lilian?*

Mother had stored her tisanes behind glass and grown several inches. Her feet were brisk now on the polished floors and she did not bother with her *constitutional*. She said, *Lilian, slouch no more*, and poked her large stomach, and laughed to see me draw it in. It was easy now to believe that photograph of her with the donkey.

Under the plumbago I fingered the smooth garish fruit for hours, seeing heroism in my future, dreaming out at the garden.

Father Takes a Tumble

You are loony, Rick explained carefully, holding the wooden rifle in the crook of his shoulder, thinking of Huns, *and so is your dad*. Rick's father was being a hero in puttees now, and his fat mother had become a sock knitter. *My father is a general*, Rick yelled, thinking of the stripes on his father's sleeve, the powerful sweat of his khaki shirts, his hard hand on his son's shoulder. *My father is beating the Hun at his own game*. John looked at me but I had nothing to say and we could only wait for the bell to put an end to lunchtime. Father lay in a darkened room, waiting to get better or die, and Mother had never been a knitter.

Father's illness could not be defined, no matter how many doctors walked up the stairs. For some weeks there had been talk of *nervous prostration*. There had been talk of hospital, but this was not kept up. Father continued to lie in his darkened room and doctors continued to arrive with square black bags. *There are no doors*, I heard one say in surprise, and Mother said, *No, there are not*, but thoughtfully. I had never seen her point with such authority as when the carpenter stood holding the door, wondering. *There*, she said, and pointed, and the door was hung on Father's room.

Behind that door, Father lay in his nightcap, silenced by facts. When Mother led John and me into the room, we tried not to look at the face on the pillow. In an excess of zeal one of the doctors had ordered Father's moustache shaved, and his face was frightening without it, his upper lip long and sallow. *Does he know we are here?* John asked in a hoarse whisper. Father stared, blinking, as if thinking too hard to be interrupted. *Of course, he knows*, Mother said briskly, but I was not sure. If I had dared to be in the room alone I would have pulled Father's ear, or stuck my tongue at where his moustache had been, but Mother herded us in once in a while, *to say hello*, and herded us out again, and I would not have opened that door at any other time.

In Father's study dust collected, and every so often a clipping would slide off the desk in a chink of sunlight between the curtains and join others on the floor. Dust puffed up in a small way, and the clipping settled in for a long spell. As Father lay month after month, the clippings yellowed and looked like rags.

Plots

Ursula loved wickedness in my company and longed to know my secret. *What is it, Lil?* she pestered. *And what do you mean, historical?* But it was still my ambition to dazzle them with the whole picture, and I would not say.

Ursula loved wickedness in my company, although in the company of her neat widowed mother she agreed with everything and was a good girl. At Rick's birthday party she had laughed in all the right places in the magician's act, and had not disgraced herself by turning green from too much chocolate cake. I had seen her there, singing "For He's a Jolly Good Fellow" and leading the cheers, and she had been next to him in the seat of honour while he blew out the candles and crossed his eyes, making his wish. She had been pleased with his keepsake and had said Thank you nicely at the end. But the idea of the jam jars was her own.

I got a secret too, she boasted to me as we rowed out in the old boat. *But it's not historic*. She giggled and had to lean on her oar until she could stop. *You got your silly secret, I think it's just nothing, you and your secret, Lil Singer*, she said, and at last she told me her secret. *We could bottle our smells*, she said and burst saliva on the last word. *And let them go in Rick's fort*. She smoothed her pinafore. *He thinks he's Christmas*, she said, and that was enough reason for anything. *Boys are silly*, she said, and flicked her long shining plait over her shoulder.

The night I crept downstairs with my satchel full of jars I discovered how easy it was to leave dark houses. A noise from behind Father's door might have been a snore or a moan, but I did not stop. Out on the headland, Ursula waited for me with her jars and together we lifted the boards away from the entrance to Rick's fort. Inside, the cave was full of a smell of damp, and old urine, and our candles only made the shadows blacker. The back of the cave tapered into a cleft full of drafts and Ursula and I did not care to turn out backs on it.

The jam jars were disappointing. Perhaps the smells had not got into the jars. *Maybe it just fades*, Ursula said and sniffed at the rim of one. *Just smells of jam.* On the rough walls of the cave, names had been scraped with a slate and under each name was a rough seat. Under the word RICK there was a chair, one leg mended with string, the springs bursting through rotten brocade. At the back of the cave, there was a sharp-looking rock with JOHN above it in letters that started big and ended small. John, with his glasses and feeble wrists, and younger than the others, was only tolerated here sometimes. When Rick had no need of our boat, or another body to swell out his gang, John returned red-eyed and silent from the headland.

Boys are dirty, Ursula said and sat on Rick's springs and brocade. *Dirty and silly.* I touched my arm, full of happiness that I was not a boy. The shine of Ursula's fringe by candlelight was good enough to eat. *Come on, Lil*, she said. *Think of something.* In my excitement my mind was blank and Ursula watched with dark eyes. *Something good, Lil.*

When I reached over her head and added a T in front of Rick's name, Ursula nodded but it was a while before she smiled. She was waiting for more and I began to sweat. *Well?* She kicked at John's sharp stone. *You got a sissy brother, she said. They all say. Rick says.* She moved aside to let me get to John's name on the wall and finally rewarded me with a laugh when I had made JOAN. *Boys are silly*, Ursula said again, *but sissies are the worst.* I gave her the slate to do something with GARY or KEVIN but she dropped it in the sand. *Won't they be angry?* she whispered. The slate lay as if she had never touched it. Our shadows wavered over the walls and shadows sprang out from corners, but turned into yellow rock when I looked closely. Outside, the bush whispered and crackled and something began to croak and would not stop.

Ursula made me go outside while she hiked up her pinafore to ease herself on the sand of the cave near John's stone. The croaking stopped abruptly when I trod on a twig and the sound of Ursula's water was loud and rude in the night. The patch of sand was still steaming when I was allowed back in to watch as she did up a last button or two. *They will not know if it was you or me*, she said.

I spoke before I thought, and would not have spoken and shocked Ursula if I had thought, but the words came out on a thought: *Books should have toilets in them.* Each word was bitten off by the dead air of the cave. I coughed, to hear the sound flatten into the crumbly stone walls. Ursula's giggle floated a little further. When it was swallowed up in the silence, she laughed again on an anxious pitch. *What do you mean, toilets?* The last word rang out around the cave. *I mean like people really do, go to the toilet and eat.* Ursula sucked the end of her plait and brushed the ribbon against her nose. *You're loony*, she finally said. *I've got to go home now.*

Pride and Its Fall

I am afraid of nothing, I boasted in the playground, but Ursula remained expressionless over her fish-paste sandwich. *I do very dangerous things and am not scared.* Ursula's eyes shifted to the side and I felt the hot breath of Rick's contempt in my ear. *You! Crybaby, and being sick all over the place!* Rick was scathing and Ursula allowed herself a small glistening smile. *You two couldn't even keep your cake down.* Rick was without mercy. His birthday party would never be forgotten, even though at home I had done my best to destroy the memory of that day. With Mother's sharp scissors I had shredded the hated cardigan with the embroidered cherries, and dropped the pieces behind the huge wardrobe in my room, where they would never be found. *And you cried at the magic. Bet you're not brave enough to go to the toilet by yourself, even.* Everyone laughed, Ursula showed banana in her open laughing mouth, pale Anne hid her laugh behind a hand, freckled Judith tittered, even George stretched his lips back, copying everyone. I was dignified as I walked away from them all, and did not spoil the effect by stooping for the orange I dropped, but let it roll. *Lil!* I heard Ursula call, and turned, hoping, but felt one of Rick's pellets hit me on the nose and could not stop sharp tears as they laughed again.

In the middle of mental arithmetic, Miss Vine was not able to suppress a snigger as she asked, *Lilian, whatever has made your nose that colour?* It was time to silence them all. John warned me, *There will only be trouble, Lil*, but I decided that there were worse things than trouble.

Under the Moreton Bay fig, where the ground was sour and black, I unwrapped the pride of my collection, the tile with the goat's face. Rick was a cool one. *So what's the story, fat-face?* he said dismissively, a finger tracing the thick embossed glazing of the beard. His finger could hardly bear to leave the smooth cool glaze.

Ursula had not quite been impressed. *Where'd you get it?* she kept asking, and would not touch it. *Whose was it, did you pinch it?* She continued to ask questions, when what I wanted was awe. *Is that the famous secret, then?*

Finally it was Gary with the pendulous lower lip who was the first to recover from the shock of the sly goat face and those tilted amber eyes. *She pinched it*, he said. *She got no right. I'll tell my dad on her*, said eager Gary whose father was a policeman in important blue. They went away at last and left me with my tile and a shrivelled fig that had fallen into my hair. *They are just jealous*, said John, and waited with me until Miss Vine came out and rang the big brass bell.

But after school, in the Bent Street lane, between the dunnies and someone's chooks behind a fence, Rick was waiting with his gang and John and I stood watching them come closer. *Show us again*, Rick said, but my nose still smarted from his pellet. *Ask properly*, I shouted. *Ask nicely*. Rick did not glance around at Gary and Kevin and Andy, but he must have known they were watching him. I saw him hesitate, and knew then what power there was in the goat face. *Well, please, then*, Rick said in a mumble, and I watched his teeth shine with spit and continued to stand with my arms folded, smug in my silence. *Come on, Lil*, he shouted then. *Please, please, please!* I saw that this was as far as he could go with Gary and Kevin watching, and made a show of accepting his humility. *But only for a minute*, I said, and took as long as I could to unbuckle my satchel, take out the tile, and unwrap it.

Where'd you get it, Lil? Rick asked while I let him hold it for a moment to feel its weight. *Where, then?* But I was full of triumph and would not tell. *It is my secret*, I crowed. *Because I am braver than anyone, and know all the dangerous places*. I watched Gary watching Rick, but Rick did not have anything to say, and he knew we were all watching. *I am an explorer and a hero*, I shouted, *and I discover things*. But before I had finished, Rick's voice had gone shrill to drown me out and a dog began to bark behind palings as he shrieked, *You ugly fatso, you ugly old maid, you make me sick*. He was breathless when he had finished, and Andy was capering vaguely and trying to start up a chant: *Old maid, old maid*, but I knew what to say. *Yes*, I shrilled, and grabbed the tile back from Rick, *I will be an old maid like Queen Elizabeth was an old maid, and Grace Darling*. There was a silence in which we all heard Kevin snuffle up his surprise. Rick was loud but not quite convincing as he shouted in a strangled way, choking on dust in his throat, perhaps, *You! You ain't no queen!* He spat and a gob of spit landed in a ball beside my shoe. It swayed, rolled, covered itself with dust. *You ain't no queen and you ain't no hero*. His voice was still thin in the sceptical sunlight. He had to go on trying to shout. *You got no right*, he tried, and grabbed at the tile. *Not yours, anyhow!* He jerked at the tile, but I was strong in my triumph, and knew that Gary and Kevin were watching, more aloof every moment as Rick's voice grew reedier with frustration.

When our struggle was over, the tile with the goat face lay on the tired dust between cauliflower stalks, its fragments already part of the rubbish of the lane, one amber eye split from the other, the beard a dozen sharp chips. There was a silence in which we could hear the squeal of distant billycarts. Rick's voice was at the end of its tether. *Go on, cry, then*, he said, but I did not. *I got plenty more*, I said, and tried to shrug, though I knew nothing would ever equal that goat.

Andy began to pick his nose and Gary could suddenly have been alone in the lane as he bent to peer at a wheel of his billycart and smear a little black grease that was leaking out of a vital part. Kevin was squatting, piecing together the beard as if it could be whole again. Rick's shadow lay alone on the dust. But his eyes grew narrow as he turned to John, who stood beside me holding his satchel tight. *It was you, Johnny. Wasn't it?* With a toe he recalled Kevin and Gary, and Rick had a gang again as he said, *Fatso girls don't get things. It musta been you, Johnny.* John shook and shook his head until the glasses slipped down his nose and he had to let the satchel go to push them up, and I heard myself grow shrill as I screamed, *It was me, I was the one.* But Rick with a hand in my chest pushed me back and with all his old swagger said, *Couldn't be you, Lil, it's man's work, see.* The gang crowded John like mates but he was puny between them and knew what was coming. *Come on, Johnny, tell us where you got it*, they said, and crowded closer. For a moment Rick's father was with us in the lane as Rick winked in a man-to-man way. *Come on, John, she's only ya batty fat sister. Tell us.* John looked as though he would have liked to start polishing his glasses or being deaf, but he could only go on standing. In Rick's hand, my brother's shoulder was like paper.

It was me, I continued to shriek, even after Kevin had been ordered to sit on me. *It was me!* I tried to stop them when they took John's glasses away and began to poke at him, but they all ignored me, even Kevin, who sat harder on my back and forced my nose to inhale the dust. *Tell us, Johnny*, Rick crowed, his voice full of power again. *You can be a proper one of the gang if you tell.* He laughed and tried flattery. *Pretty smart getting that tile, Johnny, pretty brave.* But John went on shaking his head, saying nothing and shaking his head, even after they thought of tying him to Kevin's billycart and sending him down the steep part of the lane.

That lane plunged down between the fences and dunnies like a crooked drunk making for the creek at the bottom, but John would not get that far. Without his glasses he could not see the way the lane twisted violently, or the fences he would hit when he failed to steer the cart around the bends, but he had seen it all on other days. They put the ropes in his limp hands and laughed to see him blink at the blur of the world. *Just steer her down, Johnny, she'll be right*, they said, breathless at the thought of how gravity would seize him. They could hardly speak for panting and laughing. Without his glasses John's eyes were tiny and blind and did not blink often enough as he squinted round mournfully. *Lil, Lil*, he called, and they laughed and copied him. *Sil-ly Li-ly, sil-ly Li-ly*. Kevin's knee in my back was squeezing all the air out of my lungs so I could not call out, and the dust in my mouth tasted of failure, and heroism gone wrong.

Other Games

A few hot days were necessary for the word to get around. Smells of bananas, of ink, of the sad insides of satchels, rose to the high ceilings while Miss Vine spoke and pointed and tucked the hankie into her belt. The seven-times table was hard and we were becoming familiar with the threat of algebra. It seemed that the holidays would never come to relieve us.

In the playground the heat made us shrill, the way it beat back from the bitumen and fell out of the hard-edged sky. When Gwen forgot and left her rubber ball on a grating, it shrivelled and died in the sun. *Pooh*, Ursula hooted. *It's gone and melted*.

In that playground where only the most desperate still ran and yelled at midday, I could not fail to notice the silence gathering around me or the way people under the trees became nothing more than leaf shadow as I approached. Always elsewhere, people spoke together. I sweated in my fat and felt my lips grow thick with the desire to please.

You are a thief, Ursula explained, her eyes, though, still on the pumpkin scones I was offering. *You pinch things*. Her fingers smoothed her silky fringe. *Rick says*. I could not bear the way her eyelids were sleepy over her eyes, and bit into the scone to feel the comforting crumbly dough in my mouth. *And you're a liar. Wasn't even you took it*. I could have choked on that scone, so dry with that flat pumpkin taste. Ursula was hardly interested, her eyes elsewhere, a hand idly swinging her skipping rope. *I did*, I tried through a spray of scone. *I did. It was me*. The scone muffled the words so that even I was hardly convinced. Ursula watched as I poked a bit of crust back between my lips. *I am the bravest*, I tried to say, but Ursula spoke crisply over my words. *You think you're Christmas*, she said. *And you're too rough*. As if I was not there, she uncoiled her skipping rope and began to skip in front of me, her eyes staring past my shoulder or over my head. Even when I took a step closer and filled her vision with my bulk, her colourless eyes would not admit that I was there. But when I grabbed for her wrist to make her see me, she tripped over the rope and began to shout, *You're too rough, Lil Singer, and you think you're someone special and you're not*.

She was always at a distance after that, even though I spent whole lunchtimes following her. She was always at a distance, and skipped with Anne and Judith, and moved to another spot, as if she had not seen me coming, until my feet were tired on the hot bitumen. Rick was taller and more distant than ever and the white of his shirt in the sun brought tears to my eyes. *Fatso fibber*, he called, and the playground was not big enough to hold so much laughing.

In the full blast of sun, I sat under the palm tree in the sea of bitumen and cried without hoping they would relent. Ursula walked in the shade with pale Anne as if things had always been like this, and Anne did not bother even to glance back at the fat girl who sat awkwardly on the knob of a palm while tears dripped from her nose. The heat was dark in my face as my hands gripped the trunk, shiny from so many years of backs and lunchtime fingers.

In those distant groups, John was briefly the centre of attention. They fingered the plaster on his wrist until it was grey, and one or two wrote their names on it and the date. *Does it hurt?* they kept asking, but John shook his head, and became tongue-tied when they wanted to know what it felt like when it broke against the billycart wheel, and they lost interest again. Nothing had ever been different for John, and he climbed as he had always done into the fork of the worn monkey-puzzle tree and watched everything from above. It would have been easy for him to join all those who called out after me, but behind his thick glasses John was still brave. He did not join, nor did he not join, but took off his glasses and cleaned them and when he could not postpone any longer the moment of seeing again, said, *What? What?* so many times that even shouting Rick lost interest in the end.

Father in Bed

Mother sighed over junket and said, *It is just as well your father does not have to know.* John hung his head when she said, *No one in our family has ever broken a bone before.* A spoonful or two later, she laughed so suddenly that Alma nearly dropped the cream jug. *Think of yourself as a pioneer, John, and now I remember your Uncle Harry was thrown by his gelding and broke an ankle.* John stared at his junket but did not eat, and Mother leaned down the table towards him. *It is manly, John, there is no need to be ashamed of protecting your sister.* The sound of her spoon in the dish as she finished and pushed it all away was like a sad bell. *Your father would be proud,* she decided, and bowed her head as if praying, but I could see her examining her lace for stains.

Father's nightcap appeared to have shrunk, or perhaps it was his head growing like a gourd. His eyes moved sideways in his face as Mother poked John until he was standing beside the bed. I hung back but Father's eyes slid around slowly until they found me. *He is vastly improved*, Mother said loudly as if everyone was deaf. *Is that not true, Albion?* But her shadow, as she thrust the curtains back from the window, lay like a weight across the bedcover. I watched Father blink several times and heard him hiss: *Sssssss*, he said, although I did not see his lips move.

Mother explained laboriously about the *bullies* and how John had *showed a lot of pluck*. Father did not show any sign of hearing and did not even blink, but when Mother had said it all he whispered hoarsely, *Well done, John*, and fumbled among the bedclothes towards John's hand. Mother filled the silence in which John edged away from the bed and her voice ushered both of us out of the room. We avoided each other's eyes later, and John practised being deaf when I spoke to him, and I could not persuade him to do anything.

Brothers Are Others, Too

John no longer mentioned Miss Gash and never responded if I tried to interest him in her. He hid her away with all the other secret things he knew. There was a notice on his door jamb now that said "Keep Out, Please", and he had moved the furniture in his room so he could hide in a corner. He was beginning to be someone I did not know. Everything I told him disappeared into the space behind his earth-coloured eyes.

He had become a collector. Under his bed, in the only corner of the room not visible from the doorway, was a growing pile of exercise books in which he collected hands and feet. The pages were pocked and warped with the thick collages of hands and feet of all sizes and kinds, page after page: hands in gloves from Mother's fashion journals, hands on ploughs from the farming pages, feet standing on platforms, hands demonstrating telescopes. Some were in pairs, some were single. There were puny ones, badly drawn, smudged photographs on cheap paper. One was huge, a pointing hand from a poster, too big for the page of the exercise book. The thick paste had lumped under them so that the books bulged with limbs. *No one will take them from me*, John explained when I asked. *I am the only one who wants them.* His face was enthusiastic behind the thick glasses.

John, then, was locked in his own world now, with his own passions and secrets. I became choked by such silence at school and by John's blankness at home, and I grew desperate. *I will be an aviator when I grow up*, I said, and had to shout at John's shining unlistening glasses. *I will be an aviator, or invent something important, or win the Victoria Cross.* I watched John sway in the blast of my voice, but he was not impressed by anything I could think of to tell him. *Girls cannot be aviators*, he said at last. *Or get the Victoria Cross.*

John was becoming convinced that he had no sister and was finding it easier to believe from day to day. His silences were magnificent, even when I shook him so hard his glasses hung lopsided from one ear, but he did not care, and could escape from me easily, when I was panting at last and discouraged, and he could go then and join the gang in Rick's cave.

At such times, I went away and threw stones at Miss Gash's tabby to comfort myself, but it was too quick for me and could make itself invisible in shadows, while I had to continue to inhabit heavy perspiring flesh.

When they took the plaster off John's wrist, a change had taken place there. The hair under the plaster had grown thick and black in that private darkness and I found it hard to look at, as frightening as a man's hairy leg.

Heroes

The lattice of the summer-house was peeling away from the beams in a hopeless disintegrating way and the floor had collapsed, but I stood on one of the remaining bearers and looked out over the dish of weeds that was the tennis court. I smelled salad and saw egg-shaped tomatoes growing under me where there had once been a flower bed. The plants sprawled over each other, tangled with paspalum and nasturtiums. I had only seen tomatoes cut into quarters, lying in a dish, and these were alarming, hanging secretively among leaves. Among these plants was a warped and stringless tennis racquet, and I toyed with the idea of giving it a history. The leather grip was as brittle as cardboard but the name OATES was still clear on the handle in gold, and gave me ideas. *He was a hero who died of frostbite*, I would tell them and the dark heat of the schoolyard would make us shiver as I described snow, crevasses, the way feet fell off with frostbite. *In the waters of the Antarctic a man dies in less than thirty seconds*, I could tell them, remembering one of Father's favourite facts, and I would watch Rick shudder. I would only let them look at the racquet, not touch it, and I would tell them it was an heirloom. *Heroism is in our family*, I would say in a casual way, and John would not deny it.

I thought of John's face, twisted like a shoe caught under a door, and the terrible silence of his grey lips when I had been released to run down Bent Lane to him, and in my anger I needed to make a large and violent gesture. With the white chalk from school I began to be rude on the walls of Miss Gash's summer-house. DEVIL, I wrote, then DAMN. The chalk became sticky in my fingers as I appalled myself at the thought of more words. Finally I reminded myself of the way John had whimpered like one of Aunt Kitty's pups, and wrote over and over till the chalk fell apart in my hand: HELL HELL HELL.

In the light of such rudeness, the warped tennis racquet was no longer impressive enough. Rick would sneer and pretend it was diseased. *Dirty old rubbish*, he would say, and hardly glance, and I would be left under the palm tree holding a racquet that had not belonged to anyone but a person called OATES, who was probably not a hero, but a bank manager by now.

Miss Gash's verandah gaped at the sun, and honeysuckle circled slowly around the railings, looking for a way to climb higher. From behind a bush, I watched Miss Gash digging for potatoes where they grew spindly out of compost. When she turned and looked at the bush I was crouching behind, I could see how the white powder had settled into the furrows in her cheeks, but I was sure that in spite of my bulk I was invisible. I needed something to bring gasps to those mulish faces in the playground, and waited, feeling ants crawl on my calves, trying to outstare that knowing tabby when it left Miss Gash to investigate me. Its nose was cold against my leg and its eyes were wide with disdain. I did not blame it, but had to wait behind my bush for something I could boast about, and sweated awkwardly from so much crouching.

Dirt clung to the ragged hem of the postage stamps when Miss Gash straightened up from her spade and stared into the sky with a fist in her back, but she did not notice it, even when she bent to gather up the potatoes in her hands. On her way to the verandah she dropped several that bounced and lay, and spoke to them—*Trying to get away?*—but left them where they were. On the verandah she dropped her handfuls and sat on the top step, her feet wide apart in burst slippers. When she reached into a basket on the step and brought out one of those egg-shaped tomatoes I was not surprised, but felt my palms moisten at the thought of her seeing my rudeness next time she went for tomatoes. She sat eating in the sun, and her laugh when the tomato burst red down her postage stamps was as shrill as a rusted hinge.

When she had finished she flung the stem as far as she could towards the bush I was behind, bending her elbow and throwing from the shoulder in the business-like way I had seen Rick do and that I had tried to copy. He had told me, though, that girls were missing a bone and could not throw properly. We both watched the stem lying on the grass as if it might move, then Miss Gash felt among the folds of her postage stamps, brought out a pipe, and began to smoke. The blue smoke hung around her head, trapped under the green hat, and diffused slowly in the air. That nosy tabby sniffed the tobacco tin as gingerly as if it was hot, investigated a potato with a paw, then sat neatly beside Miss Gash until she had finished her pipe, knocked it out on the verandah post like any comfortable gentle-man, and disappeared into the house. I could have thought I had imagined it all, but the thick fruity smell of her smoke drifted over to my bush, and I did not think I could invent that smell. I would have liked something tangible to take away with me, though, and knew already that no one would believe in Miss Gash's pipe.

There was a long silence when I finished telling John about how I, his fat sister, had seen Miss Gash smoking her pipe and wearing trousers like a man. The ropes of the swing creaked as John scuffed at a piece of dirt. His silence was full of doubt at my story, *Rick says you are loony*, he said finally. *Says I got a loony sister, and she makes stuff up*. The glance he gave me was swollen with painful feeling. *They all laugh at you, Lil, for being loony.* His kick at a tuft of grass might have been at my shin. *And it is not my fault you are my sister.* A butterfly the size of a bird suddenly appeared in the space between us and was interested in John's chin, then his shoulder, then was gone. John took off his glasses and began to polish them on his sleeve. *Lil,* he whined suddenly, *what's loony, exactly?*

The Consolations of Art

I was huge with secret now, in the sunlight of the playground, in the heat that smelled of hot serge and everyone's lunch. My secret was what kept me from minding when Ursula walked to and fro in front of me with an arm around Anne's waist, or even plaited that white witch hair for her when it came loose down her back. When Rick hooted something I refused to hear and Kevin made a rubber noise of disgust with wet lips, I reminded myself that I had my secret of Miss Gash, that I knew where the rest of the picture was, that I had seen a woman smoking a pipe. I had now almost convinced myself about the trousers and pictured them dark and faintly striped, like those Father had worn before he took to bed. There would come a day when I would be able to use it all. They had stopped wanting to know where the tiles had come from, had stopped wanting to know anything at all, but the time would come when they would want to talk to me again, when Ursula would offer me her date slices. I waited for that day, huge with my secret.

Miss Vine considered herself well in advance of her time, with her daring French roll and her waists. It was so progressive to give girls metal to work with rather than silks and watercolours that she was flushed the day she distributed the lengths of copper wire. *You see, children,* she said, deftly twisting her piece of wire.

Look. The shape she held up was recognisably a duck in silhouette. The class gasped and even Gwen cleared a little hair away to get a better look.

My clumsy fingers failed at my construction, but for once Miss Vine spoke to me. *What is it, Lilian?* she asked kindly, holding my snarled wire up to the window. *It is a woman, Miss Vine*, I explained, so eagerly I felt my nose beginning to run. *Wearing trousers*, I added from behind my handkerchief. *Pardon?* Miss Vine said. She was willing to believe she had misheard. *A woman, Miss Vine, wearing trousers*. I repeated it so loudly that everyone stared. Miss Vine's voice was thin with dislike as she said, *That is nasty, Lilian, and not at all amusing*. She did not quite toss my wire at me but it bounced off the desk and slithered into my lap. *Lilian, such ideas are not appealing*. I knew the wet pellet of paper that hit my neck came from Rick's desk. I also knew that everyone was laughing behind me at the red patch on my neck and probably at the way my ears were standing out in shame. With my head lowered over the desk, I spent the rest of the lesson writing in my exercise book, *I have a secret. I will not tell. But I have a secret. They would wish they knew what I know if they knew my secret. I have a wonderful secret*. If Miss Vine had made me show her what I was writing, I would have been heroic in my refusal to tell my secret, but although I scribbled in an ostentatious way and she stared at me, she did not ask.

But it could be noticed that Gwen was circling towards me across the bitumen and between the trees at lunchtime. Even when she finally sat beside me on another knob of the unfriendly palm tree, her hair still hid her eyes. I watched her mouth, that I could not remember ever seeing speak. At last she said, *I could be your friend*, and I saw her tongue flicker and lick her lips as if they were already dry from too much talking. *If you like*, she added. I did not refuse or accept, and after a while she took my wrist and led me to the corner of the yard where paspalum grew long and rank and no one went because of the snakes. Her hand around my wrist was as bony as a bird's claw and she kept her head down as if fearing trouble.

My secret, Gwen said, and for a moment I thought she had guessed and was mocking me. The paspalum waved around our knees in a sticky way and I would have liked to go home and lie under the plumbago. That was a blue I liked. I did not like the way the paspalum clung. *No, look*, Gwen said, and stopped me from going back to where the shouts of the playground already seemed far away. At the base of a young gum, a hole had been grubbed. The thin soil was grey in the sun. *Treasure*, Gwen explained. *Like Troy*. There were two nails thick with rust. *Convict nails*, she whispered, and in my confusion I saw them hammered through palms. Gwen's eyes blinked quickly under the hair as if her treasure dazzled. There was a shard of pale mauve glass. *We will find the rest and put it back together*, she said, and panted at so many words. She showed me a fragment of porcelain and was now so excited her words were hardly audible. *Probably Wedgwood*.

After that, I made it obvious that I did not care about Ursula or Rick or the silences that pooled around me, and made a point of offering my pumpkin scones to Gwen in front of Ursula. I might have invited her to Rosecroft to go out in the boat if I had been sure that Ursula would know. For Ursula, though, it was easy to appear not to care. With Anne she watched as Gwen and I walked purposefully, secretively, to the shabby corner of the schoolyard, but she never asked what was there. As Gwen and.I scraped at the dirt, I glanced behind us, waiting to see everyone finally inquisitive, but the stringy saplings hid no one.

Gwen was in love with holes. She scratched away at our hole with a piece of stick and scrabbled out the loose earth. When we found treasures, she cleaned them with spit and pinafore and hid them in another hole at the base of a wattle. *They are safe there*, she said, and considered. *Is anywhere safer than a hole?*

Lilian! Miss Vine, bending over my isosceles triangle, was appalled. *Class, I want you all to see.* My hands with their dark crescents of nails were held up for everyone to see and someone clicked a tongue in disgust. I had never thought of myself as anything worse than fat, but was now displayed as frankly dirty. *Ingrained*, Miss Vine said, and let my hands go suddenly. *Go and wash your hands, Lilian. Do not return until they are clean.* As I filled the aisle between the desks, leaving the room, and caromed painfully off the corner of one, I saw the way Ursula drew in her chair as if I was contagious, and the way her mouth had gone prim.

It would have been easy then to betray Gwen. *It is buried treasure*, I could have said in front of everyone, and Gwen would have slid further down in her seat. I could have mentioned her by name. *Gwen and I are digging up treasures like Troy*, I could have said, but both of us were saved that. *It is the colour of my skin*, I told Miss Vine, but it is hard to be fat and dignified.

Public Pride

Found a mate, have you, then? Rick said, and I tried not to be alarmed at being Gwen's mate, or too ashamed. *We have a project together, that is all*, I said with dignity. I was excited, though, that he was speaking to me. He seemed excited, too, and bumped his satchel against his knees while he examined my face. *A project, eh?* Rick said, and I wished I could think his grin was a friendly one. *You're two of a kind, you two*. There was something more behind his grin that I could not read. If Kevin had been with him, or loose-lipped Gary, I might have been able to read in their faces what the joke was. But Rick and I were alone together beside the taps, and although we were both late for school and would be in trouble, we lingered. I allowed myself the pleasure of imagining how everyone would see us walk into class together. They would all know we had been late because we had been talking beside the taps. There would be no way, though, to tell them it was Rick who continued to linger and spin out the minutes while his grin widened. I could see a fleck of spit slide down a tooth. I was as close to him as that, and could feel my heart beat as he continued to watch me.

You will be just like her, Rick said and I smiled, but wondered if he meant I would become silent like Gwen. It was hard to imagine that. Now I was beginning to become anxious at the way Rick was delaying me. I watched the water ooze from the broken tap with the clot of rust growing on its lip, and wanted to make a triumphal entry with Rick while he was still grinning. As long as the class saw it, I did not care what was behind that grin. But around us the empty playground listened and stared, and the sun was beginning to heat the bitumen, and a dog limped quickly across it, turning his head to make sure he was not being chased.

Rick was losing his temper. *You're just the same*, he said more loudly, and I felt my smile stiffening as he watched it and became angry. *Yes*, I tried to agree. I knew that if I could keep him smiling until we had made our entrance into class together, everyone would speak to me again. *No*, he yelled suddenly, and the limping dog leaped as if kicked, and ran sideways behind a tree. *No, I mean you will be a batty old maid like that Miss Gash and dirty and loony*. His words hung in the silence of the playground as if they would be there for ever and I watched Rick run with his satchel hitting the back of his knees. Just before he pushed at the big blue door into the building, he turned and under cover of the seven-times table that had suddenly started up, he called, *I would not even touch you, you make me that sick.* He looked pleased with himself, and as smooth as a peach.

Still, I ran to be in the classroom just behind him and tried to look as though we were accomplices. Miss Vine did not notice us, drawing laborious lines on the blackboard with the chalk shrieking along the side of the big ruler. I had squeezed in behind my desk before she turned and dusted herself off with her hankie. Seeing me there, where I had not been before, she frowned and began to say, *Lilian*, when a bee caused a sensation, coming in at a window and making everyone cringe. Miss Vine cowered with her hands over her face and on their side of the room the girls tried to put their heads under the desks. But Rick, waving his geometry book around his head, was taking command of the situation, and I wanted to be by his side. But by the time I had struggled out from behind my desk, not made for people of my size, and disentangled the hem of my pinafore from where it was wedged somewhere, the bee found the window again and the room was suddenly silent. There was a sigh like disappointment. *Thank you, Richard*, Miss Vine said and smiled. *Lilian, may I ask why you are standing?*

I loved my country, with its bees and sea, I loved Rick, but I could not persuade myself to love Miss Vine, with her French roll and small tidy mouth. And I could not have asked Rick how he knew about Miss Gash, and would not ask. In any case I knew that I knew already, although I would not allow myself to admit it.

Killing the Cat

Is it true she is dirty? Ursula asked me. *Is her dress really all torn? Is she really a witch with a black cat?*

I could not be haughty for long. *It is a tabby*, I said coldly, trying to be haughty. Ursula offered me a date slice; pale Anne nibbled at a pale arrowroot biscuit and watched my mouth as I chewed. *It is a tabby. And she is not dirty.* Ursula did not look at me and continued to sit sideways, as if next to me by accident, and asked her questions out of the side of her mouth as if it was not fat Lil she was talking to. Anne stood in front of us nibbling and watching nothing happen on the ground at her feet.

Gwen watched, too, but from the other side of the playground, behind a tree and behind her hair. *She talk funny?* Ursula asked, and could have been asking anyone but me, might have denied speaking at all if she had been challenged, and I decided to ignore her. But I did not go so far as to join Gwen, who was trying to attract my attention by scratching at a tree with a stick. I sat and tried to guess what had made John talk at last, and waited for what Ursula would offer next. *There's two left*, she said of her date slices. *One for me.* She popped it whole into her mouth and chewed puffily. Pale Anne, whose mother did not believe in anything but arrowroot biscuits, looked up. *Close your eyes and open your mouth*, Ursula cried to no one in particular, and I saw Anne's eyes close in the moment before I shut my own, and saw her small square teeth. I felt saliva gush into my mouth and the doughy date slice between my lips. I chewed with closed eyes, loving Ursula's present, and when I opened my eyes, Anne had moved away into the sun and her broken arrowroot biscuit lay in front of me. Ursula turned a little towards me. *That Gwen*, she said crisply, *she's got the ringworm. And she smells.* Her eyes had never been more aloof as they flickered over my face. I was the same fat girl she had farted and laughed with, but she would deny everything. I saw Gwen drop her stick and sit down, and I picked a crumb of date slice off my pinafore and savoured it.

It was your sissy brother, Ursula hissed suddenly. As she spoke we saw Miss Vine come out onto the step, holding the brass bell. In the moment before it began to clang out, Ursula said, *He spilt the beans good and proper*. I heard her mother's satisfied voice in the words, and as Miss Vine clashed the bell up and down so that magpies scattered out of the trees, I saw the way Ursula smoothed the hair back smugly behind her ears, and knew that she must have told John who had thought of calling him Joan. Why else would John have betrayed me? Ursula waited until the last peal of the bell was dying through the air. *If I come to your place tomorrow we can go out in your boat*, said Ursula, who loved our boat and Alma's pumpkin scones, and who might have started to find pale Anne dull, and too sluggish to boss. *All right*, I said, and tried to be indifferent, but could not stop a smile. *And you can show me this witch of yours*, she said, and stared at my face, which suddenly felt stiff. *You have date*, she said primly. *All over your face*.

Being Egged On

Ursula had caught only a single unsatisfying glimpse of Miss Gash and had become tired of crouching behind the bush waiting for more. Out in the bay later, she wanted to know everything, and with the sun on the water making me blink and bringing tears to my eyes, I told her.

She sings songs, I said, and had to hold on to the side of the boat for laughing. *She sings songs about bananas!* Something happened to my voice on the last word so that I roared it out across the water, and had to repeat it so Ursula understood. *She's got bananas*, Ursula said, and had to hold her side from so much giggling. *She's got bananas for brains*. My cheeks were wet with tears, but I could stop laughing at last and go on. *And she's a witch*, I hissed as if the waves might hear. *She nearly killed me one day*, I improvised hastily. Ursula stopped giggling but was not convinced at this, so I tried another tack. *She's rude and nasty*, I said. *That tennis shed thing, she's written rude words all over it*. I was so eager I spat on the words. I whispered into Ursula's coiled ear the words that I had written on the summer-house wall, and smelled the intimate smell of her hair in the sun. *She's an evil old witch, she killed her husband*. I was drunk from the smell of Ursula and being with her in the middle of so much water, and the sun winked into my eyes from the waves, and my story was inspired. *She ate him. I saw her, she sat on the step eating bits of him. Out of a basket. And wearing trousers*. As if this was the most shocking thing, Ursula gasped. *No! She never!* She wanted to hear all about the trousers and the pipe and swore that she would never again go anywhere near Miss Gash or her house.

But, Lil, she said, after scratching at flaking paint on the oar for a while, *I want a tile like that one you had. And you say you are not scared*. We had stopped rowing, and the boat rocked on the water in a way I thought might be about to make me seasick. I was hot behind the ears and wondered if my breakfast was about to come up. In the silence, I was conscious of the air passing in and out of my nose. *I am not scared at all*, I had to say, feeling flushed. *I will get as many tiles as you like*.

Now I wanted to stop talking about Miss Gash and her pipe and trousers, her tiles, the way she had eaten her husband. I wanted to be somewhere else, and in some other mood where I would not have to think about Miss Gash and feel Ursula watching me.

An Exhibition

I was beginning to dislike the way Miss Gash's lumpy lawn snatched at my feet, and the way the house seemed to withdraw as I ran over endless grass towards it. The steps up to the verandah were yawning away from each other, about to fall apart, and the shadow I saw under a leaf looked like a funnel-web. The house knew everything and was brittle in the mauve twilight. A pink cloud hung above a chimney in the shape of a puff of smoke. A pattern of postage stamps in the shadow of the verandah swayed towards me in the moment before it resolved itself into leaves and shadows, and the lace curtain in the window stirred as it always did, and fell back.

Brave at last behind lattice, I looked out and listened, and did not shrink when I saw Miss Gash walk out over the lawn with a sheet of damp painted paper held in front of her. She had to put it down to clear the weeds from the tap that stood on its pipe beside a hydrangea. At last it gushed out a ropy strand of water and she held the painting under it. For a moment I could see the vague circle of a face filling the page before the water washed the colours into the grass. It had grown thick around the tap, fed by so many paintings. On hands and knees she scrubbed at the painting and smoothed the paper like a sick-bed sheet. When she scrubbed too hard, conscientiously going into a corner, the paper tore with a wet rotten sound and she laughed in surprise. She stood for a long time when she had turned off the tap, holding the dripping paper as patiently as a clothes-line.

Later, when she had gone back into the house at last, and I had heard her footsteps and singing go to some far room, I began to creep out from behind my lattice and emboldened myself with thoughts of Rick for the climb up the verandah steps and along the boards. Miss Gash had pinned paintings to the railing to make a kind of exhibition for me alone. I did not resist, confident that she was deep in the house, and took my time looking. There were faces, crooked trees, staggering lines of bush against water. There were the washed ones whose colours had bled to death under the tap. At the end of the row of paintings, Miss Gash sat behind a post, watching me in her postage stamps. An iron bucket threw itself at my feet and clashed out in a terrifying way, and the tabby that had been watching me squealed and fled. My pinafore could hardly contain my bursting chest. Although Miss Gash smiled and was about to speak, I ran away heavily into the bushes.

It was only when I was safe under my plumbago again that I remembered I had not stolen a tile for Ursula. Safe behind my blue flowers, I was glad. I was not in a mood for stealing from Miss Gash, but wanted to watch her painting, or see her smoke her pipe again, and enjoy that rich smell.

The True Story

Alma brought in the blancmange so hastily that it palpitated in its dish. *Parer's horse*, she said, red-faced and important, *it's gone and got itself in up at the Gash place*. Mother quietened the blancmange with a stare. *Thank you, Alma*, she said, and Alma put the blancmange on the table and struck at its heart with a spoon. *Parer can manage*, Mother said, watching a bead of rainbow from her water glass. *And will deal with the old lady*.

Mother could not have dreamed that I had seen Miss Gash at close quarters on her verandah, or that I planned to keep going back there until I understood. Father would also never have believed, and would have laughed his short laugh at the mere idea, but did not have to believe anything, lying quietly upstairs and eating strengthening gruel. Nor would I have tried to make them believe, but I was curious. *Oh,* Mother said through a mouthful of white froth, *she is a bit odd, Lilian, that is all.* I stopped eating in the hope that she would go on, and felt John watching me from across the table. *There is some story,* Mother went on at last, *that she was jilted early on, and went a little odd.* She frowned with her fine eyebrows. *Lilian, you are spilling your white-eat,* she said. *And goggling.* She finished her blancmange and tossed the wide sleeves of her robe further up her arms with a gesture like a man preparing to chop something down. *It is hard for jilted women,* she explained. *Oddness is to be expected, poor thing.*

Meeting a Madness

Miss Gash came up to me where I crouched behind a hibiscus. *I thought you were a dog,* she said. *In the bush there.* Her lips had been drawn in vermilion on the withered skin around her mouth, but her voice was that of a reasonable person. I would have liked to finger those silk postage stamps, now that I was so close, but I did not. *So you had better have a dish of water,* she said, and led me up onto her verandah. *I am not a dog,* I said, and wondered what she could make me believe. I glanced at my hand and smoothed the wrinkled pinafore where a tiny spider laboured through stitching.

The water was not in a dish, but in a teacup of the kind that Alma dusted daily while Mother watched with a finger to the side of her neck. The water tasted of rust but was as cool as the sea. Perhaps it is poisoned, I thought, and met her eyes, which were dark with something applied more to one eye than the other so one side of her face seemed to recede. There was no fur on the backs of my hands, but I could hear my breath panting.

Miss Gash drank her own water in one long swallow and sat watching me and hiccupping. *I wear postage stamps*, she said at last, after we had watched a small spider let itself down jerkily between us from the rafters. *I would have liked to travel, but this is the best I can do.* She picked at a fold of cloth on her knee and held it up close to her face. *British Guinea*, she said. *Where is British Guinea?* I did not know. *Africa*, I said with more authority than I intended. The rusty water had made my voice loud. *It is in Africa.* Miss Gash stretched her arms above her head, showing me pale hairy armpits through the rent in her dress. *You modern girls*, she said. *You know everything.*

I had never seen armpits like those before. I had seen Alma's armpits, dark and matted, once when I had come across her in the laundry in bloomers and camisole, her hair a pile of lather on her head, her face mottled with steam. Mother had no armpits that I had ever seen. The hair in Miss Gash's armpits was a tiny head of well-brushed hair. She saw me staring and said, *You see, it is cooler this way*, and I began to sweat under my clothes. *Men are proud of theirs*, Miss Gash said, and winked at me like an uncle. *Hair is supposed to be virile.*

After a long silence she said, *You do pictures too*, and nodded many times. *I saw them*, she said, and pointed down towards the summer-house that I had covered with rude words. She held out a hand with the fingers framing a piece of garden in front of us. *I do a picture every day.* The postage stamps were fraying into long fringes that swayed around her arms as she gestured. *Then I wash them away*, she said. *It is the only thing to do.*

The spider had begun to build a web in a corner of Miss Gash's wicker chair, and a cicada shrilled once from a tree and thought better of it. Miss Gash stared out at her jungle, her vermilion lips smiling, but it could have been just the way they were drawn. One hand smoothed and smoothed at the cloth over her knee and she nodded now and again in agreement with someone. *Well, you have had your water, and can go now*, she said, and smiled with those savage lips. *But you are welcome any time.*

Bombast

Where is it, then, the tile you were going to get? Ursula taunted. *The old witch scared you.* I yelled into the playground, *No, I am not scared*, but I did not even convince myself. *I just have not had time yet.* But Ursula did not care what reason I might think of. And I would rather her think I was scared than for her to guess that I did not want to steal any more of Miss Gash's tiles, and did not want to hear about her being a witch. I had enjoyed Miss Gash's postage stamps, and could still feel the taste of that interesting water. *Next time I will*, I shouted unhappily. *I will get you the best tile there is.* Ursula stared from her cool blank eyes. She had eaten all her date slices herself today, and had rejected pumpkin scones. Behind her, almost hidden by a tree, I could see Gwen watching me. She had seen me offer my scones to Ursula, had watched Ursula refuse them. Now I knew that she was watching as Ursula left me and joined Anne and Judith at skipping. I moved away too, although I had never got the knack of skipping, and came down so hard my fat shuddered. But Gwen followed me and was by my side before I could get away. She said nothing, but watched my face as closely as if I was speaking, and at last the silence was too much, and I had to speak. *You have the ringworm*, I told her, but then I could not believe I had said the words aloud. Gwen showed no sign of having heard, but stood tossing a pebble in her hand. When she dropped it at last and bent to pick it up, I saw the hair part at the back of her neck and expose the pale secret tendon there, and said it again, louder, *You have the ringworm, and you smell.* This time there could not be any doubts that I had spoken aloud. I did not watch Gwen's back as she walked away, but counted the revolutions of the skipping rope in the sun, until I was dazed by the numbers.

A Vanquished One

Gwen, you are very green, Miss Vine said, and everyone turned to look, Gwen's pale lips opened, but she said nothing. *Gwen, go at once to Matron if you are feeling sick,* Miss Vine ordered, but Gwen had never stood up in front of the whole class and would not start now. By the time the lesson was over, the afternoon blowflies buzzing against the window, Gwen could not move from her desk, but sat shivering and twitching with a face that was grey and puffy. One finger was swollen to three times its normal size and the hand itself was swollen tightly like a sock full of sand.

Gwen never returned to school, although we were told she did not die. The girls' lavatory was boarded up and Mr. Pinnock warned us again about *venomous fauna*. When Ursula, in between two bounces of her ball, said, *You made her do it,* I let out a terrible trumpeting that made everyone in the playground turn and stare.

Lazarus

When Father recovered, everyone was surprised and no one was pleased. *It is a miracle,* Mother said, and ripped the lace of the handkerchief she was twisting in joy. Her mouth shook and she smoothed her dress as if it was a bed. *We must give thuds*, she said, but I knew she meant *thanks*.

In this crisis, John spoke to me. *Are you pleased he is better?* he asked me, and I thought of all the things I could say: *Yes*, or *No*, or, *I don't know*. He stared at my silence and said loudly: *I am not.* He sniffed. *Tell them if you like.* We sat under the plumbago in silence for a long time. It was cramped in there now, for John was getting taller each day. *By Jove but you are filling out*, jovial shopkeepers exclaimed. As if telling the time, John said, *I wish he would die*, and tears began to roll down his face so that he had to put his glasses on the ground and smear his face with his sleeve.

I did not hold a grudge, and brought him hands and feet later for his collection. He sat on his bed staring at a blank piece of his bedcover. *These are Raleigh's feet*, I tried to cajole him. *He discovered potatoes. And here is King Henry's finger, pointing at a wife.* John had gifts for me, too, and we did not mention Joan, or Miss Gash, or even Rick or Ursula. *Here, Lil*, he said, and handed me a cigar box full of dead moths. *Here*, he said, and hurried away from me. From behind, his clothes seemed to be strangling him, and Father's voice was all around us in the house again.

There was no convalescence, only Father better, carving the leg of lamb at the table and being mean with the mint sauce. There were no more facts now, but many questions. *Lilian, I have a question to ask*, he would say, and pounce: *What is the length of the Amazon?* Or, *John, pay attention and answer this: what is the population of Somerset?* John, who had begun to eat meat while Father was ill, went back to carrots and celery, and the Japanese ladies were astonished at so much noise.

Fan Mail

I probed further and further into the chinks in Miss Gash's crumbling walls, looking for snail shells. Finally I arranged my collection carefully under the plumbago. Even John was impressed. He wanted to know what I would do with them. *I have done it*, I said. *I gather them*. But as I continued to sit under the plumbago and think about British Guinea, which I had discovered was not in Africa at all, I decided what the shells were for.

John watched from the doorway as I crept into the darkened room where Mother was sleeping silently on the chaise longue, her mouth ajar. A slipper hung from a toe and trembled with her pulse. When I pulled her tangle of silks out of the embroidery basket, yards of every colour in a beautiful bright clot, I found a skein at the bottom I could use, and a needle. In threading the snail shells into the silk, I shattered seven of them between my fingers, so it was a necklace of one hundred and thirteen shells that I finally held up for John's admiration. *A few more*, I decided, and John nodded and went away. He came back with a handful of snails and held them out to me. They crawled over each other, sent out eyes on nervous stalks, and one left a shining trail along John's sleeve as it made for his elbow. *They will soon die*, he explained. *When they are threaded, they will die*. But I left John with his crawling handful and crossed the fence into Miss Gash's garden.

Another green shutter hung askew now on its hinge so that the side of Miss Gash's house had a rakish look, like someone who had been winking and got stuck. A kookaburra eyed me from the top of a chimney with a lizard in its mouth. As I crept across the lawn it began to caw and titter, and I made a dash to the verandah. The dry snail shells made a fine fragile sound as I ran. When I had coiled the string of shells on top of the wicker table I had to stand back and admire. It was a beautiful gift.

Back under the plumbago, John was still watching the snails crawl across the dirt. *Why'd you give them away, Lil?* he asked. I had not wondered about this before and it stopped me. I made a small cairn of pebbles beside me before I thought of an answer. *It is a gift*, I said at last. *Just a gift.* John snickered so loudly that his glasses suddenly steamed up and he took them off to rub them on his sleeve. Without them, his face looked blind and happy. When he put them back on he stared at me for a long time and I could see that he was planning large action. He leaned over and hit me once, quite hard, on the fleshy part of my shoulder so that I rocked off balance. *Like that is a gift?* he asked. The punch made my shoulder tingle and I knew I would carry a yellow and purple bruise there for a week. *That is a gift, too, if that is what you are giving*, I said. His eyes were large with tears about to fall as he squirmed out from under the bush, but his glasses made it hard to be sure, and I could not think of anything more to say.

The Power of Words

The biggest blackberries were all in the middle of the bushes and I was stuck on thorns again and again, and became hopelessly tangled in pinafore and brambles. My billycan of blackberries spilled and I had to crouch among thorns and pick them from the ground under the bush *where all the snakes are*, Rick said casually, and Ursula, balancing neatly on the board he had laid for her across the thorns, giggled and popped a berry into her mouth. *You look funny*, she said without smiling, *with all blackberry on your face, Lil*. Then Rick, in a voice bursting with something, said, *You're all caught up at the back, fat-face*, and I discovered the hated pinafore was caught up in itself and was exposing the backs of my dimpled thighs and my green bloomers.

Miss Gash took us all by surprise, standing there suddenly in her postage stamps with a saucepan of berries in her hand. *Oh*, she said under the green hat, and I tried to become invisible or make her forget, but I saw her teeth in the shadow of the hat, and there was no denying that it was me she was looking at, smiling and saying *Hello, Lilian*, as if it was normal. I felt Ursula staring with a berry on its way to her mouth, and saw Rick straighten up from the bushes and stare first at Miss Gash, then at me. It seemed they would never stop staring, and waiting for me to do whatever I was going to do. *Catching many?* Miss Gash asked, and lifted her dented saucepan at me. I heard a snort from Ursula that was her holding in a snigger, and I knew that I could not escape, but had to decide. Rick was standing now with his hands on his hips and they were all waiting, and would go on waiting until I turned on shameful Miss Gash who was being so familiar with me. I thought at last that she would realise I was not going to answer her, but she went on standing and shaking the saucepan at me, and the stamps and the rips of the dress fluttered at me, and I felt Ursula forming the story of how Lil Singer was best friends with loony Miss Gash, and I saw Rick wink at Kevin. I could hear the taunts in the playground, if they knew that I did not hate and fear Miss Gash, but had spoken to her like an ordinary person. I could see, too, how John's face had gone blank, and how he was trying to blind himself with a web of thorns.

If Miss Gash had gone away I would not have had to say anything, but she stood, and took a step closer as if to make sure it was me, and smiled again, and was about to say more, when my mouth opened and I heard myself shrieking. *You're a silly old loony old maid, you got a face like a prune, go away.* There was a long shocked silence in which we could all hear something slithering in the depths of the bushes, but finally Miss Gash went away with her sad saucepan.

I turned to Ursula, ready to join her snigger now, but she rattled her billycan and said, *I got plenty, I'm going home now.* Rick would not meet my eye either, but heaved up the plank onto his shoulder with more grunting than necessary, and I was left alone in a great silence. Even John had vanished. I took a step forward, following Ursula and Rick, or perhaps to go after Miss Gash, but stopped with my shoes purple with the blood of my spilled blackberries. I wished I could be like John, blind, or deaf, but the best I could do was to see the bushes and the sky shake and break into rainbow-edged fragments that swam in front of my eyes and threatened to drown me.

Sickening Escape

When Father became insistent over the lamb and asked us all question after question, John could no longer believe in the god of his deafness. *Lilian, what is the longest river in Britain?* Father asked, and when I said, *The Darling*, stuttering on the word, his laugh shook the lamp. *Darling! Whose darling will you ever be?* he shouted, so that his long white teeth showed.

John stared at a carrot as if he wanted to become one, but it was not enough. *Euclid's second theorem?* Father asked silkily, and continued asking until John shook his head. *Euclid*, Father bellowed. *You clod, you clod!* John's nervous grab at the carrot might have been to give himself a weapon. *You will answer*, Father said. His neck was engorging like an angry cobra's and his eyes were becoming small. *What is your name?* he asked, and John put down his carrot in defeat. *John Singer*, he whispered. Father became as outraged as if he had said *Talleyrand or Robert Louis Stevenson.* He asked again. *What is your name?* and John tried once more: *John Thomas Singer, sir.* Father rose half out of his chair so that it fell backwards on the polished floor with a silly clatter. *What is your name?* he roared, and we heard Cook in the depths of the kitchen drop something. John was the colour of raw pancake. A muscle in Father's cheek was jumping and making his mouth wink. *My name is John Singer,* said poor John, and Father lost interest suddenly, and picked the last chop out of the dish and stood at his place at the end of the table, ripping the meat off the bone with his teeth.

On the patch of bare earth beside the swing, John began spinning in a circle until he was suddenly sick. When he stopped retching he began spinning again. When he had started, I had asked, *What are you doing?* but he had not replied. I sat on the stone and watched until he had been sick three times and had fallen into the dust and lay curled there. When I turned him over so that he lay on his back, he stared up into my face and smiled. He was in bliss. *I cannot hear you,* he said. *I am deaf.* I did not tell him I had not said anything.

Some bird flew in and perched on the branch over our heads, blinking at us out of one eye, then the other. When the sun had slid behind the roof of Miss Gash's house and the sky began to turn pink, the bird flew away with a twitter and insects began to croak. Out of a lantana bush Miss Gash's tabby crept, stared at us with a paw raised, and crept on. John lay in his vomit and I watched pink dusk die into grey. Somewhere, streets away, someone was practising the bugle, sending sad, random notes into that shallow pink sky like something lost.

2

A Young Lady

Lawn Lovelies

At the tennis parties for the young folk on the serene lawns and courts of Kissing Point Road, I was the fat girl who looked like coconut ice when she blushed. I had not been kissed at any point. Some boys, gallant by nature perhaps, or attracted by Father's rumoured money, or most likely doing it for a dare, attempted conversation. No one attempted tennis. There was one with hair the colour of autumn who held my hand and told me I was gorgeous. When I watched him later, laughing with a girl whose tan was as smooth as a leaf, I wished I could hide, but there was no place to hide in those sunny gardens.

In the shade, under the jacaranda where no profane kookaburra ever perched and cackled, white-clothed tables were spread with food and there I could at least console myself with another slice of cream pie. I surreptitiously eased the satin sash choking my waist and stood legs astride to feel the cool air between my thighs. The hated pinafores had long since become dusters, but now I had to prickle and sweat in layers of silk, and white stockings that did their best to suffocate me, and I had not accustomed myself to a handbag, and the gloves Mother insisted on.

I had never seen myself smile. There was nothing in the mirror, when I stood in front of it, to make me smile. Others smiled, I saw them out of the corner of my eye, smiling.

But I was a person of brains, and still hoped for the best. *She is bright, of course*, I heard the mothers tell each other as they fanned themselves under the jacarandas. *She is ever so clever*. I gulped down the last of my cream pie and filled my mouth with noisy ginger beer but nothing could stop me from hearing. *It is just as well*, some mothers said languidly, and loudly enough to carry. *Is she feeding those brains of hers, do you think?* The tinkling of so many titters, and their faces all turned towards me behind their fans, drove me like a thwarted cow back out of the shade and onto the terrible sunlit stage of the lawn.

On the lawn, all the young folk were at ease with their futures. The girls were fragrant, slim, good enough to eat in their pale silks and their sashes of pink and yellow. Their feet were small, their shins straight in their white stockings, their hands inconspicuous. Boys did their best to fill their striped blazers and live up to the joviality of their straw boaters. Laughter and a sense of a tidy future lay over everything here, where everyone was graceful, leaning on a croquet mallet or swinging a tennis racquet. They were not troubled by much, these confident people, and most troubles could be washed out in soap and water, or laughed away.

Ursula had the prettiest laugh of them all and the most winsome way with her croquet mallet. Boys watched for the dimple in her cheek, and the pink shell of her ear that showed if she tossed her hair a certain way. They watched, and would try anything to make that dimple appear. At these parties it was hard to get close to Ursula through the group of boys around her, and scones were no longer of much interest to her small pink mouth. But there were times when she saw the fat girl unhappy on the edge of the group, holding a mallet like a weapon, or a ball as if she wanted to crush the life out of it. Ursula would put her hand on my shoulder and smile up at some hero in a boater. *Lilian and I were at school together*, she would say, and become adorably dreamy.

Rick was so tall now it made my eyes water to look at him. *Such a manly jaw*, I had heard some mother say, watching Rick pile Ursula's plate with cakes so that she protested and laughed prettily. His jaw was square, with prominences under his ears that gave him the look of someone who knew what he wanted, even when what he wanted was just another scone. He tried to be kind because it seemed clear that he would get what he wanted, and although Ursula protested at all those cakes, she did not refuse them. *Well, Lil*, he would say, and stand clenching his jaw, thinking, and finally add, *Life moves us all along, doesn't it?* and smile at me. His flannels were crisp and dazzling, his blazer was from the approved tailor, the boater shaded a brown muscular face and those pebble-coloured eyes. No one was going to know that Rick had fought among dunnies and cauliflower stalks, or that his father had made his pile from rubber. *On the manufacturing side,* Rick might admit if pressed, but never *in rubber*. His mother, fluttering vastly in a rather loud blue, had sat under the jacarandas once or twice. But the other mothers had seemed not to hear her comfortable advice about tea leaves on the ailing azaleas or the best way to deal with bird droppings on flagstone. She had stopped coming, and Rick lost his congested look.

I had not been allowed to stop coming. Mother's distress when I said each time, *Mother, I do not want to go*, was too much for me to deal with. And Father had decided it was time I readied myself for my position. *The daughter of a gentleman*, he said. *A young lady*. In the end it seemed easier to buckle the tight shoes on, hook up one of the dresses, and avoid my eyes in the mirror. *You look very nice, Lilian*, Mother would say when I stood ready to go. She was a kind woman, and always hopeful of a miracle.

Lilian, your future is in your hands, Father had said more than once, and looked at his shoes. *You will have to marry money*. So John and I set out every Sunday for one of the lawns where we would suffer for a few hours. John, being young still, was not expected to be suave or to deal skilfully with the yellow voiles, the pink muslins. With a spare mallet or a broken hockey stick, or whatever he could find in the games room, he spent his afternoons playing some private and solitary game in which a bush was the nearest thing to an opponent. *He is a bit shy*, the mothers agreed, watching from the shade, but they could find no excuse for me.

Although I had tried every colour and every kind of laugh, nothing eased the lawn parties for me. Yellow made me look bilious and my laugh always showed too many teeth for prettiness. In white I was sallow, and pink made me look as if I was trying too hard. I heard a mother defend my choice of something with spots that made me look aswarm with insects: *But she is trying*, this charitable mother said, *you must grant her that, Olive*. Olive shrieked and said: *Oh, I will grant you that she is trying*, and could not resist adding, *very trying*.

Proud Mama

Mother was a kind woman, and always hopeful of a miracle, but she had become a person of important preoccupations. She had begun to rise earlier and earlier each morning until she was sitting in her scarlet dressing gown at dawn, waiting for the newspaper to sail over the privet. Newspapers were still concealed from Father. The doctors had been unanimous about that, even after he was better. *No newspapers*, they all agreed. *Newspapers may bring on a relapse.* So Mother arose at dawn each day and crept downstairs and out onto the porch, and when the newspaper arrived she folded each page separately until it was small enough to be slipped under a plate or the embroidered parrot.

She smiled like a sage through the steam of her tea as she read every word on every folded page, from the date on the top to the printer's name at the bottom. The glasses she wore for reading had rims of an unpleasant flesh colour like a false leg. When John and I came down for breakfast, tiptoeing so as not to disturb Father, who had become a late riser, she was waiting for us, one hand warming its palm against the bulge of the teapot, with the news. *Ninety-five dead*, she crowed in a whisper and shook the newspaper at us. There had been an earthquake somewhere, or a volcano. *Two hundred dead in that epidemic already*, she hissed, and her flesh-coloured rims danced with delight. She brushed her hands together with a dusty sound. *Two hundred dead, just like that.* She was becoming robust on all those she was outliving.

By the time Father came down, the sun was high above the trees and Mother was fortified by all those deaths. *Good morning, Albion*, she said, and hid her glasses in her pocket. Father frowned at the morning and rang for fresh tea while Mother traced a finger around and around the plate under which a page of the newspaper was hiding. *What is the point of getting up, Norah, if you have nothing to say?* Father demanded in his irritable morning way, but Mother remained tongue-tied with so much news, and smoothed the silver blade of her butter knife, and smiled to herself, but did not share her dead with him.

Narrow escapes excited her, when Father came down the stairs in the silent way he sometimes did. *He nearly caught me red-handed*, she would tell me, and her eyes would shine. *I was caught up in that fire, seventy-seven dead and ten missing.* Her smile stretched her lips so that they became colourless and showed the darkness of a missing tooth at the side.

The dead could have her full attention only in those pearly hours just after dawn. For the rest of the day she had taken to timing the ferries as they steamed across the bay from one jetty to the next. She sat back against the cushions of her favourite wicker chair, the smooth silver stop-watch in one hand, and on the table beside her, the little gilt book where she recorded pages of figures. *Seventy-two*, she would announce triumphantly to anyone who was near, or to the air if she was alone. *Seventy-two seconds with a head wind*. It was unwise to interrupt Mother as she sat with her thumb on the watch, ready to record the ferry. I would stand behind her, looking at the secretive way her hair grew in a whorl on the crown of her head, and heard the boom as the ferry's engines shook into reverse, and the tinny ping of the captain's bell carrying clearly over the water to us. The gangplank was shot out onto the ferry and a few seconds later we heard the rattle it made.

He thinks it is my diary, Mother said and giggled, holding up the tiny gilt book. *He has no idea of its real meaning*. I nodded, because what she said was no doubt true. Not since she had stood trying not to giggle, with a hand on the gritty back of a stuffed donkey, had she looked so happy.

Mother had become a woman who lived behind a curtain drawn across her face, and she spoke most happily when she thought no one was listening. Between the dead, the stop-watch and the pleasures of narrow escapes, she spent serene days in her chair on the flagstones.

My Golden Future

It was impossible to believe that nothing would come of all those hours I had spent dreaming out at rain on the harbour. I would have liked to be Wilberforce, anxious about slaves, or Dickens, bringing tears to everyone's eyes. I would have liked to be Socrates, and was certainly better at asking questions than at answering them. I, too, could have quelled Cossacks in an astrakhan cap. I also could have called the distance from the tip of my nose to my thumb a yard. I was sure I would not find it hard to be great.

Women do not need education, Father pronounced regularly over the leg of lamb. *Women's aptitudes lie in other directions.* But it was easy to convince Father that I was not much of a woman. *You will need something behind you*, he agreed, holding the newspaper where my name appeared towards the top of a list, between Huggett, J.P., and Stroud, F.J. He shook the newspaper and peered at Singer, L.U., as closely as if he found it hard to read, and perhaps he did, since it was the first newspaper he had been allowed to see for a long time. When he looked at me, I could feel him inspecting my shiny forehead, my wide nose, the chin that was beginning to look pointed above a roll or two of fat. My forearms were freckled, my hands scaly from so much sea water and exertion. I had looked long into the mirror and knew what he was seeing. My teeth were white and straight, fine teeth. But teeth are visible only in a smile or snarl, and with Father I neither smiled nor snarled. *You will need resources*, said Father, and between us over the rose-patterned carpet a string of young men approached, looked at me, and moved on. *Otherwise you will be left high and dry.*

Had I had those ringlets and peach-like cheeks, those dimples, all that daintiness, there would have been no danger of my being left high and dry, but as it was I planted my feet further apart in their thick shoes and was glad of my trunk-like legs. *Then I will be going to the university*, I said. I did not want there to be any misunderstandings. *Yes*, Father said like a kettle going off the boil. *Yes, I suppose you must*.

Mother would have protested if she had been able to concentrate for long enough. *Oh, but, Lilian*, she began. *Before you do this, let me have my say*. There was silence while she timed the ferry, slow today because of waves. *Ninety-six*, she said. *And fifty-five dead. That makes forty-three*. She did not have to think to arrive at this figure, but nodded and made a note in the little gilt book. Her head continued to nod for a long time after she had closed the book and slipped the stop-watch into her pocket. Her grey dress shone in the sun, her hair was beginning to slither out of its combs. Her vague eyes, shaded by her hand, stared out into the bay and the sky without blinking quite enough. *Your Aunt Kitty and I did nothing of the sort*, she said with sudden indignant animation. *But you were pretty*, I said, and she smiled, remembering. *That is true*, she said, and said nothing more, but smiled and nodded, smiled and nodded, at the silky oak and the bay.

You will be a bluestocking, John said. *Will you, Lil?* He was not sure of the implications of any of this, and squinted at me, showing his teeth. *What about nursing*, Father had asked without hope, *or teaching?* I answered John the same way I had answered Father. *I will be a doctor*, I said with pride, *or a philosopher. Perhaps some kind of scientist*.

Poor John had got all the looks but after a rashly promising start he had gradually turned into a dunce. Father was already wondering who he could *have a word with* about his son's future. *You are too clever*, John said, and spat out the apple pip he had been sucking for an hour. *You are brilliant but unstable, Sir said*. John did not know whether to be proud of his sister or ashamed. *Brilliant but unstable*, he said again, and I pictured myself as a spluttering green firework.

Photographs now showed a fat girl who took herself seriously. It began to be important to list twenty-seven reasons for happiness, fifteen prerequisites for wisdom. When Jimmo finished building another set of shelves in my room, I arranged my books on them alphabetically, and had ambitions to possess the complete works of everyone.

Lilian, Father said, while I stood with heavy new textbooks under my arm. *You are about to start a new phase.* From where we stood at the top of the terrace, we could watch Alma toiling up the hill from the ferry. *Success comes in many forms, Lilian*, he said, and crushed a snail underfoot. *There is no need to excel in your studies, other things are important.* His hand was rough and smelled powerfully of citronella when he brushed the hair away from my forehead. He thought better of this and brushed it back down. *A few new dresses, perhaps*, he said without faith. *And a hairdresser.* I could have told him none of that would make a difference, but I did not.

Choices I Have Made

The admiration of strangers must be a stimulus like no other. Sometimes I was allowed to walk beside Ursula like a friend, down our street to the bus, or to the shop that had spawned on the corner. I would see the way strangers glanced admiringly. Ursula's hair had never been as sleek and as casually ringleted, as gleaming in the sun, as it was that summer. *I am helping Mother out for a short time*, she said, but I knew, and she knew, that when she had finished *helping Mother out* she would be married. Her hems were straight, and even the bag-like dresses of that year, and the hats that made us sweat and look bulbous, did not make her any less beautiful. *You are like a cat*, I said, impulsively, and she slapped me with her newspaper. *Oh, Lil, what kind of compliment is that supposed to be?* But she knew me well enough to recognise a compliment. *And you?* she asked, smoothing the golden fuzz on her forearm. *What are you?* On my own forearms, which never tanned, but went the colour of clay, the hair was dark and stubbly. *Oh, I am a dog,* I said, and barked to prove it.

Ursula was not a bad person and she had the generosity that sometimes goes with being beautiful. There was not much Ursula was uncertain of these days, but she was uncertain now, and looked at the ground as she said, *I could advise, Lil.* Her kindness was almost more painful than the titters of the mothers, but she did not want that, and went on. *I could help, perhaps. A diet, and my dressmaker, she is a genius.* I imagined myself dieting and being measured by Ursula's dressmaker, and appearing at last on those lawns, radiant, graceful, a person who did not have to console herself with the thought of her brains. I imagined those boys in their blazers drawing around me, bringing me cakes which, like Ursula, I would squash with a fork but not eat. I could imagine the way Ursula would smile at me, and wink encouragingly if no one was looking, and the way she would teach me what to say, and how to laugh daintily, and how to encourage the boy you wanted. It frightened me to think that I could also have that kind of future. Ursula watched me as I thought, and she was also afraid, because fat Lil was someone she did not understand, and she could not imagine what it might be like to live in my flesh. She was afraid, but was kind enough to be brave. *You do not have to be the way you are,* she said resolutely, and we walked a block in silence, and I watched her small feet taking step after step.

Ursula loved the admiration of those strangers who would go home and tell someone about the *ill-assorted couple* they had seen, and I, too, was beginning to love something like the admiration of strangers. At least if

I did not have their admiration I had their attention. Clothed in my bulk, I was free to try for other kinds of admiration and other kinds of attention. *You are a good friend*, I said finally, and touched Ursula's arm, where the skin was so softly downy. *You are a good friend, but this is what I have chosen.* Ursula did not understand, but touched my hand as if she liked to feel our skins together, and I tried to explain. *I would be a mediocre pretty girl*, I said. *And I am too arrogant to be mediocre.*

We arrived at the gate of 7 Allambie Crescent, but I could not think quickly enough of something more to say that would stop Ursula going in. It was not often that I was able to speak like this with her. Ursula led a busy life now, of morning teas and those tennis parties, and fittings with the dressmaker, and trips in to Mark Foys for gloves. It seemed she was always with other people, who did not understand fat Lil even as much as she did, and who did not mind being cruel. She pushed the gate open suddenly enough to take me by surprise, and was standing on the other side, latching it carefully between us, when she said, *They say you are loony, some of them.* The gate between us made her brave, and she leaned over and kissed me quickly on the cheek. *But I always tell them you are simply a genius.* She waved as she ran up the path to the liver-coloured house and turned to call, *I tell them you will go far.*

Pursuing Wisdom

That first morning I was made dizzy by the vertiginous lecture hall, and everyone was pushing from behind so that I nearly stumbled on the steep steps and went plummeting down towards the lectern. I sat down on the nearest bench and the boy there slid along it as if I needed the space of six people. I was still trying not to topple forward into the well of the hall, clinging to the cracked desk top in front of me, when he slid back towards me. *Good morning*, he said. *I am F.J. Stroud*, and began to finger my brand-new textbooks and the book bag I had bought with pride the day before. I was still too frightened of this steep hall and the violently carved desks, and the knowledge of being at my first lecture, to look at him, and saw only a freckled hand sorting through my books. When I did not answer, he jogged my elbow and said, *I am F.J. Stroud, I am officially a genius*. On one of the words he sent a fleck of spit flying that landed unnoticed on the head below. I nodded and said, *Good morning*, and as I spoke into a sudden silence I saw that the lecturer had entered by a secret door and was standing behind the lectern. In my alarm at hearing my voice ring out, I dropped my pencil. From this height in the hall the lecturer looked as foreshortened and puny as a bad photo. In the silence he stood easily behind his notes, smoothing his sleek grey hair with a palm and glancing up with a pleased bright look, and in this silence my pencil slowly and methodically rolled from step to step down the hall. Its progress was as stately as a pavane. I reminded myself that no one could know it was my pencil, but under my new dress I could feel the trickle of sweat slide down from an armpit.

The pencil stopped at last, somewhere near the front, and there was a gust of nervous laughter from everyone. *And now, perhaps*. Professor Noble's voice was urbane and experienced and I heard a girl behind me whisper, *Wouldn't he looked distinguished in tails?* F.J. Stroud nudged me and handed me his own pencil. *Again*, he said, and I held it, looking at tooth marks in the wood, until finally he snatched it back and began to scribble in his notebook.

I was in no state of mind for wisdom and heard nothing that I wanted to write into my own crisp new notebook. I watched Professor Noble, but his upturned pale face, with its dark mouth hole opening and closing, was as unimportant as a scrap of paper under a desk. At last I felt that I must write something and join all those who were filling page after page around me and I glanced at F.J. Stroud's book. He had filled several pages already, and was about to start another. I read, 'Tis a far far better thing to be brillig or enter the breach dear friends for there is a season for every man jack of them? Before I could see more, F.J. Stroud closed the book with a smack that made Professor Noble glance up. When he had gone back to his notes and smoothed his hair again, F.J. Stroud whispered moistly into my ear, *Hot air rises*. I nodded, but when Professor Noble turned to the blackboard and drew a big diagram of lines and circles, I copied it carefully. I listened while he explained, but could not decide what was important enough to write down. Professor Noble enthused in an urbane way, and jabbed at the diagram with the chalk until it was freckled with dots, and I sat listening to all those pens writing it all down.

What Matters

What is it like, Lil? John wanted to know. *It is not wisdom*, I had to tell him. *It is more like school.* I could see he was disappointed, but I did not want to mislead him. I felt it should be possible to spare him something, since I had those four extra years under my belt. *It is all right*, I said finally, *but it is not wisdom*, and John nodded as if he had expected nothing better.

He had become adenoidal, and enunciated badly. He sounded on the point of tears at all times. *The tuba is bad for him*, Mother thought aloud in moments of clarity, but Father had hopes that the tuba might make a man of him. In the evenings, when John came home from school, he ripped off the tie and jacket before he came in the gate, and tore off even the socks that were part of school before he wrapped himself in his tuba. His face became red, his eyes closed, and nothing existed for him except his vibrating lips puckered against brass. When I tried to produce a note from the tuba, I failed. He did not try to show me how, but took it back and blew a long sad note. *It goes right through me*, he said, *it shudders me*, and shivered to demonstrate. It seemed that the world was nothing but tuba for my brother. He made breathy hooting noises for hours, the sound drifting across the water when I rowed out into the bay in the grey dusk. It was a soft incompetent sound that travelled like a current through the air to me, resting on the oars.

I do not care about wisdom anyway, John said. *I would like to be rich. And have a motor car. And a twelve-piece brass band of my own.* Those who thought him backward had not heard him become passionate about what he believed, and only I had heard this, because he had missed out on friends, somehow, and only had his tuba and sometimes his sister. *There is nothing that matters*, he told me. *And even that does not matter much.*

I could not agree. There was nothing that did not matter. The way leaves fell and turned into earth, the way sun caught an eyelash or showed the bones in fingers: all this mattered.

Kitty Again

Someone brought a pup to a lecture, and it got out of its bag and made straight for Professor Noble. He did not seem to know what to do, and everyone became tense on their benches when it looked as if the pup meant to be sick over the Professor's shoe. A girl with dyed red hair that had gone a kind of green ran out and stuffed the pup back into the bag, and smiled up at the rows of students as if it had all been on purpose, and I was reminded of Aunt Kitty and decided to visit her.

Father mentioned her sometimes, when warning me about things. *A wasted life*, he said. *Not a bad-looking girl, but a wasted life*. At these times Mother would twist her wedding ring around her finger and say, *Aunt Kitty has had a difficult life*. When I said that I was going to visit Aunt Kitty, Mother nodded as if it had been her idea all along and said, *Yes, yes, she has had a difficult life, and your father has done all he can*. Father shook his head and looked solemn. *I will not forbid, Lilian, but I discourage*.

I was not discouraged, but found Aunt Kitty's house, where the front lawn was gay with nodding paspalum and the paint of the front door had gone powdery with age. *I am your niece*, I said when Aunt Kitty, in white frills that had once been smart, opened the door. She showed no surprise. *You are Lilian*, she said, and I nodded in the draught of the hall, smelling whisky and old chops. A tiny spider descended calmly on its web beside my aunt and settled on her shoulder, but I felt I did not yet know her well enough to say anything. *I am glad to see you, Lilian*, Aunt Kitty said at last, remembering how language worked. *Very glad*. She lost interest in me then, and turned a dead plant in its pot on the window sill as if it needed only a fresh view to come to life. *Follow me, Lil*, she said then in a sudden loud commanding way, and led me through the smell of chops to the back garden. When we were standing there among cactuses she began to smile and exclaim over me, and offer me barley water and arrowroot biscuits as she always had.

But, Lilian, she said finally, *you are fat*. Few people were so blunt. Aunt Kitty stood, thin and wrinkled, her hair drawn into a bun that was uncurling like a blown rose. It was easy to see that Father was right. She had once been pretty, but she was not pretty now. In the web of broken veins on her cheeks, her eyes were a weak blue and her wrists were knobbed as she gestured with her glass.

But her smile was sweet, and none the worse for its missing tooth. *I had taken a drop*, she said, confidentially when she saw me looking, *and I woke up on the floor with my tooth in my ear*. She fingered the gap and said with sudden robustness, *It could happen to anyone*, and I agreed.

She continued to smile, so that I finally asked, *Aunt Kitty, are you always smiling?* She brushed at my jacket, stroked back a strand of my hair, wet a finger with spit, and smoothed my eyebrows. *I have few visitors*, she said at last. *And I smile for all of them*.

We sat in her garden, which was many rockeries, many cactuses squatting on sand. *I like spikes*, she remarked, topping up my barley water, and sat looking dappled like an old stone under her lace parasol before she said. *But, Lilian, why are you wearing black?* I suggested, *Perhaps I am in mourning*, but Aunt Kitty declared, *I am the one in mourning*, and shook the white frills of her dress at me. *In China, the deepest mourning is white*. She made me sit on a rock, balancing my arrowroot biscuit on one knee, while she disappeared into the house. She returned with a tiny metal tin with a picture on it of three moustaches arranged like a flower. *Not just for gentlemen*, she said. *For us too*.

For a long time she stood in front of me, blocking out the sun as I sat on the rock, sipping my barley water and nibbling my biscuit, while she smoothed and smoothed my thick eyebrows with moustache wax. Her finger was infinitely smoothing, the barley water warm, the biscuit stale and soft. Near my foot a cactus was producing a single outlandish red flower. *It flowers once every hundred years*, Aunt Kitty said. *Like a really first-rate wine*. The barley water was confusing her, but I would be dead next time the cactus flowered. Aunt

Kitty and her confusions would be dead, my eyebrows would no longer be a problem.

And how is John? Aunt Kitty remembered when she had had enough of smoothing my eyebrows. *He is blowing into brass*, I said. *Trapped in a tuba*. Aunt Kitty lost control of her laugh and it went careening and shrieking away across the cactuses and startled birds out of the trees. I saw that children were looking through the fence at her, where the palings had fallen sideways, and she saw, too, and reached into the cactus pot and threw pebbles at the fence until the faces disappeared. The sun was becoming oppressive. On Aunt Kitty's face concentration and the pressure of an audience had worn off the red lips drawn shakily on the skin round her mouth, and the lace parasol was ineffective now among the barbaric cactuses.

A Hungry Beau

When I discovered new corners of the university I enjoyed the satisfactions of Cook or Leichhardt, even though others had been there before me. Cook and Leichhardt had not worried about a few natives, and nor did I. There was a small damp courtyard where palm trees grew out of bitter clenched soil and gnashed their fronds overhead, and I thought I was alone there, and might have spoken to those busy fronds or smiled in an unguarded way to the square of sky they played in. Two boys leaned, watching me, against a wall. Their grey jackets had pretended to be stone. They were as sudden and chilling as a spider under a leaf. I also pretended: I pretended that my smile had been a cough, my words a sneeze, and walked by them with dignity. They stared at my body as I walked by so that my steps stiffened as if I had forgotten how to bend at the knee. *Not worth the time of day*, one of them said just after I had passed, and in a stiff voice like my knees I said, *Pardon?* They straightened against the wall as if preparing to be shot. *Nothing,* one said and blushed mauve. The other made a gesture like brushing away a fly or a bad dream. I walked on and heard their laughter behind me, echoing in sniggers around the courtyard. *Not at me,* I whispered like a prayer. *Not at me.*

But there were always the consolations of food. In the refectory I was undaunted by the greasy walls and putty-coloured busts of ancient scholars, and sampled everything on the menu. When F.J. Stroud sat beside me there, in the steam from my stew, he introduced himself again. *I am F.J. Stroud,* he said, and this time I was ready for him and said, *You were the one ahead of me in the Honours list. I am Lilian Singer.* Strengthened and comforted by my stew and mashed potatoes, today I could look at F.J. Stroud. He was a pale skinny boy, and short, with the poor complexion of too much bread and dripping. With a shaking finger he pointed to my stew and said, *What's that you're eating?* but did not wait for me to answer before saying, *Looks like entrails.* His laugh was shrill, like a cry for help. I saw how dry and cracked his lips were, and the thinness of his wrists. Through a hole in the shoulder of his black shirt, his skin was pale, bloodless, cold-looking, and it was not warm enough to wear so little. I said, *You must be cold, F.J. Stroud,* but he did not seem to intend to answer. He breathed in a wisp of steam before saying on a sigh, *I never feel the cold.*

I could feel the grease warm on my lips and the cosy peppery taste on my tongue, and felt him watching as I put my knife and fork together and pushed the plate away. His scornful smile and his hunger made me angry, and I could have been shouting when I said into his pale face, *Not eating?* He pushed my plate further away and spoke quickly over the rumbling of his stomach. *I have a delicate constitution,* he said loudly, and as his stomach went on rumbling he went on talking. *I cannot possibly eat in such oily public places.* Beside him I felt myself the size of a battleship, felt my whole face to be shining with greed. I could not remember the last time I had allowed myself to feel hunger or heard my stomach rumble. I sat wondering how I could offer to buy F.J. Stroud a plate of stew when he said, *You must be clever.* I was willing to agree, and had begun to smile and nod, but he went on, *I like clever women.* He sat staring at the table and cracking his knuckles one by one, as if to conceal the blazing blood that had risen into his face, his neck, even his ears where they showed through his ragged hair. Only his hands stayed pale, freckled, awkward. I remembered repartee I had heard on the lawns, which I had never attempted before, and tried to make my reply sound witty: *And I like clever men*, I said, although I did not know if I did, hardly knew if I had ever known any clever men. F.J. Stroud replied immediately. *I am a clever man*, he told me urgently. *In fact, I am officially a genius.* This was no attempt at repartee but a statement of fact. I wanted to laugh, but knew what other people's laughs could sound like and I chose instead to nod, and examine the flecked hazel eyes of my first genius.

A Beau up a Tree

In spite of my alphabetically arranged books and my notebook becoming dog-eared from my bag, although not filled with notes, I was still not permitted to decline those tennis parties. *You must not close off your options*, Father said, and tweaked at one of the unflattering frills on my dress. *Options should always remain wide open, Lilian.* With a tearing sound he ripped his fingernail out from where it had become caught in a frill of bodice.

On the lawns, fringed by every colour of azalea, lives were beginning to be arranged. The mothers looked away now when Ursula and Rick disappeared into the shrubbery to look for balls, and after so many years Ursula's mother had put away her black dresses and had taken to mauve.

There were new faces on the lawns now. Duncan was someone's cousin from the west, learning something at the university. His vagueness about his studies was pathological when the urbane young men, secure in their well-fitting striped blazers, asked him jovial questions. He was the kind of victim to whom fathers could hold forth as the ice in the whisky melted, but they did not respect him for that. *A feeble kind of a lad*, they would say impatiently later, tipping back the glass for a last drop. *Not much get up and go.*

Duncan's smile reminded me of the country. It was probably so many freckles. Even his lips were freckled, and his mouth was a wide one. Duncan was tolerated on these lawns because of all the cows his father owned. *A big man in beef*, I had heard someone say of his father. Duncan had been to one of the right schools, although it did not show, and wore the right kind of blazer, but was as awkward and sandy as if fresh from the bush. His hair was the colour of the dust of a dry river. When Ursula asked him for a lemonade or Rick joked about tennis with him, Duncan brushed the hair back from where it hung, and exposed a forehead so pale and bare of freckles it was like something shocking and private. I saw that he hated the lawns and lemonade as much as I did, and was no better at banter than I was, but he hated it all with the recklessness of someone who would come into beef in a big way one day.

In the meantime, the girls pointed at the way his wrists showed below the cuffs of his blazer. He was the only young man to slip and come up with a green bottom during the desultory cricket game. He did not run languidly like the others, but panted as if he really cared, and pelted up and down the pitch, losing his cap as he ran, becoming red in the face, sweating visibly under the arms. When he spilled the pink ice over a section of Ursula's new daffodil-yellow dress, it was easy to see he would have liked to be dead. But he had to stand and dab hopelessly with a napkin until someone stopped him. Later, Ursula could laugh it off and speak to Duncan again, but it was the first time she had worn the daffodil yellow that everyone agreed did so much for her, and she could not forgive straight away.

We were paired off together at croquet more than once, Duncan and I, but we did not take to each other any better for knowing that we were together in failing to meet standards. On the wide sloping lawns, lace fluttered in the afternoon breezes, shoulders were very straight in stripes, and pools of light gathered around each mallet. When Duncan picked up one of those clumsy tools and took a crooked swing at a ball, he struck a hoop instead, somehow caught his thumb painfully, and stood holding his thumb and swearing. Ursula, who had smiled and approached, preparing to be gracious, changed her mind. I heard a clucking noise from someone. *Pardon the French*, Duncan said to me, as being the closest. *But it hurts like buggery*.

But Duncan was the one who spoke to me when I dropped my slice of cream pie on the flagstones. Someone's mother tinkled the bell for someone to come and clean up the mess I had made, and everyone looked away and made a circle of silence around me and the shameful spatter at my feet in which shards of expensive plate could be seen. But Duncan stood beside me and said, *Where would you like to be, Lil?* I tried not to shout as I answered, *Up a tree*, and felt my nose beginning to run, and remembered that I had no hankie. Would I ever be invited back if I wiped my nose on the hem of the white dress that made me look like a badly wrapped parcel?

The maid cleaned cream pie off stone and put shards of plate into her dustpan as if gawky girls did this every day. She was no older than I was, but pretty, like some small night creature with tidy habits and paws. *Here you are, miss*, she said, and handed me another slice on another plate, and in the moment that she took me by surprise and I fumbled for the plate, it was easy to imagine how tight my hostess's mouth would become at the sight of another slice of cream pie and another plate lying on the stones. I could not eat it now, although cream pie was one of my favourites, and stood holding the plate tightly by its edge. Duncan took it out of my hand while the mothers watched, frowning for their daughters who were unwilling to overlook enough for the sake of prosperity in beef. *Then we will do that*, he said, and ran with my hand across the lawn. His feet came down heavily on the grass, loose on their ankles, his knees seemed about to poke through his flannels. He was all awkward corners like a hard problem in geometry, but he urged me up into the silky oak.

In the tree it was possible to feel better. The mothers shaded their eyes and made gestures up at us, but we looked away at where the shrubbery was like moss from this height. Behind bushes, invisible to everyone but us, John sat in the depths of the vegetation, picking his nose. *That is my brother*, I told Duncan, in case he did not know. *My brother John*. Duncan nodded and spurred his branch into a canter. *He is picking his nose*, he said, and the day had so far been so bad that it was no anguish to agree. *You and me, we are the ringers,* Duncan said, and up on my branch I agreed. He was not ashamed of the truth.

He had let me climb further into the silky oak than he had, to leave all those giggles behind. *Lil*, he said when we were settled on our branches, *you are a real sport*. He was flushed with this declaration, and when he handed me up one perfect leaf as a gift, I realised I had an admirer. *By Jeeze, Lil, it is better up here*. The girls in white, in pink, in daffodil yellow, and so many straw boaters, seemed miles away. There was a breeze up here, and if Duncan cared to look up my skirt to the white bloomers, I could not have minded. He did not, however, but handed me perfect leaf after perfect leaf until I could hold no more. *Stop, Duncan*, I had to laugh. *I have too many now*. Duncan laughed, too, and was a happy person there on his branch. *I wanted to give you*, he exclaimed, and I held them all tightly, not having been given too many tokens before. His shoulders were very wide from my view above him, and the sandy hair grew up straight on the crown of his head so I could see pale scalp. His freckles, when he looked up and grinned, were the kind that are with a man for ever. *Duncan*, I said, teasing, *why are you not with one of the pretty ones, eh?* Duncan spent a long time showing me the crown of his head, while below us the pinks and the whites strolled and tittered hand in hand. *You are pretty to me*, he said at last, looking up at me. He met my eyes fiercely, as if alarmed by my bloomers. *You are preferable*.

The Stroud Diamonds

F.J. Stroud was officially a genius but, although he understood the logic of the distributed middle and I did not, he impressed the men in tweed no more than I did. *I am a scholarship boy, I will go far, I am officially a genius*, he said, and I bought him another lunch. Watching the gravy run down his chin as he gobbled, forking food into his mouth desperately, cleaning every speck of food off the plate with a last crust, I was tender towards him. *If I was a real man I would call you a mate*, he said, and wiped off his chin. After a good feed, his smile was not as pinched as usual. *Of course you would also have to be a real man.* At other tables in this chilly hall, girls in summer pink copied things from one book into another. Others filed their nails or looked serious with friends in powder blue. I saw familiar faces at times, faces I had seen at school, and they would smile at me because my name was up in gold now on a board somewhere in the school, but their smiles failed to charm me. Behind those smiles, too much thinking was going on. Words would be flowing too easily. I preferred something clogging.

My father is in diamonds, F.J. Stroud said rather loudly, and the sallow boy clearing plates looked around in a frightened way. *He is a millionaire.* I did not try very hard to hide my scepticism, but F.J. Stroud was not put out. *You do not believe me*, he said. *That is one more sign of your intelligence, Lil.* When he laughed he exposed long grooved teeth like an old dog's and a pale tongue, but in spite of those hungry teeth his smile was something I looked forward to. *I do not often tell people, Lil, because they usually laugh. But I do not mind your laugh, and you will believe me in the end.*

In the end it was not quite that I believed him, but any tale is real if it is told well enough. F.J. Stroud drew lines and circles in the greasy film on the table between us, and told me about the diamond mine full of sweating black men. *They try to smuggle the stones out*, he said, *in orifices of their sweating bodies*. He watched me until I blushed, then said, *One orifice in particular, of their sweating bodies.* He told me about the house with verandahs and bougainvillea and the way the neighbours rode over for gin rickeys, and about the pet monkey, and the black nanny who burned feathers when he was sick. He showed me evidence when he could. *My pony threw me one day*, he said, *and Father had it put down. Perhaps you have noticed the way my shoulder-blades protrude?* I had, but had thought it was just another part of him being a short skinny boy, the way his shoulder-blades moved like wings under the faded black shirt. *But they fought bitterly, Mother and Father*, he said. *I would be under the table listening and wishing I was not there.* I did not know what sweating black men looked like, and had never smelled burning feathers, but I, too, had been under furniture listening when I would have preferred to be somewhere else. *Mother sacrificed everything when she left*, F.J. Stroud said, and stared into my face as if waiting for a sign. His eyes were almond-shaped, almost the eyes I had wished for as a child, and were the colour of certain flecked greenish stones under water. *F.J. Stroud, I do not believe a word of it*, I exclaimed, and heard myself laugh, and F.J. Stroud laughed, too, so that I saw his long old dog's teeth. The girls in their yellow and tidy pinks paused in their copying and looked around at us laughing too loudly in this echoing refectory, and that made us laugh even more loudly, until the woman behind the tea urn looked as if she might come over and tell us to leave. But in spite of so much laughter I did not disbelieve F.J. Stroud, and watched the way his shoulder-blades moved. When I stopped laughing at last and said, *It is a sad story*, I had to wipe away a tear of laughter from my cheek, and watched F.J. Stroud do the same. *You need not believe me*, he said, and stared at me with his hands behind his head so I could see how bumpy and red his wrists were where they came out of the cuffs of his shirt.

The Person with the Pup

The person with the pup was called Joan and we had somehow become friends. Up close her hair was no longer a kind of green but more a kind of purple shot with light, and the roots were brown. It was cropped short at the back like a man's so that her neck shone with the clipped hairs and the strong pale tendon was exposed. Her bobbed hair was miraculous for me and her trousers a scandal. Joan was not like anyone I had ever known. Joan did not ask me what school I had been to, or show interest in Father's profession or Mother's family. She did not copy her lecture notes neatly into a bound black book, did not admire anyone's dress or exclaim how well blue suited them. It was not possible to imagine Joan knitting baby clothes for anyone's sister.

In the mornings, when Joan and I sometimes caught the same train, we walked together through the slums to the university. Grey-faced children wiped the snot off their upper lips and stared, or shouted at us in hoarse voices. I had been shouted at before, but it was different in company, and Joan made the quite street ring when she shouted back, and exchanged banter with men who came to doorways to stare. *Smile and wave, Lil*, she said, and nudged me, and smiled and waved when women looked over the shoulders of the men, frowning. *Come on, Lil, smile and wave, like royalty*.

Joan's smile showed no dimples, but short pointed teeth. She showed me her teeth as we crossed the quadrangle. *I have vampire teeth*, she said. *My grandmother is from Transylvania, do you believe me?* I would have believed anything of Joan, and admired the long sharp canines she was baring at me. *I had an ancestor who was burned as a witch*, I told her, but did not add, *Do you believe me?* in case she said, *No*, in her blunt way. But it did not seem to matter to Joan whether it was true or not. *Lil, there are women of destiny*, she cried, *and we are two of them!* She shouted at a man in tweed who had stared, *We are women of a different ilk!* The carillon tried to silence her, snarling out from the bell tower, but she did not wait for the

114

din to stop before she shouted, *And fuck the lady with the lamp!* There had been no one like Joan before.

What Duncan Said

On the lawn below, everyone posed and sauntered. Sometimes, when there was nothing better to do, they would stand underneath our tree and try to coax us down. *Come on*, Ursula's thin voice floated up. *Be a sport, Lil*. At this height, Rick, beside her, looked as squat as she did while he echoed her. *Yes, be a sport, Lil*. Duncan and I found that they lost interest in the end, and we would continue what we had been discussing when those below had started to shout.

Well, Lil, Duncan would say and flush, his neck mottling like marble. I watched the delicate skin of his ears fill with blood, like a soft wafer of something that would taste good. I waited as he thought of another word, more at home astride a branch chewing the end of a leaf than on a lawn. The blood glowed under his skin as he remembered another word. *What is it, Duncan?* I insisted each time, and explained each time that I would not be shocked, and that I would not think worse of him for knowing such words, but better. *Come on, Duncan*, I had to wheedle, *be a sport*. He had begun by whispering when the words had not been too much for him. Now, when only the worst of the words remained unsaid, he was unable to utter them in cold blood. *Here, Lil*, he would say, and would hand me up a leaf on which he had scratched the word with a twig. Or he would hold out his hand for mine, and write the word letter by letter in my palm. *Now, Duncan*, I would have to say, *that is too fast*, and he would start again and spell the word out, letter by rude letter.

But what is it, Duncan? I asked. *What does it mean?* In the beginning the words had been enough, but after a while I wanted to know what they meant. *Well, Lil*, Duncan would finally say in a thin voice, trying to be matter-of-fact, *it's when they do it in your arsehole*. I had to keep asking, *Do what, Duncan?* because Duncan could not believe I remained so ignorant at twenty. *Oh, come on, Lil!* He would shake his head like a reluctant animal. *It is just that you want me to talk dirty, eh, Lil?* His grin up at me from under his sandy eyebrows was the nearest I had ever been to intimacy.

I had words for Duncan, too, that he enjoyed, and understood as little as I understood his. *I do not know one of my sex! no woman's face remember, save, from my glass, mine own; nor have I seen more that I may call men, than you, good friend, and my dear father.* Duncan watched my mouth carefully as I spoke and nodded and nodded, so that his branch shook under him. *That is beaut, Lil*, he would exclaim when I had finished. *Just beaut.*

When we slid down the trunk at tea-time for scones and lemonade and I prepared myself for all the comments on the rip or stain that was inevitable on my dress—*Oh, Lilian, and it was so pretty*—it was reluctantly, drawn only by those scones, those crisp Anzacs, the succulent cream pie. *Bit of a let-down, eh?* Duncan said when we stood together at the table, eating steadily. It was unusual for us to speak together, though, unless we were in the tree.

Sometimes I met Duncan under the arches of the quadrangle at the university, but so much stone and so much tweed, all those purposeful scholars striding along the paths, made us uneasy. *They make me feel dense, most of them*, Duncan confessed, *with their long words and Latin*. His smile stunned the too-green when he spread a large hand over his heart and exclaimed, *I am just a simple bush bloke, you know, Lil*, and that smile stayed with me through a long afternoon.

A Jealous Beau

I was too large and loud for those studious young men with a row of fountain pens in the pockets of their jackets, and heads full of facts. They looked around like startled birds, and were careful not to meet my eye when my laugh echoed under the clock tower or among the cloisters. I walked with my books in the company of others who did not want to be rude to the fat girl, and who let her walk with them to the next lecture, and sometimes they laughed in a discouraging kind of way at my jokes, but mostly they smiled without showing any teeth, and began to look around for rescue.

F.J. Stroud seldom laughed, but I could tell he was often amused. *What are you, Lil?* he asked one day out of a long silence in which we had fed pigeons our crusts. *I am a fine figure of a woman*, I said without hesitation, and laughed so that pigeons scattered into the air. F.J. Stroud sucked a knuckle. *And what am I?* he asked. *Am I a fine figure of a man, like that flannelled fool you speak to?* Surprise silenced me and pigeons took advantage of my absence of mind. *Stop*, F.J. Stroud said finally, grasping my hand and sandwich. *That is your lunch.*

An ugly childhood is a bad preparation for success. I did not know what to say to F.J. Stroud about that flannelled fool, Duncan. *Duncan?* I said, and F.J. Stroud blinked. *With a name like that,* he began, but did not go on. I heard him gulp, and stared at the possibilities of the sky. *You are a fine figure in your way, too*, I said. If my hair had been long and silky enough, I would have tossed it as I had watched Ursula do, being a coquette. *But he is no fool.*

F.J. Stroud showed me swans as though they were his, and picked forbidden flowers and thrust their stems into my button-hole. *My estate*, he said, and swept a thin hand around the gardens to include the swans, the palms, the view of the blue harbour, gardeners kneeling in soft earth. *Feel free, won't you, to suggest alterations.* He went down on a knee so that I could see only his dun hair. *One day this will all be yours.* His laugh made a gardener stare with suspicion. He spoke recklessly: *I would like not to be poor. Even poor and honest, much less simply poor, which is what I am.* He could not stop the flow of words. It seemed he had unlocked a torrent when he had spoken the word *poor* for the first time. He ripped a red bloom from a shrub and tried to force it behind my ear. When a gardener approached and spoke, F.J. Stroud replied in Latin until the gardener was driven to snort *bloody dagos*, and walked off with his fork over his shoulder. *I have no beef,* said F.J. Stroud, watching him go, and I wondered how he had found out so much about Duncan. *But I have beauty, and beef is not beautiful.*

We walked for hours in the gardens, touching sometimes by accident so that I was afraid of knocking him over like a chair. *Lil, you are so big,* he exclaimed querulously. But he admired my bulk, too. *It would be hard to lose you, Lil,* he said. *There is so much of you.* We walked and walked as if wanting to arrive somewhere, until even my strong feet were tired, and until the Latin labels on the trees had stopped being amusing, even when they were called after someone's wife or mistress.

A Green Thought

Only Duncan could have steered me through that first dance. Dances had been threatened before, and I had felt sweat on my palms at the thought. I had developed rashes, headaches, even once a short-lived loss of voice, in the face of dances, but Duncan's freckles gave me courage. *We will show them, Lil,* he said. *And you will be the belle.*

No yellow, Aunt Kitty said with decision. *You will be as appetising as an old flounder in yellow.* So Duncan ushered into the dance a mass of green, *which young girls do not wear, dear,* Mother had warned, but I had insisted. In the bright room where the dancing was going on, Ursula and everyone turned to look. *It's Lil*, I heard someone say, *in green!* Duncan had presented me with a red corsage which I felt was too small. In the powder room, looking with surprise at the majestic figure in green, my impulse was to brush off her shoulder that accidental debris of red. But Duncan, awkward in a black suit, had whispered, *You look delicious, Lil,* so I left his corsage where it was.

With Duncan I found dancing possible, but with other partners I became again an ugly blushing girl. Rick was endlessly surprised to be refused his offers of waltzes and foxtrots. *Don't hold all that old stuff against me, do you, Lil?* He was handsome and his smile could have melted stone. He and Ursula were a couple whom people looked at. Duncan did not mind that people looked at us, too, even though he knew their looks were not of admiration. *I do not care, Lil,* he said, and held me more tightly as we danced. When the music ended and I saw that my pink stocking had slipped down around one sturdy ankle, I could not hide it from him. *That is why they were looking*, I said, and the green dress felt puckered and hideous. I was again a fat red girl. *They were admiring your aplomb*, Duncan said, and I permitted myself to be restored.

No Fury Like a Father's

Duncan did not meet Father, but saw him. From our height in the tree, Father was puny and stalk-like. Duncan was not impressed. *So that's the old bloke* he said, without admiration. It was pointed out to Father that his daughter was in the tree above and he craned up, shading his eyes with his hand. He said nothing, turned away, walked over for a scone, and left.

Lilian, you disgust me, he said later in his study. He was a cross silhouette in front of his window. *Up a tree with a lout from the bush, even if he will be rich*. He turned away and opened the small window as if suddenly stifling. *Showing the world your drawers*. He could not fasten the catch, and flung the window out in the end so that it swung in a frenzy and banged against the frame. *Has someone told you that this is the way to catch a husband, showing him your vile drawers?* I said nothing and hoped he would lose interest, but he tore at the trousers around his crotch, loosening something, and went on and on. *What do you think you are up to? What are you up to, up there?* Finally I tried to answer. *I am not up to anything*, I said. *With him or anyone*. But Father could not accept this. He had not heard me, and began to bellow, *I will not have it!* But was there anything he could do? *I could forbid you, Lilian, to go at all*, he pointed out more calmly, and sat at his desk. I could see the light from the window pink through his ears. *But it is your future at stake there*. If I had thought that was my future, I would have rowed the old boat out into the middle of the bay and somehow made myself sink. I would have needed a few bricks, or at least pocketfuls of stones. But I knew that futures came in all kinds, and would not give up on mine just yet.

What do you get up to there? Father asked again, *Lilian, I will have answers*. The pink roses of the carpet were chaining me to the spot. I held the edge of the desk with my fingers, watching the nails go pale as I pressed harder, and wondered why it was not possible to turn away, leaving Father's questions hanging in the air of this stuffy room, and leave. I would close the door carefully behind me and seal in the unfinished questions, and Father might sit there until he atrophied, waiting for answers.

The silence finally wore me out. I was becoming bored with this room. *We get up to Shakespeare*, I said, and did not expect him to believe me. *We recite Shakespeare*. This was exaggeration, of course, since I recited Shakespeare and Duncan listened, but it saved me having to confront in Father's company the words that Duncan did recite. Exaggeration or not, it was enough to enrage Father. He rose from behind his desk and spilled the paperweights in front of him. *Shakespeare*, he snorted. *Expect me to believe that story, Lilian?* He looked at me for long enough to realise how funny I was, and began to laugh. His laughter filled the room, flattening the roses, beating at the window to get out, and I stood in front of him. *Come on, Lilian*, he said at last. Tears twinkled in the corners of his eyes and he wiped them away with a sigh. *Wonderful*, he said, *let's hear you, Lilian*. His rage and shouting could not have made me recite, but his scorn and laughter were provocations of the right sort.

I did not look at him as I recited, but at the window where a branch swung backwards and forwards, applauding. Father did not stop laughing. *Oh, Lilian*, he crowed. *You are like one of those apes, taught to do things*. Then I could not stop, but felt my mouth shaping word after word, faster and faster, and on those hated pink roses saw page after page slipping over, thick with words. *Stop, Lilian, stop!* I heard Father shouting, and felt his hands on my shoulders. *Shut up, Lilian*. His voice was only a distant interruption to the words it was vital to keep reading from the roses. When he slapped my face I saw startled points of light before my eyes and a great ringing began in my ear.

I lay with a headache like an axe between my eyes, and did not remember how I had arrived in my own room, stretched on the bed with my toes towards the ceiling, a wet cloth on my face. *You were upset, Lilian*, said Mother from a chair beside me. *And so we brought you here.* Mother's eyes wandered over my face and settled on my chin to speak to. She winked laboriously at it. *I told them it was your time of the month,* she whispered. *And they believed me.*

Healthy girls with broad feet recover from most things. It took a week or two, though, for me to find that the heavy leather Shakespeare that had been a gift from Father when I was a child had been taken away again. *Who has taken my Shakespeare?* I asked John, and he looked more stupid than necessary in denying everything. I would not cry in front of anyone so dull and mulish and did not bother to hit him. Later, though, he came to find me. *Father took the boat out,* he said, *and drowned your book.* I cried, but it did not matter, because I had enough in my head to last me a lifetime.

Scandals

Lil, they are saying you will do anything, Ursula said. *They say you are after him.* Ursula herself was not required to do anything now, and smiled smoothly at the world from safety. There was nothing Rick would not do for her now. *I am your friend, Lil, and I understand,* she said, and smoothed a wisp of hair. *I am happy, and do not care what anyone else does.* Something in Ursula was ripening and sweetening in the light of requited love. *But others are talking,* she said. *It is the business of being in the tree with him all the time.* Of course I had noticed the way they looked when we came down. They saw my flush, too, and did not know it was just from all the words I had been taught. Their faces were prettier than mine, but bitter above their voile.

A Mother's Work Is Never Done

So much scandal even reached Mother as she sat with the stop-watch on the terrace. *Sit, Lilian, there is something I must say*, she said briskly, and I sat opposite her in the deck-chair, and watched her face forget what she had had to say. Nodding, she followed the course of a ferry as it steamed slowly across the bay. The chair creaked under my weight and the canvas strained at its stitches, but held. Mother's eyes were fascinated by the crescents of dark cloth under my armpits. *Lilian*, she said, reminding herself who I was. *Lilian*. I could see her labouring to say something more, and at last, smoothing the stop-watch like a cat in her palm, she said, *Your brother is a boy, and girls are not like boys*. She stared at me closely as if to make sure I was following. *Yes, Mother*, I said, and waited.

Her face was hidden behind its curtain of frown and it was hard to see the face of the smiling young woman who had married Father. I had pored over those old photographs until the breath wheezed through my nose from crouching on the floor so long, trying to see something more. She had married in Valenciennes lace that curved behind her in a train like a whirlpool, and her flowers had wilted in her hands. But although I could see every bud and trace every fold of the lace, I could not see what had happened to Mother.

I was willing to blame myself. No one had warned Mother that a daughter might grow into a fat watchful girl with thick red cheeks and tiny triangular eyes. She could not have imagined that her own daughter would be so clearly unsuitable to wear the Valenciennes, now packed away somewhere in tissue paper and lavender. She would not have thought any daughter of hers could sweat so profusely, would so often have morsels of food on her clothing, would have hair the colour of buried bones and as lank as grass.

But Mother was not a shirker, and she loved me enough to try to warn me. In her thin papery cheeks a terrible flush had risen and her fingers were turning the stop-watch over and over. *Lilian, when a woman becomes a woman, there are changes*. I could not think of the words to tell her that she did not need to go on. We sat listening to a blowfly drone between us and away, and I tried to forget the way Miss Vine's face had been full of disgust, those years ago, when she had suddenly snatched at me as I ran out into the playground, and hissed, *Go to Matron at once*. She had been so close to me that spittle had landed on my face, and she had been so disturbed that she had brushed it off with the side of her hand, and said *Sorry* as if she had forgotten who I was. *The back of your skirt, Lilian*, she had whispered at me with horror, and when I looked and saw the ugly blob of purple on the back of the green skirt, I had been horrified, too, and afraid.

I am twenty, I told Mother, and saw her flinch as if I had shouted. Had I shouted? She twisted her wedding ring as if to unscrew her finger. *That is why it is time, Lilian*. I watched her stare out over the bay. The ferry had disappeared around the headland, leaving a dirty thumb-print on the sky, and a gull was wheeling and plummeting into the water. From a bush near us a bird sang the same three notes over and over like a practising soprano. Mother's eyes glanced quickly backwards and forwards across the bay and the sky as if reading an interesting page. Her lips moved silently and her right hand sketched tiny gestures. When she turned to me again, the furrow between her eyebrows was smooth and I saw a canine catch on her lip as she smiled. *You see*, she said happily, *it is all very simple*. I nodded and said, *Yes*, thinking of the hopeless feeling, standing behind the screen in the sick bay, shivering in camisole and bloomers with a thick wad of cloth between my legs. When Matron had returned with the sponged green uniform, she had stared rudely at my thighs beneath the bottle-green bloomers and I had been conscious of how mottled and dimpled they were. *Next time, Lilian, be more careful*, she had said, and watched me as a I struggled with buttons.

Mother had fallen into a doze, her knuckles pink as she gripped the stop-watch even in sleep, and I left her there. Later the breeze would come across the water and blow wisps of her fine hair across her face and into her nose, until she would wake up with a jerk and the curtain would be drawn tightly back across her face. But in sleep, with her duty done by her daughter, she could be recognised as the young girl proud of her husband and her Valenciennes.

Being Conspicuous

I had looked forward to reading all the wisdom ever written and to thinking deeply about important things. I had planned serene hours with fearless minds who would help me resolve problems of good and evil, and what everything might mean. I had been excited by my future.

In the lecture hall, I watched the men in tweed mouthing, smothering a yawn before turning to the next page in their notes. F.J. Stroud and I stared down at so many heads bowed over tricky considerations of philosophy, so many pens flying across lined paper. In the first row, right in front of the man in tweed, was the deaf boy who was going to go far in philosophy in spite of his handicap, and the pretty girl who did not know that she did not have to work so hard at understanding. She pressed hard, putting words into her book, pressing each word into the paper as if otherwise it might run away.

But what did any of it have to do with me? Did any of it have to do with the stars that hung low near dawn, or the way the sun came up dripping out of the sea? The notes I took meant nothing: a few facts about enclosure laws, a list of the dates of battles. My notebook did not fill like other people's, and what was in it was largely illegible. Even when it could be read, there did not seem to be much sense in these lists of denuded facts, dates, names. Descartes was a man with a ball of wax, I knew that much and Philip of Spain had died an unmentionable death, but what else? Even Napoleon seemed boring.

Here up in the back of the hall, where the hot air gathered, and the smells of ink and feet, the fat girl with the red cheeks sat beside the thin ugly boy in black. The man in tweed had not wondered for many years what all this had to do with God, but he was annoyed by so much whispering in the back row. *He that has ears, let him hear,* he boomed out suddenly, to his surprise as much as his students'. The pretty girl dropped her pencil, the deaf boy showed his teeth with the pleasure of having heard for once, and the thin boy and the fat girl stopped their whispering to stare.

I often wanted to stand and yell down into the ring. *Where is size?* I would have liked to shout. *What have you done with the grand and ineffable? Where is the life all around us?* I stood in my place, balancing against vertigo with a hand on the bench. The men in tweed stopped what they were saying and stared up, waiting. There would be a long silence which gradually filled up with shuffles, titters, things dropped with a bang or tinkle, during which I struggled to formulate one of my questions. The men in tweed became embarrassed. My formulations evaporated as I stood with my mouth trying to open on words, and watched them toss chalk from hand to hand. One pushed a long hand into his trouser pocket and drew out a gold watch on a chain. He laid it in front of him on the lectern as gently as a soufflé. *Yes?* They would ask, their faces turned up to me in a moonlike way. *Yes?* The silence would deepen and finally splinter with a snicker from somewhere. The men in tweed prided themselves on their poise and silver temples, and smoothly turned to the board when they had waited long enough.

On the board they enumerated a few more facts about the movements of centuries or battles or philosophies, and when they turned back to the class they continued speaking as if the tall girl was not still standing, her mouth ajar, blocking the view of those behind, but still full of undelivered questions. They would learn to expect her and would finally look around at the beginning of the lecture to see from which bench she would rise, and would recognise her in the quadrangle, and nod, and smile a watchful smile to show they knew but that they would not be impressed.

It is a shock to me, I confessed to F.J. Stroud, who continued to be willing to be made conspicuous as the boy in black beside the standing girl. *I expected something else.* F.J. Stroud sneered, but did not intend cruelty. *What did you expect?* he wanted to know. *Wisdom?* The bedlam of the lunchtime bells strained after a melody—it might have been "Greensleeves" or just as well "Ye Banks and Braes"—but could only produce clamour. *Wisdom*, he said when we had passed out of the quadrangle. *You will not find it here.*

I was not sure that anything as complete as wisdom, or an answer, was what I was after. Even one satisfying question would have done me.

Father and My Beaux

When Father was not cross these days, he was smiling too sweetly. *How are your beaux, Lilian?* he would ask. *When will they start beating a path to the door?* His smile showed all his front teeth in a row like a fence. That long upper lip had not stopped frightening me, ever since it had been shaved clean, because of the

127

way it exposed so much of Father's mouth. His lips were rosy, turgid, glowing with blood, as he showed his teeth and waited for an answer. But I pretended to be more mulish and unwanted than I really was. *You are a woman now, Lilian*, he told me, and laid an arm so suddenly along my shoulder that I staggered. He pressed me against him, but we had not much practice at this and I stood in an ungainly way in his arm, holding my breath. *You must tell me, Lilian, if anyone is forward with you*, he said, and gave me a final squeeze that made me gasp, before releasing me. *The world is full of bold forward men who will try anything*. He ran a tongue over his teeth so that they glittered, and glanced over his shoulder at where Mother sat with the ribbons of her hat trying to whip her awake. Father's shadow on the grass reached out towards her in a dark way and the ribbons danced and fluttered urgently. *Fixated, Lilian, is the name for it*.

But I made many mistakes. I told him, for example about the short swarthy man who spoke to me each day in the park, a short man who left his bench each morning to walk towards me. The leather strap of my book bag squeaked conversationally as we approached each other. He was my Napoleon, his teeth shone like an animal's, and he was never properly shaved. *Good morning, miss*, he said every day, and showed his wet white teeth. His accent could have been Corsican. And he was clearly in exile, even though this was not Elba.

It had been a nasty mistake to say anything. *A man, eh?* Father said, and got up and poured me a glass of wine. *Better start sometime*, he said, and I watched the wine in my glass shake a bead of pink light onto the tablecloth. *No, Albion, no,* Mother said in a general way and I saw how her fingers trembled as she held them spread over the top of her glass. *Please, Albion, no.* She laid her other hand over her fingers as if afraid he would pour the wine through them into the glass. Father watched me as I drank, and I saw his Adam's apple move energetically under the skin of his throat as he tilted his head back to empty his own glass.

Across the table, John's glass was still full of water and untouched as he watched Father and me drinking. His eyes receded further and further into his head as the wine in my glass disappeared and was refilled and my face became hot and happy. The Japanese ladies above the sideboard had flinched in a gust of my laughter when Mother got up, still holding her glass tight in both hands, and left the room, but John stayed to watch like a Buddha in glasses.

He is Napoleon, I heard myself stutter and giggle. *He waits for me every morning in the park*. Father's eyes grew small and cunning. *What Napoleon*, he said. *What park?* His voice was as smooth as a grape. I was old enough to know better, but I told him.

I think he told the police about my Napoleon. *Dissolute and cunning*, he said with a hand in his trouser pocket, jingling something. *Corrupting my daughter. I will not have it*. He thrust the other hand into a pocket and glared at me. *I will not have you corrupted by any dago in a park, Lilian*.

The police, when they came, did not believe anything. They hardly bothered to conceal how sceptical they were that anyone would want to corrupt this fat, frowning girl.

Aunt Kitty Advises

Ah, your beaux, Aunt Kitty said when I told her about Duncan and F.J. Stroud. *You see, you are like all of us, with beaux*. She smiled dreamily at the memories of her beaux and straightened her spine in the chair. *It is not everything, Lilian, but it is a lot*.

I had never been closer to being ordinary, and lay back in the wicker chair, feeling another strand snap under me, to enjoy it. Aunt Kitty turned the rings on her knobbed fingers. *Forbes was not my favourite beau*, she said. *But he was the best husband.* I watched a leaf shudder. *Oh, husbands*, I said, and could picture nothing but frowns. *I am not sure about husbands.* Aunt Kitty finished her barley water in one gulp. *Neither was I*, she said and laughed. *It is all so grave.*

But she brought out the wedding dress, packed like Mother's in tissue paper. The sleeves seemed big enough only for twigs, the shoulders so narrow it could have been a child's dress. I had not thought before how frail Aunt Kitty was. I had always been wide-shouldered, staunch-thighed, and my arms needed plenty of room to move.

A man likes a good listener, Aunt Kitty advised. *A good listener with a bad memory.* She sucked deeply at her barley water, which was a darker shade than mine. *A memory is unforgivable, no one's jokes are infinite.* I asked, *And what does a woman like?* But even Aunt Kitty had no answers for that. *Fun*, she suggested at last, and slopped barley water on her knee. *Perhaps.* She smothered a belch that escaped through her fingers. *Forbes was fun, but he died.*

In Aunt Kitty's living room, curtained against the heat, we sat in armchairs in which mould had become personality. Crickets were loud on the verandah and a bird in some bush yelped like a hungry pup. *I would like to wear an outfit like a cactus*, I said, and Aunt Kitty was immediately interested. *That ill green*, she said. *Paler points. Pale green lace, perhaps.* I never wore lace, but the idea of having an outfit like a cactus was pleasing. *And one red flower under an armpit*, I said. Aunt Kitty agreed. *You are right, Lilian, they do grow their blooms in their armpits.* She had become dreamy. *And a hat made of banksias.*

I never wore lace, never wore anything but my tartan skirt and the black coat that knew every one of my secrets. But Aunt Kitty continued to hope for me. *My own days are nearly over*, she said, and held out a trembling veined hand to inspect the old skin. *But it is just beginning for you. And for girls now it is all different.* She was silent for a long time, making each of her starched flounces lie tidily beside the others. *But I would have loved an outfit like a banksia.* She laughed a sudden robust laugh from the depths of her white frills and lavender water. *All those mouths. I love them, Lilian.* After so much animation she slipped into a reverie while the glass of barley water tipped more and more perilously in her hand.

It was time for me to go, time to leave Aunt Kitty in her chair with her mouth slipping ajar for her afternoon stupor. But I found it hard to leave. At home, cold leg of lamb awaited me, and the unread books that Father reminded me he had paid for. *You are letting opportunity slip*, he said tiresomely. *Opportunity is passing you by.*

A Sad Street

Although there was so much of me, there did not seem enough to go around. Duncan saw me as I strolled among old stones with F.J. Stroud, and waved in an uncontrolled way. He never mentioned what he had seen, but held my ankle tightly as we sat in our tree, and threatened never to let go. From a distance, Duncan in his white flannels looked like someone at ease. Anyone who had not seen him blush purple over lemonade and cream pie would assume he was just another crass boy in beef.

I was embarrassed when F.J. Stroud met me in the Gardens in his own white flannels. A pale blue stain in the pocket of his white shirt had been patiently scrubbed by someone and the cuffs had been carefully turned and darned. The flannels were too tight, too obviously left over from small days at school, strained at the waistband, and showed too much black sock at the ankle. F.J. Stroud was waiting on our bench, looking sardonic for the benefit of a gull, when I came over the grass towards him. He grimaced and held his lined palms out towards me. *Kindly pretend I am not here today*, he said. *That other man's clothes do not fit me.* I could see how much he wanted to return home and rip off those sad white clothes.

You are my secret vice, Lil, he told me after a long silence, broken by a gull rudely shrieking at us. *I think of you at night like a drug*. I watched his finger knotting together in a desperate way as he spoke at last. *In a year I will come into my trust account*, he began again, and smiled at the thought of that trust account. *Then I will buy you things, Lil, and take you to dinner*.

I could not refuse then, to visit the street where he lived. *Come along*, he said, and gripped my wrist. *There is nothing to be afraid of, or not much*. It seemed that the failure of his flannels had made him determined to see how far humiliation could go.

In his sad street the terrace houses crowded together with teeth missing from their railings and sheets of iron leaning askew. Everything smelled of milk gone bad. Thin dogs nosed along the gutters and from every gate lack-lustre children stared with pale faces. It would be important to have a secret vice in such a street.

Mother sacrificed everything when she left, F.J. Stroud said, *and she would not accept a penny*. In that street he looked bigger, stood straighter, beside so many dustbins and dog turds. *This is where I live*. He pointed at flaking green paint. *That woman, do you see, is my mother*. He pointed and tried hard not to be ashamed. His mother was one of the three women standing in aprons and hairnets talking at someone's railing, but I could not guess which one she was.

I was not breathing properly in this street of such poverty, but F.J. Stroud continued to grip my wrist and when I looked down at my own shoes rather than face those grey children, he tilted my chin up. *I am poor*, he said, *but I can be just as ruthless as anyone else*. He was thinking of Duncan as he squared his shoulders at the street, but was not used to standing as if he was proud of something, and began to cough. *That man is too healthy*, he said through his cough, so he sounded frantic. *He cannot be any good, so bursting with health*. When he had finished coughing he stood staring at a dead sparrow that lay beside a rag in the gutter. *You will be a young widow, though, if you choose me, Lil.* He coughed his sharp cough once more, demonstrating. *Do you wish to make old bones, Lil?* he asked, and nudged the sparrow with his foot. *Are you aiming for that telegram from the King?*

Proposals Abound

We were all quickly getting older, and thinking about marriage and death. People in shops called me *Miss* now instead of *Dearie*, and Duncan had been given a manly cut-throat razor for his birthday. On the lawns below us all the boaters and voiles were becoming serious about their prospects.

Duncan had never spoken about his beef, except to say he had eaten enough of it for a lifetime. He spoke about card games in the dry river bed with the abos, about how skinning a rabbit was like taking off a sock, about some dog he was fond of that was half dingo. *But it is dry there, Lil*, he said, looking around. *Nothing decays there, it just dries up like snakeskin.* We were silent for a long time as I thought about that kind of dryness. *You would like it, Lil*, Duncan said, and I thought of how pleased Father would be, so that I had to lean over and watch a shining gob of my spit spin down to the grass. Duncan laughed and compared his own spit on the way down, stringier through the branches, hitting a leaf and dribbling. *I promise you would like it, Lil.*

It was a day of recklessness and everyone's mother was a little shrill and inclined to tears under the jacaranda, because Rick had proposed to Ursula and been accepted. Ursula sat now in a chair with the mothers, turning the diamond on her finger so that it shot points of light. There were moments when, surrounded by the other girls exclaiming and blushing with envy, her smile seemed to be exhausting her. From the sedate depths of her wicker chair, she watched the girls in voile who were still creating their futures in a web of smiles and glances, and seemed to feel she had arrived at hers too quickly and by too direct a route. Some transformation she had been looking forward to had not taken place.

Duncan and I were made uneasy by the mood of panic and by so much wishing. We filled our hands with buns and lamingtons and climbed the tree again, awkwardly, with them. From high in the branches we could not see Ursula, but we could watch Rick standing in a group of boaters. We could not see his face, but we could watch as his foot drew patterns on the grass as he talked. Duncan swallowed lamington and said, *He is a husband now*, and I thought about husbands and wives and wondered if there was any alternative. Duncan coughed on a shred of coconut and said, *You are a mate, Lil.* When he looked up from his branch, no man had ever looked me so straight in the eye. *A good mate*, he said. I wanted to cry with pleasure, but felt a mate would not cry. I had seen mates, slapping each other's shoulders, shouting, spilling beer on each other, but I had never seen them cry with pleasure or anything else.

You could be a bloke, Lil, Duncan said obscurely, through a mouthful of bun. He hardly knew what he was saying, but the gigantic bite he had taken, and the vigorous chewing that made the muscles of his face stand out, did not retract what he had said. I had not been happier in company for as long as I could remember. For those few minutes while I listened to Duncan chew, it became possible to imagine futures. I broke pieces off my bun and rolled them around my mouth, unable to swallow for the pressure of a future and happiness. I would see all the skies I wanted to, sleep on all the kinds of earth there were. I would be able to experience every dawn, and storms by the sea and in mountains. Duncan would rip buns apart with his short strong teeth and I would be his Lil, his mate.

Duncan on the Beach

Blue Gods wait outside some women's doors, but Duncan waited outside mine. In the moonlight his face was the colour of paper and by night he was warmer than by day. When he took my hand and led me down to our beach, I could feel that my whole large being was contained in his warm palm. On the cold sand Duncan warmed me with his side against mine, and we counted stars and kissed, while small waves toyed with the rocks. In small quantities, on quiet moonlit nights, the sea was very tame.

Other men did not kiss me. F.J. Stroud would have been welcome to, in spite of being so skinny and having cold hands, but he had never tried. And the young men doing well in law or medicine, who reached my name on the list of young ladies to be invited for a drive, did not try either. They took me out on Sundays in their new cars, opening the door for me, helping me up with an indifferent respectful hand. We drove and they shouted facts about the car, about the scenery, about the full dull history of some spot named after some colonial governor. They had good futures ahead of them and in the meantime they were willing to be respectful to fat Lil Singer. Their futures were full of boots up on brass fenders, of smiling serene wives and endearing clean children. But kissing and feeling cold sand slither between fingers and toes like something alive, that was something no one but Duncan tried.

You should not let me do this, Duncan said, and let go of me so that I rolled away on the sand. *Do you let other men do this?* Our mouths had been fastened together for so long my lips were tender and faltering. On the second try I could still not form words, so I abandoned the idea. *Lil, you are crazy*, Duncan whispered, his hair grey in the moonlight, his eyes in shadow. His tie lay like an eel on the sand between us, but he still wore his shoes. When dew began to fall and the stars retreated in their sockets until they were tiny sharp points of light, he sat up and emptied sand out of his shoes. *You*, he said, looking at me as sand poured out. *You devil*. His smile was wet by moonlight. *You are trying to egg me on, eh, Lil?*

I was hungry for each next step, each new shape of skin waiting to be discovered. I was hungry for the grit of sand between our naked skins. *Lil, you cannot do this*, Duncan said with a hand on my thigh, and removed it. *You cannot do this*, he said, and turned away.

But I was a bold girl, and hungry for everything. I took Duncan's hand and put it boldly on my breast. *I am an innocent*, I told him, although I knew he already knew that. *But you, have you done this?* Drunk with the feel of sand on the back of his hand, I listened for an answer for so long I thought he must have fallen asleep. But under his eyebrows I could see his eyes shifting in thought. When he looked at me, it was a plea. *Look, Lil*, he entreated, *you are a good mate. I cannot take advantage*. There was more, so I did not allow myself to answer. *You are a good mate, and a person of class*, Duncan said in a confused way. There was still more and I waited for it to make sense, but Duncan could not find any more words. The silence between us began to congeal and something cold crept up my spine. My lips felt puffy now and Duncan sat hunched under the moonlight as under a weight.

Aunt Kitty had warned me against boldness, but I had laughed at her. *It is said they lose respect*, Aunt Kitty said. *If it is respect you want. Do you want respect?* I had experienced respect. The boys with good prospects had treated me with respect. After they had handed me up into the car, I watched their faces as they walked around the nose of the car to the driver's seat, and their faces were full of how pleased they were with the way they respected me. *Respect is not much my line*, I told Aunt Kitty. *What is, Lil? What is your line?* she asked. It was a natural question but a hard one. Finally the silence between us gave up the effort. Respect seemed a subject that could reduce all of us to silence.

Answers from Joan

Joan had the answers to many questions, so I tried her with the one that was troubling me. *What is it all about, Joan?* I asked. *How does it all work?* I could not find a better way to ask than that, and trusted Joan and her understanding. She thought for a long time, shredding a leaf until she held up just the stalk of its spine, and then knotted it back onto itself. I had been thinking about F.J. Stroud when I asked, and his skinny nervous hands under the fig tree, and about Duncan sighing in the knots of his clothes, but Joan could not have known any of that. *Well, Lil*, she said at last, *it is all about whatever you like. It is about kittens and roses, if that is what you fancy.* She poked her stalk at me until it squirted up a nostril and I squealed. *Or it is like that, if you like.* Joan's small green eyes watched me closely, as if she was thinking about purchasing me. Up so close I could see how her

137

skin was different from mine, from all the Annes and Ursulas I had gone to school with, not pink and white, but brownish, olivish, with a sheen as if water would run off it smoothly. *Does that satisfy you?* Joan finally asked, and I nodded and said, *Yes*, although I did not know if her question was about her answer or the way I had been looking at her skin. *Look, Lil, if you want to see something*, she said, and suddenly raised an arm and pulled at the loose sleeve of her blouse until a beard of kinked black hair sprang out at me. *Now, that is worth a look*, Joan said. *That is one of the things it is all about.*

Joan did not impress Father as she impressed me, when I invited her home. *A skinny sort of girl*, he said, *with not much in the way of womanly graces*. His hand began the sketch of something in the air.

Joan and I went out in the boat as Ursula and I had, but Joan was less afraid of everything than anyone I had ever known. *It is too nice not to be in*, Joan cried one blue morning when the water was like a living jewel. *It is a scandal not to be wet*, Joan said, and was naked, diving off the stern, before I could gather thoughts or words. *Come on, Lil*, she called, looking like a seal with her dark hair streaming over her skull. The water ran off the sheen of her skin as I had always imagined it would. Of course I would not budge, and certainly would not remove my clothes. *I will watch*, I called primly. *Someone should watch for sharks*. The truth was that I thought the sun might fall out of the sky if I removed my clothes.

In the struggle I was afraid the boat would tip us out and sink. Joan was as strong and slippery as a hooked fish as she pinned me to the boards of the boat and began ripping at my buttons and hooks. My own bulk held me spreadeagled under her and finally it seemed easier not to resist. My eye was filled with puckered nipple as Joan reached over my shoulder for a fastening, and I smelled a sharp animal smell from that hair-filled armpit. When my breasts lolled out in the sun, Joan sat back so that the boat rocked sickeningly. *Now, Lil, I will not ask again*, she said, panting, and I watched her pink tongue lick the salt from the corners of her mouth. I heard my voice say, *I cannot, Joan, I cannot*, even as I was standing up to remove my skirt. I outraged myself, standing naked in the sun with the boat rocking beneath my soles, but Joan was not outraged. She leaned back so that her sallow breasts became as flat as a boy's, and admired me. *You are a fine figure of a woman, Lil*, she said sincerely. *I like the way there is so much of you.* I had not thought about myself in such a way before. My bulk had always been an appendage, but now, looking down at my smooth pale breasts in the sun, I was prepared to reconsider. *Your skin is as smooth as rabbit's fur*, Joan admired, and leaned forward to touch. *Mine is more like suede*, she said, and laughed so loudly that I imagined the sound ringing across the water until it reached the shore and entered windows. *You feel, Lil*, she said, and put my hand on her shoulder. Her skin against mine was foreign but not at all unpleasant. I could not tell what was happening, but knew that there had never been anyone like Joan before.

Bringing Home the Bacon

There is the Milton lad, Father said dismissively over roast chook, meaning Duncan. *He does not look as if he knows which way is up.* Father laughed his angry laugh and hit the table with his palm, because he had already finished several glasses of wine. *You would wait a long time for enlightenment with that Milton boy*, he cried, and winked at me from each eye in turn. I did not say anything about the enlightenment Duncan had already given me, but watched the way Father's eyes had grown small and hard, like olives in their sockets. *What about a real man, Lilian, who can show you what is what?* He leaned forward at me. *You would be the better for it, take it from me.* He laughed again and repeated, *A real man*, and Mother pushed back her chair with a terrible scraping noise and left the room.

F.J. Stroud was not what Father, or perhaps anyone, would have called a real man. But it was F.J. Stroud whom I brought home to meet Father, and he promised me that he would enjoy meeting the man he called *my sire*.

Yes, sir, I am in Law, and think I will have a good chance at the Medal, F.J. Stroud said sincerely and with modesty. Sitting down, with a glass of Father's sherry in his hand, he looked taller, looked like someone in Law who had a good chance at the Medal. Father took another glass and was not sure whether to be impressed or not. *Splendid*, he said vaguely, and we could both hear him swallow a mouthful. F.J. Stroud met my eye, but neither of us needed to wink. *One can never be sure, of course*, F.J. Stroud said with even deeper modesty, and added with inspiration only a fraction too late, *as my father always used to say*.

Father asked, as he was supposed to, about the father, and F.J. Stroud, with the promptings a modest person required, told about his father, his brilliant record at Oxford, his glittering rise in the diplomatic, his tragic early death. *So it has been a struggle*, F.J. Stroud said modestly. *Mother is frail, but we have done our best*. His modesty and lies were beginning to nauseate me, but Father was looking grave. *Just you and your mother*, he said, and could not stop himself winking at F.J. Stroud. *Just you and her*. As we watched, he winked again and a corner of his mouth jumped uncontrollably.

Shocking Joan

Joan's back was pasty and pimpled, but she did not care, and showed as much skin as she liked. In the quadrangle people stared and clucked, but Joan swung her book bag at them or made a face like a rabbit, and they steered well clear. She knew more swear words that Duncan had ever taught me. *Oh, how droll!* she exclaimed when I told her what I knew, and she taught me another. *Lil, what an innocent you are*, she said, but her smile did not make innocence contemptible. She took my hand in both of hers and squeezed it. *Do you speak French, Lil?* she asked, and I was surprised, but said, *Well, we learned at school, "La plume de ma tante est dans le jardin,"* and her laugh made birds take off in fright from the grass, but I was not displeased. *I enjoy you, Lil*, she said, and was not like anyone I had known. She pulled me close to her so that she was near enough to fill my ear with her tongue. *You are good enough to eat*, she said after I had first squirmed, then enjoyed the feel of that outrageous tongue, and she nudged me as if it was all a good joke I had not grasped.

How about a cheap Chow feed, Lil, she shouted then, *and a bottle of plonk, eh?* A boy with four fountain pens in the breast pocket of his suit stared at us, smear of ink on his cheek. *He would like to join us*, Joan giggled into my ear so that her voice was huge and moist. *But he is not invited.*

Few people had dared to encircle my wide waist, but Joan did. Her arm was hot and heavy around me and I could feel her hip jostling against mine at each step we took down the hill towards our cheap Chow feed. Men came to the doorways of pubs and stared at us, whistled, made comments that were too thick with beer and bashfulness to be understood. *You are only jealous*, Joan turned and called, and a man with a large red nose snatched the hat off his head and flung

141

it at us in rage, but could not seem to find words. With the sad countryman's hat lying on the pavement I would have liked to separate from Joan and hurry away with my head down, and let them laugh at the way my bottom looked in haste. But Joan took another handful of my waist and made me slow down. *Between us, Lil, we could launch every ship in the world*, she said, and the man with the red nose heard, and his eyes changed in fear, thinking she was mad.

And what do you think of boys, Lil? Joan asked later, refilling our glasses with the urine-coloured wine they had brought us. *Boys*, she said again, making it sound ridiculous, and laughed. Behind her a Chinese waiter stared at her bare back and seemed to be waiting for the scarf she had tied around her chest to slip down. *Boys*, I said, and tried to concentrate, but under the table Joan's leg was warm against mine. *Some are thin*, I heard myself saying solemnly, *and some are more robust*. Joan did not laugh, but winked at me. *Yes*, she said. *Go on*. I thought and finished my glass of wine. *Some of them smell chalky*, I said, *and some of them are mates. There is Duncan, he is a boy and a mate*, but I did not add that F.J. Stroud, up close, had the chalky smell of cotton washed too many times. I had seen Joan speaking to Duncan, and knew that she knew him, and now she nodded and showed her vampire teeth. *Duncan*, she said. *Duncan is a mate of mine, too. He is good at being a mate, eh?* Her smile was asking something I did not understand, but I nodded. It was a miracle that the world now was full of mates, of women in trousers and scarves tied around their chests, of men who were mates. I looked back with pity at the tennis parties and the hated croquet, the filmy dresses, the long afternoons full of wet cucumber sandwiches, when the dew condensed on the tall jugs of lemonade and my hands sweated against my dress.

I belched and did not even think of excusing myself, while Joan picked her teeth behind her hand in an experienced way, and I was happy that life could provide such riches. *It will be you and me together*, Joan promised and leaned forward across the greasy plates and kissed me on the mouth. When she sat back in her seat the scarf over her breast was spotted with rice grains, and I reached across and brushed them away. The watching Chinese faces did not reveal what they thought.

Those Trousers of Father's

Father was beginning to object to it all. *Too much gadding*, he said excitedly. *And who knows what you are getting up to with those lads of yours?* His ponderous reminders of the money he was spending on my education, the price of each book he thwacked down on my desk, did not reform me. *But Father, you said other things mattered, too*, I ventured to remind him. *And my gadding is other things.* But Father became red and loud. *With those feeble lads!* he exclaimed. *Midgets! Wordless oafs! Are there no real men these days, Lilian, or are you trying to taunt me?* He stood over me as I sat at my boring desk, with the wood grain that was the pattern of boredom for me, and gripped my shoulder. *You are a tight little vixen*, Father said as if his teeth were clenched on the words. *A tight and seamy vixen.* I sat staring at the wood grain and at my hand lying on it, hearing Father breathe above my head and feeling the heat of his body against the side of my arm as he stood over me. His nearness for such a long time made me itch but I could not move, and sat feeling the blood pound in my face, and a great heat and congestion radiating from Father with his dark hidden trousers at eye level.

A Foreign Prospect

Since we are such friends, Lil, you had better come home and meet my parents, Joan said with her arm around my waist. I did not wish to meet anyone's parents, and sit being fat and drinking tea on some alien parental brocade, but could not refuse Joan, and in any case she had run the gauntlet of Father, and had seen tremulous Mother with her stop-watch, so I agreed to meet Joan's parents.

Joan's house was not a house, but a flat in a box-like building of liver-coloured bricks. I walked up stairs through a sweet smell of cabbage, past doors behind which dishes clattered and babies cried. Joan had not told me any of this and I felt brave, reckless, to be climbing stairs to see someone else's home. I did not know anyone who lived in a building full of flats. There were polished brass bells and knockers on the doors I passed. When I stopped to read a name beside a bell, I had to peer closely: "Zbynski," it said, and the next one was in green ink, in a script I could not read, with letters back to front. I walked up more quickly then and tried to be silent as I moved so none of these people would guess I was here. There were no names here like the ones I was used to, no Greenwoods or Abercrombies.

Joan's mother smiled and showed gold teeth and it shortly became clear that she did not speak any more English than, *Yes, please*, which got me as far as the living room and into a deep chair that made me feel sleepy. Then Joan's father came out from somewhere and closed a door carefully behind him. *She is not yet ready*, said this completely hairless man in a thick accent. *But soon she will be ready*. In the depths of my chair I smiled and nodded, confused by such accents and foreign furniture. Joan's father said *Drink?* with his back turned, clinking bottles, and I found myself holding a glass too big for my hand, full of whisky and water such as Father drank. *Smoke?* Joan's father asked, and I found that a cigarette was in my hand and I was obliged to light it from the flame that he held too close to my nose. Joan's father smiled like a smiling egg and finally sat down opposite me. His skull was good enough to toss from hand to hand. The ears were the only decorations on his head, and like tastefully concealed machinery his eyes moved smoothly in their sockets. *You are studying what?* Joan's father asked from his mouth that ate English words as though they were something tough. The cigarette had mercifully gone out and I leaned forward, making the chair creak symphonically under me, and put it in the ashtray. *Oh*, I said, and stammered through a list of what I was studying. *And you will become what?* he persisted, and did not smile when I shrugged with difficulty, for the leather chair was as hard to shrug in as a bed, and spoke vaguely of seeing the world. *But your career*, he said, and the surprise in my face made him elaborate and chew a few more bits of English. *Your future. Your livelihood. Your prospects.* F.J. Stroud had responded better than I. The glass tipped in my hand, I held it with both hands, felt then as though praying, and experienced a sudden pang for lemonade and yellow dresses. *I will teach*, I said wildly, randomly, and he nodded. The light glanced off his head in a way that was fascinating. *What does that pay, now?* he asked, and there was no escaping his well-oiled eyes. When Joan came in I was on my knees, wiping at the whisky I had finally been able to release onto the table and down the front of my dress.

Alone Together

It was the year Mother was bullied into her cruise. *You are a bad example*, Father shouted at her, and snatched her stop-watch away. *Your daughter is full of woman-*

liness, he roared at her so that, upstairs, I blushed for myself. *And you cannot see what is under your nose!* I could imagine Mother looking at what was under her nose, sinking her chin further and further into her chest under Father's voice. When the doctors were called, Father stood over them all like a revenge.

Rest, complete rest, and a change of scene, the doctor said mournfully and pulled at a nostril. *A cruise, for example.* Mother's headaches and indispositions were squeezing her face inwards as if it was straining to turn inside out. The furrow between her eyebrows grew deeper and deeper as the plans were laid. *Pago Pago*, Father said with authority. *You'll love it.*

Well, Lil, Father said when the taxi had borne Mother away among boxes that made it hard for her to wave goodbye. *Well, Lil*, he said, although John was there too. Behind us we heard Alma sniffling. All goodbyes are sad, but Mother among her boxes and trunks might have guessed that Alma was taking advantage of the occasion to allow her nose to become red, her eyes to disappear into damp puffy flesh. No one would ask, *Why are you crying, Alma?* and she would not have to make up any stories about a dead cousin or aunt, and try to pretend it was not because Rob the milkman stood passing the time of day with her among the dustbins but would not offer her anything more.

Well, Lil. It seemed that Father could not stop himself from saying this, and John slid off to his room. *It is just us, now.* We watched the ferry glide across the bay and puff black smoke from its funnel. Mother's stop-watch had been packed carefully away somewhere, but the gilt book lay forgotten in the sun, its cover arching like something in agony. *We still have to see how we manage, Lil*, Father said, and above us a lugubrious note with a head cold wobbled out of John's window. *The food of love*, Father said, and laughed. I noticed again how long and grooved his teeth were.

Mother's postcards reminded us that on other beaches, with water the blue of glass, brown people smiled and put flowers in unlikely places. *Having a wonderful time*, the cards said. *Wish you were here* was written with a different pen, a paler afterthought. Father smiled more than necessary as he propped each one carefully on the mantlepiece. *We are managing nicely, considering*, he would say.

From behind the door of his study I could hear the whirr of the globe spinning and the thwack of Father's palm on America or Turkey as he gave it more speed. Sometimes he wrote fast with a squeaky nib and snickered to himself. At other times the silence was profound and nothing was visible when I looked through the keyhole. *The creative life, Lilian*, he would say through a mouthful of lamb. *We who are creative*. He would chew and swallow. *We artists*, he would say at last, and smile greasily.

I was twenty-one that year and did not know what to expect. *Do not let anyone take advantage of you*, Mother's letters told me. *You are a woman now*, Father said like a threat.

All My Futures

That summer, nights at Rosecroft became harder and harder to bear. Father sat turning the pages of one of his thick books, or was shut in his study with his squeaky nib. Even shut behind his door he filled the house like a smell. *What are you up to, Lilian?* he would demand, appearing suddenly in a doorway if I began to leave the house. When at last he fell asleep in an armchair, sitting up on guard, or in his bed, his snores followed me as I crept out.

Yellow moons rose into the window of my bedroom and lured me out into the night. Grass stuck to my feet in the dew as I made my way down to our beach.

The water drew me like a promise and I rowed and rowed through the soft darkness, thinking of Duncan's freckles and F.J. Stroud's flecked eyes, and wondering just how far Chile was, and what my future held. It became harder and harder each night to turn the old boat and head back to the beach, away from Chile and the future.

Out there in the private night with water making sucking noises at the boat, my body was transformed. I became an envelope of sensation, nothing but skin, as I thought about those men I loved. The boards of the boat were hardly enough to contain so much passion, which seemed about to turn the whole world into a mist of bliss. Finally in my ecstasy, and remembering how Joan's skin repelled water like a feather, I could not resist lowering myself over the stern while the boat lay quietly on the black water. My feet felt the depths as I hung there and the water became an extension of my skin. My body was terribly white and flickered in the black water like a flame. Something began to throb through me and finally it was hard not to let go of the boat and allow any current to toy with my tremulous white body. When I dragged myself back into the boat at last, weak-kneed, mouth ajar on breathlessness, I lay for a long time feeling the salt dry on my skin.

Penetrating Secrets

It was the year of the eclipse, and the prize rams were bigger than they had ever been and some hen had laid an egg of record weight. Father made me look at a photograph of this egg, filling some man's bumpy hand. *The lay of the year*, Father cried. *Can you imagine, Lilian, laying such an egg?*

At the Show these wonders waited to be seen. Father was looking forward to it. Animals were beginning to fascinate him: *The beasts of the field*, he expounded at the table to John and me. *Geldings grow muscles as thick as trees*, he told us, *and a pig has an organ of generation that is curved, and as sharp as a knife*. All these wonders waited at the Show and it was arranged for us to *make up a party*. Father said, *and remember the animal in us*.

But I did not want to see all those congested bulls. Instead, I stayed out on the beach for a whole night and was not in the house in the morning. I had often crept into the house at dawn, feeling my skin glow from another sunrise, but I had never before stayed on the beach until the sun was hot in the sky and the birds became quiet. I was becoming a bold girl, and full of defiance.

I watched from beneath the plumbago, a cramped space now but enough to hide me, as the house awoke and found me gone. *Lilian!* I heard Father roar from room to room, then heard my name sound different as he shouted it from every window, and finally stood on the terrace where Mother's wicker chair stood forgotten. He kicked that mild old chair so that it staggered across the flagstones as if trying to walk, and finally fell, ridiculous, onto its back. *Lilian!* Father bellowed across the water, so I could imagine the commuters on the ferry looking at the lawns and the azaleas, and the houses hidden among trees, and wonder who could be so angry at such an early hour. John was sent to look, too, and I saw Father point around the garden, and straight at my plumbago. When John peered in at me his face was blue in the shade of the flowers, and although he blinked a few times, and licked his lips, he said nothing.

Father was a splendid black figure, as solid as onyx in the sun, in his dark suit, when at last they left. Beside him John seemed shadowy, as though the sunlight almost penetrated him. I was powerful, watching Father stride in his darkness and rage, because for all his darkness and rage he could not find me, could not make me admire the swinging tassels of bulls, or the jars of honey arranged in the shape of a map of Australia.

Someone less cunning might have come out from under the bush then, but no one was more cunning than I. I swelled with the feeling of having made Father foolish, and continued to be cunning, waiting for what I knew would happen next. I heard bees drone and felt the blood stagnate in my legs, but at last I saw Rob come to the back door for Alma. Her boots shone painfully under her white skirt and Rob's smile was as stiff as cheese. I could have told her that this would not last.

When Rob and Alma had left, I continued to squat under my plumbago. The house had never been mine to explore before. It was not something to be done lightly. There was power waiting for me when I took the house into my own hands, and I did not wish to rush or fumble such a delicate matter.

On the hall table a note from Father lay accusingly. *Lilian, I will deal with you on my return. Ensure you are here.* It was signed, *Your father.* I screwed up his note and hid it in the drawer and tried to forget that it existed.

The house was nervous when I went into its shadows at last, still tremulous from all the situations it had held. I took my time and spent as long as necessary in each room. In each one I had to still the frightened air that thundered in my ears by breathing long loud breaths that began to sound like groans. My droning filled each of the downstairs rooms in turn and calmed the envelope of air that clung to each object. When the air relaxed and hung loosely under the moulded ceilings, I sat for a long time on the stair carpet, listening to silence like a symphony. When the house breathed quietly along with my own breaths I climbed the stairs to all the private rooms above.

In Mother's room the shutters had been closed when she left, and the room was wary. My own reflection tried to startle me in a corner, but I was bold and went to her dresser. Her corset of pink satin would hardly have contained even one of my massive thighs, but I could not bear to put it back in its drawer, and hung it over my chest like a carapace. In Mother's mirror my face was shadowed and veiled with tenderness as I watched myself above her armour.

My fingers smoothed that pink satin like a pet as I walked bravely into Father's bedroom. It smelled of paper, and powerfully of starch, although everything in this room seemed limp as if exhausted: the curtains hung in a listless way from their rods, and the bed cover trailed on the floor like something dying. Near the window, a single dead rose seemed to have been in its wall bracket for years.

In this room I could not touch anything, and barely breathed. I had almost left when I remembered boldness, and strode to the wardrobe to jerk it open. Father's suits swung together in the disturbance and tried to frighten me by being alive, but I stared them down until they subsided. Their pockets were slippery and secretive when I slid my hand in. I could not breathe, and the air of the room roared at me, but I felt in every pocket, coming across handkerchiefs and coins, until I was sure those pockets were nothing but cloth. I was becoming reckless and breathing again, feeling Mother's corset swing on my chest as I bent and reached, when in the last pocket of a coat Father never wore I found a photograph. I stared at my own face, which smiled in a dazed way at the camera, caught for once in a moment of brief beauty. The photograph was heavily creased from being folded, so that my mouth was blurred in a way that made me look abandoned. This was a photograph in which the light had been kind for once. I looked like a woman with a future, and my eyes were full of mischief as I stared at where Father was holding the Brownie very steady, frowning hard, pressing the button. The start of a rip on one side of the photograph showed where someone had wanted to destroy it and thought better of it just in time. I slid it back into the darkness of Father's pocket and tiptoed out of the room as if the suits might chase me.

Alma's room did not frighten me, but I was ashamed. Large underwear hung drying from every projection and under the bed her other pair of boots sat side by side, prepared to wait for ever. The tiny mirror above her dresser gave back a pocked and leprous reflection that could have explained all her stony gawkiness. Alma could not have believed that she was less ugly than this glass made her. My face was too big for this scrap of mirror and I had to turn away from the one eye it reflected back at me.

At last I had penetrated every room except Father's study, which I left to last, wondering if the thoughts of violating it would be less frightening if I waited. I studied the door without touching it, standing in the hall, hearing a despairing fly buzz at a window. I could not imagine examining Father's secrets. My palms grew damp at the idea, and when at last I touched the knob I knew that the door was locked, and I was glad. Secure in knowing that, I could rattle the knob and push a shoulder against the door as if I really wanted to get in. The door did not open, of course, and did not even shake in its frame, as if held tight by a weight on the other side, and something dark obscured the keyhole. When I abandoned the room, I did my best to pretend it was not there, breathing quietly behind its door, listening to me, holding air between its walls, and the stiff silence which I had not been able to violate.

But in spite of that obstinate room, I could still enjoy the house. The luxury of an empty house cannot be exaggerated. A beach is very fine, and I have no objection to sharing my privacy with periwinkles and a few sleepy gulls, but a mirror in an empty house is a pleasure like no other.

There were so many things I wanted to do, I hardly knew where to start. Mother's corset had to come off first, but I laid it gently beside me on the floor, and saw in the long mirror how it lay beside me like a small incomplete person as I sat staring at my reflection. At last it became obvious where to start, and once I had started the rest was as easy as a smile. While my breasts eyed me from the mirror, I watched long enough to see the red marks of my underclothes fade from my flesh. Air was like water on my skin and the long mirror held beauty in its frame. Even my back smiled and dimpled.

When I sat on the floor in front of the mirror and spread my legs, the silence became frightened again and roared at me. It filled my ears with thick noise that ebbed and flowed like surf on a distant beach. When I met my own eyes in the mirror I thought I might be about to faint. Was this ecstasy? I filled the rooms with sounds like a storm in treetops, like rivers, like horses galloping, and was preparing for the moment when flesh would be transformed.

But Father could not let me achieve that, and filled the doorway before I could break apart and fly free of my body. All sound was drawn away into the tiles and past the windows. I watched as everything else fled and Father and I were left with each other. The brown buttons of the cardigan that Mother had given him made a small tinny noise like rats' feet as he took it off and let it drop to the floor.

In every room of the house, the air that I had stilled fled, and was replaced by trembling and fearful vibrations. I could hear my voice, a thin reedy cry like something choking and not being rescued. Father said nothing at all, but the sound of his breathing was like a thudding machine in the silence. All around us the house stood shocked, repelling the sounds we made.

My cries carried no further than the carpet of the stairway. The silent rooms would take no part in my struggle, but swallowed the sounds indifferently. *No!* I heard myself cry with a feeble piping sound. *No! No!* The house gave back only silence, and the panting of the desperate machine that was Father.

Telling

Mother was back then, and might have wondered at her corset dangling on the knob of the bathroom door, but was busy giving us pieces of poker-worked wood that said "Voolalu" and coconuts all around. She smiled often now, at last a happy woman who had left all cares behind. *I have done all my duties*, I heard her telling her friends in the parlour. *No one needs anything from me now*. I had seen her take the gilt book and rifle through it wonderingly before dropping it into an empty flower pot on the terrace. *I am as free as a breeze*, she told me with her eyes vague, but seemed to me more like a stagnant puddle. Than a breeze. Somewhere on her cruise she had lost a tooth and her smile now showed the blackness of that missing tooth in the side of her mouth.

I tried to begin. *Mother*, I began, and stopped. I could not start the sentence that would tell her what had happened. My mouth and tongue were someone else's now and even the words that rose into my mind had nothing to do with me. Whatever had happened— and I would not ask myself just what that had been—had happened to a mass of flesh called Lilian, not to me. I cowered in that flesh, my self shrunk to the size of a pea, but still I tried to speak to Mother. Perhaps she would release me from it all, or take me over, or save me. So I began again. The sentence I had to say began with "Father . . ." so I tried to begin. *Father*, I said. Mother turned with the smile that showed the blackness of the lost tooth. *Lilian*. She smiled so that I could not bear to look, and was about to make a joke. *I am not Father, Lilian, I am Mother.* She was pleased with her joke and tapped my knee with a bony finger. *Smile, Lilian, such frowning all the time is bad for your complexion.* She lost interest then, and took out her stop-watch and watched the seconds passing. *So, Lilian, what were you going to say?* she asked at last, but I took the stop-watch from her, feeling it warm like an egg in my hand, and timed the flight of a gull. *I have forgotten*, I said, and it was almost true.

Father laughed at the bulls' pizzles, John told me, *then he gave me money and left me there.* From behind his dull face, John's eyes watched me and almost knew what I had to say, but he did not want to hear me say it. *I did not spend it*, he said with cunning. *Oh no. I have kept it, and am saving up.* Those were more words than John liked all at once, and he took up his tuba and entered its embrace.

I could not make the words come for Aunt Kitty either, but she did not try to joke. *What is it, Lil dear?* she kept asking, and the barley water she gave me was as dark as her own this once, and made me cough. *Drink up, dear, and tell me.* But all the words I had ever learned did not seem enough, or the right ones. *Father*, I gasped into the barley water, slopping it down my chin. *Father*. When I woke up later on the mould-smelling couch, a headache behind my forehead, I still believed that everything mattered, but I now also believed that some things were better forgotten.

Too Much Skin

What is up, Lil? Duncan asked on our beach, and held my knee. *Something is up with you, Lil.* I felt his breath on my neck as he bent close and tried to examine my face by moonlight. My face was not my own and I did not want it examined by one who had been my mate. I did not belong to myself and could not give even my knee to Duncan. *Nothing is up*, I heard my voice say in an unwelcoming way. *There is nothing up.* But his hand on my knee was intolerable and his face was too close to mine. He was about to enter my skin through my face and knee. He could breathe too deeply and scatter me into many fragments. Nothing was keeping me together now.

When I stood up, my knee continued to tingle where his hand had been on it, and my face was numb where he had been so close, looking so hard, watching each pore for its secret. *What is up, Lil?* he asked again, Duncan, that man of few words. But I did not answer, had no story to tell him, but rubbed with a handful of sand at my knee until I felt the skin raw and cold. Duncan, who had been my mate, sat watching the water while I was a housewife on the beach, smoothing the sand where we had disturbed it. I felt tears like gravel in my eyes but I could not cry, or tell Duncan what was up. He stood, and was taller than I was. His chin was manly. *Well, Lil*, he said, and did not try to touch me again. *Better get along back, eh?*

Things were closing down like lights going out. I looked at the skin of my hand in the daylight and it was alien to me. My sturdy feet tramped over grass and dust, carrying a large stranger to whom people spoke, mistaking her for me.

Lil, F.J. Stroud said, and there was a long silence while he blushed. We stood in the draughty gallery underneath the clock tower of the quadrangle while rain poured down beyond the doorway and filled the air with cold and damp. At last he said in a dull voice unlike his own, *Lil, I find I am in love with you.* His voice was dull as if too much practising had jaded the words. *In love*, he said again, and tried to sound more convincing. Around us, cold stone was no help, and puddles were forming around the spikes of our umbrellas. I said nothing, but stood in that stranger's flesh, waiting, and listening to where some gargoyle had snapped off and was sending water cascading down over the doorway. *You are the only person who is real for me*, F.J. Stroud said in a different way, and fumbled until he was holding my hand. *All the others are fictions, and I am, too.* He had never held my hand before, and I could feel his fear. But I was full of fear myself and it was hard not to yell.

Don't, I said, wanting no hand to touch mine, no one to be as close as he was to me. *What, are you betrothed?* F.J. Stroud exclaimed, and jumped backwards as if bitten. *Did that flannelled fool beat me to it?* When I began to cry he cried, too, but I did not want such closeness, or crying together. My tears stopped when I saw how wet his cheeks were, and the way his hands looked so white as he clenched them. *It is not that flannelled fool or anyone*, I said. *It is just me. I cannot bear it.* F.J. Stroud caught at my arm and cried, *Lil, Lil!* and I tried to pull free, cruelly wrenching my arm from him, wanting silence and nobody near. *I will do anything, Lil*, F.J. Stroud shouted so that a man in a mackintosh stared. *And I will have those diamonds soon, remember.* His voice echoed wildly from the stone and was caught in the dark beams arching over us. *Stop crying*, I said, but I whispered and F.J. Stroud did not hear over the rain. *Look at me*, he said, and gripped my elbows so that I could not avoid his blotched wet face. Nothing had ever repelled me as his face so close to mine did then. All faces close are distorted and made hideous with emotion, and it was hard not to panic and flail. I tried to remind myself that this was just F.J. Stroud, whom I knew, who was my friend, who had shown me swans and ripped flowers off their stalks for me, and was not an enraged stranger, too big for me, with a face I could fight, thrust against mine and shouting.

Running Away

It could only be temporary, but it was necessary. *I am going bush*, I told them. *Joan and I are going to collect specimens*. No one asked, *Of what?* and no one knew that Joan was not coming with me. Even her smooth sallow skin would have been more than I could bear. Under a country sky I needed to greet myself alone, like a stranger.

I was eyed as I mounted the bus at Central, but the boys with the wet-looking hair decided that, although I was young and pink, there was something about me to be avoided. They whistled instead, insolently, jeeringly, as my large blue behind laboured up the narrow steps into the bus. I wished then that I was old and immune.

Further north, over the sea, I had heard that the buses were full of brass spittoons into which old men spat red juice. On this bus there were not spittoons, only curling sandwich crusts in brown paper bags, and a ginger beer bottle that rolled backwards and forwards along the floor until the woman behind me stopped it and put it in her basket.

As the bus snarled around sickening bends, northwards, I decided that I would get down only when instinct dictated. It dictated, and I obeyed, in a flat ochre town and I crossed the road unevenly, my bag hitting the back of my knees, to the hotel. The shadow of a lizard was huge on the wall where men in hats stood with beer and stared. I knew that I had guessed right, and stopped in the right place, when I looked out of the window of the room they had given me. I stood wiping my face with a corner of the dampened towel, wiping my face with the word CALEDONIAN and staring out above an expanse of grey tin roof. Beyond that I could see some sheep moving tentatively across a paddock, watched by a man in a hat. *My country, right or wrong*, I told the towel, and changed to go downstairs.

It soon became clear that trousers on young women had not been seen before in this calm town of wide streets. On a young woman of my bulk they silenced everybody. To one man, whose blue eyes were brave enough to meet mine, I said, *It is men like you who are the salt of the earth.* Perhaps it was pompous. He blushed thoroughly so that his angry eyes were sharp flints of blue in his red face. His jowls, where the razor that morning had not been stropped for long enough, became mottled and purple. He shifted the beaded glass of beer to his left hand and hitched up his trousers so that for a moment his genitals bulged through the cloth. He would have liked to hit me, I thought, or perhaps kiss me, but could not do either.

Who do you think you are, young lady? said the publican, safe under his grey hat. *Just who do you think you are?* I told him, *I think I am Boadicea*, and watched him frown. *But in fact I am Lil Singer.* He had no answer and I saw him turn in the doorway, filling it like an outraged cow. Behind him a girl, too young to know better but tall, peered at me until her father's shoulder rose up and herded her away.

From the nearest glass I took a long swallow and gave it back to the hand from which I had taken it. *This is how I became fat*, I lied to the man whose hand it was. He was a comfortable older man with thick veins like vines that threaded the backs of his hands and a face that had once been surprised, perhaps, when his first corpse fell headless at his feet in the trenches, and had never been surprised since. *Which way?* I asked, and he thought slowly, while I watched the stubble grow on his cheek, before he pointed down the dusty road. *Crik's that way.*

I had not often swum in fresh water, the sea had always been my element. This was thin water. It did not cling to my skin or buoy up my body, but let me drop into its still depths like air. The clay of the bank squeezed between my toes like something slippery and good to eat. A duck skidded across the surface and a few reeds bent into the water. I could see nothing of my body in this yellow pool. I could have disappeared from the neck down and been a head like John the Baptist's, floating upright and reproachful on the surface.

The first small boy was no higher than my thigh, and he stared with one finger up a nostril. His stare and snot were pleasant enough companions as I stroked to and fro in the yellow water. But he was joined by bigger boys, whose grey shorts hung below round bellies and whose lizard eyes flickered in contempt. I did not wish to shock them with my bulk and staring nipples, and stayed stroking and stroking under the water.

A bigger boy, whose face came to a point like a badly made puppet, finally yelled, *What are you doing?* and I called back, *I am being wet*, which silenced them all for some time. They shifted from foot to foot, brushed flies away, scratched their armpits. Mainly they stared. When they spoke again, it was with stones. They flung them loosely, not aiming at me, and the splashes freed them to shout again. I did not allow their words to enter my mind. Noise jogged my eardrums, but it was not words. And in any case the stones were forcing me further away. At last I was behind a slime-covered sunken log where small creatures with legs scuttled under the bank as I grasped it. There the stones could no longer reach me and I massaged on my shoulder and neck the tender places that would be purple tomorrow, yellow next week.

I gave them a long time to lose interest and leave. My body became wrinkled like a sultana, my fingers puckered and white, my feet numb. Behind me the bank of the creek rose up, thorny, dense with aggressive bushes on this side. Aborigines know how to insinuate themselves through such bushes but I, with my large white body, soft as a grub, could not. When at last it seemed the boys had all gone, I never wanted to see yellow water again.

I had planned to wait until night would hide me completely, but by now I was hungry and looking forward to the publican's wife's corned beef and cabbage, and thick yellow custard over jam roll. In addition to being hungry, I was too angry now to wait for darkness on this unpleasant bank of slippery clay.

It was a beautiful walk in the gathering mauve dusk. Cockatoos screeched and flapped laboriously across the sunset and Venus twinkled for me alone above a sapling. Crickets became agitated in grass stems but fell silent as I passed. Under my feet the dust at the side of the road was velvet.

I entered the town at nightfall. On the verandah of the CALEDONIAN, men sat on the steps or perched their bottoms on the railing. Yellow light lit up a patch of man here and there, and somewhere inside many men were laughing. When I appeared and stepped up onto the verandah, the silence spread out from me in ripples. As I entered the hallway, someone snickered uncontrollably behind me. It was a young sound which could have belonged to the man with the blush. Perhaps he had seen the large dark mole, like a beauty spot on the cheek of a beauty, on my buttock. I accepted the snicker as a tribute and began to climb the stairs towards my room.

The publican's daughter had swung around the knob of the banister and was half a dozen steps down before she saw me. Her momentum carried her down further before she could stop so that she was close to me when the smile stiffened on her face. Perhaps she had not seen breasts before, or a tuft of springy hair between thighs. Or perhaps it was just the way the angry thieving faces behind me were staring up in lust and outrage. *You will always remember this*, I told her, to fill the silence as I passed, but her eyes were appalled and it was hard to know if she heard or whether she would remember.

I retreated further after that, and walked for days in bush no one else wanted, comparing gum trees. Is any tree like any other? I was finally soothed by the infinite variety of trunks and leaves. On my back I carried a blanket, a billy, bush tucker. It was enough each morning to watch the way the leaves hung like hair from their twigs while the blue smoke of my fire drifted down to the creek and hung there. I hoped for Aborigines, undiscovered perhaps, or at least a secret painted cave, but I found the skeletons of birds, termite mounds, shed snakeskins, and I made do with those. There was a hollow log that could have been a didgeridoo, but although I blew until I saw stars and was nearly sick, I could not create any sound except my own breath whistling through a hollow log.

How I loved so much dry prickle. How I loved all that raucous noise, shrill birds, cicadas that made my head ring when a treeful of them vibrated together, and the heady smell of eucalyptus leaf mould under dew. How full of blue and gold promise those dawns were, when some insistent bird on a branch overhead woke me, or a hot ray of light between leaves that warmed my eyelids. Mornings then were so good I cried, so that goannas and birds blinked at me and tried to drink my tears where they fell. The blue smoke of the breakfast fire floated over the grass between smooth trunks, and the tea in the billy glinted gold. I spent hours reading the scribbles on gum-trunks, and was sometimes within a dream of understanding everything.

The Value of Words

You are no daughter of mine, Father shouted when I came back, thinner and browner from so much bush

tucker and tramping over stones. *No daughter of mine.*
So many kookaburras so early every morning had
taught me how to laugh, so many nights under the
stars that became as familiar as wallpaper had emboldened me. *Then you are a cuckold*, I told Father, and
laughed. *And Mother is a whore.* It was not a word I
had ever heard said, and it did not sound quite right
as I said it, but I did not care. Father's study was very
silent when I had spoken.

Father picked up that belt of Mother's which had not
been used for years, and smacked it lightly on his palm.
You are a disgrace to me, he said, *and to your sex.* He
stammered on the last word and repeated it in a loud
clear way, *Sex, sex.* The belt flapped against his trousers
as he tried to make it snap like a whip. *There is sand on
your skin*, he said, and raised the belt suddenly as if to
strike my face. When his arm was raised, and his cheeks
were flushed with rage, it was suddenly clear that he was
on tiptoe to reach me. *You are reprehensible*, he said,
making me sound like a reptile, but his words did not
conceal his fear. *Bend over, Lilian*, he said quickly, as if
afraid of changing his mind.

Days of watching the sun melt along horizons as it
rose, flattening through the atmosphere before it pulled
itself up and burst free, made it hard to move quickly,
and I did not move quickly, but was gathering myself
to move when Father startled me by flinging the belt
down between us. *Intolerable*, he shouted. *Vile, vile!* I
was turning in my slow way to present my behind to
Father at last, planting my fat legs apart to balance,
when I saw that he had left the room. The belt lay on
the floor in a great silence.

Other Endings

I had not been away long, but my men had changed.
Everyone seemed to feel there was not much time left.

Lil, Duncan said on the beach, *I do not know how to say this*. I did not know how to listen to whatever *this* was. The sand between my toes was still hot from the day, Venus was sliding up into the sky, birds had given up for the day and had handed over to mosquitos. *It is about marriage*, Duncan blurted and I nearly cried out, *But we are mates!* It was what I wanted to say, but I knew that nothing could prevent me hearing what he was about to say, no appeal to mateship would do.

We have been mates a long time, Duncan said. *Haven't we, Lil?* I did not bother to nod, as he was not looking towards me, but at a bobbing shape that was probably a gull asleep on the bay. *We have had a lot of good times*. Duncan held his own ankle tightly, preventing escape. *My mate Lil*. The waves were mocking me, the sand had become sharp. If we could manage without skin, I wondered, would we be happier? I thought about being flayed and tried not to hear Duncan. *Marriage, Lil, we all come to it, it is part of growing up*. Venus twinkled at my despair. *I do not want anything but a mate*, I practised saying to myself while Duncan continued to speak. *A mate is all I want*. Duncan laughed suddenly at his ankle and said, *Joan and I were lucky for a long time, but we have been caught now*. I was staring at that gull, feeling my eyeballs dry in astonishment, and heard him go on calmly, *But we want you to be the bridesmaid, Lil*.

Moments to Remember

I did not want to see Joan again, and see her pointed teeth flash at me, thinking about beef and Duncan and some wild life smelling of horses and half-tamed dogs. I did not wish to see anyone again. Duncan was a stranger now, with his new responsibilities, and a life mapped out. The stone quadrangles were oppressive with so many individual futures and plans. I had no future, no plans, I had nothing but the present and a memory of the smell of eucalyptus leaf mould under dew. The weight of so many individuals was unbearable, their eyes monstrous as they watched me walk towards them, their voices the assertive cries of alien creatures. I did not go back to those buttresses of stone and the men in tweed, and I hoped to escape a future, but Duncan found me, and F.J. Stroud did at last, too.

I waited for him, as he had made me agree, in the black shade of a Moreton Bay fig that had sent out deep spines of dusty bark over the grass. It was a tree that drank light like a pocket. In the sun at a distance three small girls with dirty faces threw sand at each other beneath the monkey bars and around my feet ants ran drunkenly from one squashed fig to another. I went on waiting for F.J. Stroud although I did not want to see him, but there was no point in leaving either, or in doing anything in particular.

Desperate convicts ate them, F.J. Stroud said, suddenly appearing, and tripping over a root, holding out a fig to me. *Are you that desperate?* When I did not reply, but only shifted my bulk on the grass, he smacked his hands together with a noise that made me jump, and held them out to show me the squashed fig that covered his palms like a birthmark.

And now, he said, and sat beside me. It was hard to remember how his face had been hideous with tears and pleas. Today he was as smooth as butter. *You had something to say?* he asked in a chilling way. *Something you wished to impart?* The effort of making my thick lips and tongue move was almost too great but I brought out at last. *No, it was you*, and then, as silence fell again, continued in a rush. *Who had something to say. To me. You said.* F.J. Stroud smiled neatly to himself, swinging a foot to and fro and watching it. *Did I? Perhaps, my dear, you are mistaken.* His foot stopped swinging and he cracked his knuckles one by one in the silence between us.

I am going to tell the truth now, he said suddenly, in an unsteady high voice. *This time it is the truth*. There was a long silence in which I watched the three little girls, who were sitting on the grass now, picking at the scabs on their knees. F.J. Stroud said suddenly, and rather loudly, *I have nothing*. He coughed and picked a fleck of fig off his palm. *That is not true either, you see*, he said crossly. *I have some things*. There was another long silence in which I began to be bored. The three little girls were moving closer to us across the grass. After a large sigh, F.J. Stroud held up his stained hand and bent down the fingers one by one as he spoke. *My father is not in diamonds*, he said. *Or anything. He is just dead, that is all, and I have never been on a horse*. He was going on and I was interested at last, but the three little girls were in front of us now and one said in a plain conversational voice, *Ask her to marry you*. Behind her the other giggled, and she slapped at one without looking. *Go on*, she said bossily, *ask her to marry you*. Her bare feet were planted in the grass as if she was prepared to wait for hours. F.J. Stroud was staring away past the palm trees and the grass, to where blue water twinkled, like a man alone with his thoughts. Finally, he said, *This isle is full of noise*, and a fig fell loudly through the leaves above us. He said again, *I said, this isle is full of noise, or noises. Go away, little girl*.

From deep in my chest, under the flesh that imprisoned me, I felt welling up a gigantic yawn that twisted my face and brought tears to my eyes. Trying to keep the yawn in, I must have looked congested and strange, and the little girl hopped from one foot to the other. *Kiss her, then*, she shrieked. *Go on, kiss her*. F.J. Stroud stood up, rammed his hands into his pockets so hard I heard stitches give, and kicked at a fig on the ground. When he turned to me again I saw a large tear hanging under one eye. I began to gather myself to stand up, even touch him, perhaps, if I could, or at least help him walk away from this situation, but he brushed my hand away. *All things do conspire against me*, he said, then went on in a different voice, *That's not Shakespeare, I just made it up.* He stared at me as closely as if counting my pores and I was frightened. The tear had been real, like those of my own that goannas had tried.

Creaking, F.J. Stroud knelt in front of me. *Will you marry me?* he asked, and the little girls stared. His hand splayed towards mine and grasped it clumsily. *Will you marry me?* he asked again, and it sounded horribly sincere. I sat in my skin, watching, and it seemed that nothing could put an end to all this. At last F.J. Stroud dropped my hand and looked down at his knees. *There's fig on my pants*, he said, and cackled. When he stood up, pieces of fig fell around his feet and one of the little girls tittered. I was stuck to the ground and could not help anyone and as I watched I saw F.J. Stroud put himself back together again from the fragments into which he had broken. *Hell is empty*, he said to the park in general, *and all the devils are here. I'm going home.*

The sight of a young woman releasing slippery tears held the interest of the little girls for a few minutes but when they had watched for a while and heard my ugly gulpings, they began to pick their noses, and after a while they went away and left me alone with my glorious past.

Running Wild

My feet have always been broad. *Nigger's feet*, Father said suddenly one day, seeing them up on a chair, and looked shocked. Later he felt it necessary to apologise. *It just slipped out, Lilian. We are all human.* His smile was tortured.

Those feet became broader and stronger now, carrying me out of the house at night to find something I had lost. The weight of Rosecroft was too heavy on those summer nights, and I was impatient to escape from it, and had to pretend to be sleepy, and go to my room yawning. The route out the window, from ledge to vine, from verandah roof to drainpipe, was awkward. The size of my thighs left no room for mistakes; the crash I would have made, falling, left no margin for faintness of heart. Under moonlight the lawns looked like seas. Trees sailed from shadow to shadow and took strides when the moon slid behind a cloud. There were no owls, but many hoarse crickets.

As soon as Rosecroft's high fence was behind me I began to run. My shoes were loud on the stones of the road, and panting burned in and out of my chest. With each year that had passed since my birth, another rash of houses had encroached on the bush of the headland. Now it was necessary to pass endless neat lawns, red brick fences, windows with venetian blinds. Where the road ran out of bitumen and finally tapered away into a rough track through bush, there were old mattresses now, iron drums, wheels that would never roll again, beer bottles. I would have liked to close my eyes, but needed them to steer me through. *It is progress*, John said when I complained. *I welcome progress*. I did not, and forced my lumbering body at a run past so much progress, until at last only bush stood amazed and silent at my noisy breathing. The track became less and less certain as it wandered out along the headland, and I grew more and more comfortable as it became harder to imagine that anyone had been here before. Roads by moonlight unfolded like a dry snakeskin and the fine dust was damped by dew. There was a rock at a certain point, a rock like a face, with a fern sprouting from a nostril, and when this rock was behind me I felt safe enough to hum. There had never been anyone but myself here on this road between scrub. It wandered more and more like a tune someone was making up from moment to moment, and bulged with boulders and roots. Harbour teased in glimpses of shining water between bushes, moonlight misled with shadows, branches looked alive. I could have been someone slim and black, noiseless as water over stone, breathing the cool air. I could have been someone slim and glossy, in love, hurrying to my love.

Finally I left that track and plunged down through cut grass and prickles until I reached the beach. From there I could look back and see the dark blob of Rosecroft across the water, where a light burned until late in Father's room. I sat on the flat rock with the buttock-shaped depression and watched that feeble light flickering on all night, until at last it winked out. Then I could sigh and lie back, feeling cool sand in my hair, and watch the stars swinging low over me, until finally I was released from my flesh into dreams.

My broad feet and thick ankles carried me many miles at night, and in the end so much shoe leather drew attention to itself. *It is the way I walk*, I had to say when Father shook the bill from the shoemaker in his hand. *I walk heavily*. Father savaged the leg of lamb with the carving knife until the blade struck bone. *I cannot be expected*, he began, but lost interest.

I could not be sure whether Father knew that I escaped at night, and did not want to be betrayed by the worn soles of my shoes. I could not put an end to those long walks by moonlight, either. Nature, which I watched so closely suggested what should be done.

My feet hardened quickly. Father said no more about shoe bills, and although I could never be some slim and glossy black person, eyes alone shining in the moonlight or my teeth gleaming in a grin, my feet could pad as silently as theirs over stones and spikes. My feet renewed themselves endlessly. Such hide was enviable. I wondered if it could be encouraged to form all over a body such as mine, that had such need of armour.

The Invention of the Wheel

Rob with the thick ugly horse that knew where to stop, dropping a steaming pile while Rob jingled from house to house with his cans, Rob had seen me walking miles. *Why, Miss Singer*, he said calmly when in the pearly dawn his horse clattered along the same road that brought me back from my beach. *Fine morning, Miss Singer*. His milk was not more placid than his brown face. *Saving your shoe leather, are you?* he said, and then I knew that he had spoken to Alma. Alma would have stood, red hands twisted in her apron, and listened to Father fling the bill across the room, smack the new soles of my shoes together so hard that dust flew out from between them, and shout until even John would hear and begin to blink. Rob's horse stopped and lowered its head to the dust, tickling its muzzle hairs against the fine powder of the road, while I realised that Rob had spoken to Alma. Rob stared at me, but I could frame no way to say, *Keep my secret*. I would have preferred no one to know anything.

The horse relieved itself with a loud liquid sound. Yellow urine balled in the dust, ran and shone in drops like escaped mercury. *All right*, Rob finally said when all the noises had stopped. A bird warbled in a liquid way from a tree. *She'll be right as rain*. He jerked the reins and the horse moved forward joint by joint and I had not been able to say, *Keep my secret*.

Next time he passed me, on some other pearly morning, he made a noise to the horse that made it stop, and I stopped, too, and watched while he moved milk cans and tugged at something in his cart.

The bicycle had been black before it had been painted white and the effect now was like the bark of a gum. A wheel was twisted, a pedal gone, the saddle a skeleton of metal. *Might be too far gone*, Rob said, *but you could give her a burl*. He wiped his big hand over his face, tweaked at his nose, coughed. *Just between you and me*, he said, and slapped the reins over the horse's back.

Finally the bicycle rolled. I had hit the wheel with a hammer until it was close to round again, had stolen from Mother's purse for tyres. The blue felt hat that Mother had always told me had a *softening effect on* my unpromising face, made an adequate saddle. The blue felt became warm as I pedalled slowly mile after mile. Father did not know that it was now in my power to go where I pleased, and Mother would only have nodded and nodded if I had told her. John had no envy, but when I had cried for lack of a pedal, he had brought me one the next day. *That Rick*, he said in his adenoidal way. *That Rick has everything he needs.*

The Wildness of John

John also ran barefoot in the dew across the lawn while the sun rose. But we did not run wild together.

John had abandoned his glasses after breaking so many pairs, and had become a purblind, blank-faced boy. He was a boy who could be heard breathing when everyone was quiet, but no one could guess his thoughts. *Now that you are a man*, Father often began by saying, John stared with large dim eyes, smiling a dim smile, and Father would shift on his chair like something on a leash. *Now that you are a man you will understand me*, Father said loudly, but John seemed to understand nothing.

At night I saw his shadow on the lawn. Crossing from the shadow of the roof into moonlit grass, I could see something beside a chimney that was not a chimney. *Are you planning to fly?* I asked one day when something had made me cruel. *Are you planning to be Icarus, or God?* But cruelty did not interest John. *No*, he said, and said no more, but if I remembered to glance up at the roof when I left the house, leaving another shred of nightdress on the sharp corner of the gutter, I would see him standing, face to the moon as it tanned his cheeks, swaying, one hand on the chimney, the other conducting an orchestra of thousands. Those weak eyes, even if they had not been closed in the rush of music, would not have been able to make out the foreshortened stubby figure of his sister trudging over moonlight into the bush.

At other times on those pale summer nights, when the sky had no colour at all, or the colour of wood-smoke, John ran in the opposite direction from me, towards the train line, where powerful black metal made loud noises. *It is the future*, he explained, and could not wait. *It will be quite different, then*. He bided his time, and began to shave his downy upper lip in secret so that he would be able to hide behind a moustache as soon as possible. At dawn when I crept into the house I heard sneeze after muffled sneeze from his room, and saw how serene and spent he was over breakfast.

Many a girl on early death has been praised into an angel, but that was not my problem. There was never any possibility of early death for me. Plain health ran out of every pore. So much walking, so many heavy-pedalled miles through moonlight, seemed to make me immune to death. *Have you ever wished you were dead?* John asked, and I could not say *Yes*. His face was just beginning to look like a man's, and he had grown tall, but stopped. *I would like to be dead*, he said once. *Or at least short*. But I could not wish for anything so definite. I carried my bulk around with me like someone else's suitcase full of unknown things, and I did not want to die just yet. To John I could say only, *It will not always be like this*.

Threats

Only those of us who know dawns know the thick fug of houses before anyone is awake. From every room come stale smells of sleep and warm sheets, grease that has gone cold in the kitchen, a tap that has been dripping sadly all night. Things creak in a bored way and there is not enough air.

Father bided his time. He was listening now when I crept into the house. Sometimes I tiptoed past his room and knew that he was lying there awake, his hands folded over his stomach as if keeping something in. At other times he stood at the top of the stairs in his striped pyjamas and shouted, *Lilian, I will not have it*. I was running wild, but I was too much for him. *You are a slut, Lilian. And you are running wild, and I will not have it*. He shouted, and went on shouting until everyone was awake and staring.

I did not bother to laugh, but I did not stop running wild. Dogs barked steadily as I squeaked along bitumen towards my headland. In each house that I passed, another animal began to warn me off. *Vile mongrels!* I yelled sometimes, or, *Curs! Reprehensible curs!* When I stopped the bicycle to hurl a stone or two they became hysterical. Men in shirtsleeves and women with curling pins in their hair came to their doors and windows, sometimes to the gate, to stare. But the sight of the fat girl forcing a creaking bicycle along their street was enough to silence them all.

Lilian, you do not understand. If you will not stop this—there are complaints—I will have to take action. I did not ask, *What action?* but Father, playing with the acorn on the blind, seemed to hear the question. *There are appropriate actions*, he said, and it was a threat.

I did not send you to the university to have you run wild, he shouted when everyone was listening at dinner. *I am sick and tired of it, I have paid good money and*

173

I am nauseated. Those heavy, shiny books, for which he had paid so much good money, sat on my table unopened now from week to week. I knew that the men in tweed and the thick books had nothing to teach me that I wanted to know. The pencils in the pencil case that Mother had embroidered were still sharp and new. There had never been much that seemed worth making a note of. *I know what you are up to at night, Lilian.* Father's moustache twinkled where he had been sucking at it. *And I am warning you I will not tolerate it.*

The End of One Life

There was no point now in even pretending that I was going each day to listen to the men in tweed. Those stone quadrangles made me cry, too, in unexpected places, and I did not like the way people stopped, stared, sometimes laughed aloud at the sight of the fat girl running her hand over a block of stone in the wall and crying. Too many corners of the university brought tears to my eyes, and I seemed to see them everywhere. Duncan and Joan and F.J. Stroud, and my tongue became thick in my mouth, trying to talk to them. They all seemed very far away as I stood waiting for them to stop talking to me and leave. I could not meet their eyes, and they seemed all eyes. Their hands reached out for me and I drew back, and even their hands seemed all eyes. I knew how truly F.J. Stroud loved me when I saw him, in his shabby black, speaking seriously to Duncan. F.J. Stroud's fist beat into his palm as he made a point, and when he jabbed Duncan in the chest, asking something over and over, Duncan pulled back, but F.J. Stroud followed. I watched Duncan shaking his head and denying, but he did not become angry although F.J. Stroud came closer and closer, until from where I stood watching it seemed that they were hugging each other. I left them and cried more, knowing how truly I had been loved.

Father laughed at F.J. Stroud when he came to ask for my hand. *She is unbalanced*, I heard Father say, and laugh. I continued to sit on the stairs and heard it all. *No one can marry a mad girl*, Father said. *And she is unruly, she is running wild*. F.J. Stroud said something I did not hear, and Father exclaimed vigorously, *By Jove, boy, she is rutting every night like a cat in heat*, and F.J. Stroud left soon after that. Although he held my wrist tight, and pulled at me as I sat on the stairs, I stiffened my ankles like an obstinate cow and would not go with him. When he was gone the hall was very silent. I knew I would not see him again.

It was a house full of tears. I heard Alma crying and saw how red-eyed she was, handling the potatoes. She would have refused any suitor now.

When I left the house in the mornings I did not bother to carry those shiny books under my arms, or only if I needed money. I became known to those men in shops where they gave me a pound or two in exchange for one of those books, and they laughed with me. *I know it all*, I explained while they waited, for the fat girl was often good for a laugh. *I do not need books*, I announced loudly so that other customers stared. *My brain is in direct communication with a higher power*. They laughed, but it was true. I did not care if they believed me, and they did not. I liked their stares, liked the way they laughed. These men in grey dustcoats behind their counters, these other men with their hats on, thumbing through old books—these people stared and laughed and thought they were stronger than I was, but I knew better, knew that it was I who was making them laugh and giving them a story to tell their wives that night. I put my pound in my pocket and walked the streets, inventing things to say to keep them laughing. I tried them out on anyone in the street, and although they did not often laugh, it was satisfying to see the alarm on the faces, trying to remain polite while being alarmed, and visibly hoping I would not follow them home, or hug them to death in the middle of Elizabeth Street.

Pictures of Lives

In the darkness of the picture theatres I could live the rich life I had always had in mind. Men with swimming eyes and thin moustaches gestured and strode, and I could forget that I was Lil who had lost the knack of living, and for a while be a man with a thin moustache or someone on a horse, or even a tremulous girl in a hat with flowers and a mouth like a rose.

But before the lights went down I remained Lil and was beginning to love defiance and being the centre of almost any kind of attention. I swelled then so that my being filled very cell of my bulk. I was huge, colossal, magnificent, when all the heads had turned, everyone was staring, a few were shouting at me, and the manager was hurrying down the aisle towards me. I belonged to myself then, and I loved the glare of public life.

If it had not been someone else's National Anthem playing when the red plush curtain jerked apart, I might not have minded, but I did not fancy foreign bombast. Beside me a wooden old man levered himself out of his seat and stood shakily to attention. He glanced at me and, when it became obvious that I did not intend to stand for this music, he jabbed my shoulder with a bony old forefinger. *The Anthem, young lady*, he said in a hoarse whisper, but I sat on, huge in my seat and unmoving. The old man was remembering parade grounds now, where boots had trampled the dew and kookaburras did not dare to laugh. *Stand up, stand up, girl*, he cried so that people turned to stare. *Show some respect, girlie*, he cried, and grunted as he tried to raise his stick at me, but failed because it had become entangled in the legs of the seats, and he began to pant as all around us, people were sitting down again and putting patriotism behind them. *Down in front*, someone began to call. *Down there!* The old man finally freed his stick with a jerk that made him stagger and in the darkness stumbled out between the seats. I sat on stolidly and laughed louder than anyone when a villain was unexpectedly hosed from behind. It gave me satisfaction to think of that old man taking his revenge home. He might spend the evening composing in quivery pale-blue ink, an indignant letter to some Editor or other: *Dear Sir*, and use his old tongue, pale like something overcooked, to stick on a stamp. In his rage he might even err so that His Majesty would stand on his head, and that would make him angrier still. He would open his paper so eagerly for the next few weeks that he would rip the Foreign News page one day, Rural Matters the next. His sad old letter, full of hollow fury, would never appear, but he would tell the story to his friends at the Mitre in such a way that this would not be apparent, so that when at last he would *pass on to the higher service* he would be remembered as *Old Jerry who wrote to the papers that time*. I sat on in the darkness, laughing and crying as it seemed appropriate, and could hardly bear to leave my seat and go home, it was so tight and warm there in the darkness.

Up Father's Sleeve

I should have seen that Father was waiting for his moment, but I did not. *I did not send you to the university to have you run wild*, Father said, but did not sound as if he cared much. He was gathering evidence, and was becoming silent on his feet in the

177

house, so that more than once, when I was conducting a conversation with myself, I looked around and found Father watching and smirking. *Eloquence, Lilian*, he would exclaim. *Ah, what a future you have as a statesman!* he would shout at me, and laugh so that it hurt my ears. *Perhaps you are thinking of becoming Napoleon, are you, Lilian?* he cried, and laughed to see me flinch.

They were waiting for me when my hair still held the dawn. Father was fully dressed in spite of the early hour and his boots were as black and shiny as spiders as he stood on the front step, waiting for me. If I had turned back then, gone back to the beach, lived on gull eggs and kelp, I would never have known what there is to know about the nature of man.

There was a lot of smiling going on on either side of Father, where two men in black jackets stood showing their teeth at me as I walked up the driveway. Mother was standing in her dressing-gown, confused by these smiling men greeting her daughter and by Father appearing at this hour. *Lilian,* she hissed at me, *get them away quickly, the paper will arrive any minute* and smiled and nodded, and winked at me, as the smiling men took my elbows and walked me to their car. Mother nodded and waved, and Father withdrew into the house and did not wait to see me driven off. It happened very quickly and I did not struggle with the silent smiling men, because I was confident that nothing could be done to me that I did not wish. For this moment, it was something like an adventure to be sitting between these men driving through the bird calls I knew so well. We passed John, hurrying back to the house, and I tried to lean over one of the men to wave, and called out, *John, John, they are taking me away!* so he could share the fun.

It was a surprise to me how quickly the smiling men had me crushed back against the leather of the seat. *It is my brother*, I tried to explain, but they were leaving me no air to speak with. The fun was crushed out of me in that moment and a hot fear began in my heart. This was not an adventure, I saw suddenly. This was a trap, and from one moment to the next, unknowing, I had become a prisoner. I saw that the smiling men had stopped smiling now, and looked as if made of stone or metals.

I caught a last glimpse of John watching the car as it passed him, but I knew he could not see me, and I was helpless, pinned against the springs, and knew that I could not hope to enjoy the next part of my life.

3

A WOMAN

Behind the Walls

Days in the institution were all the same colour and time's flow was sluggish. I could watch my cheeks becoming pasty with institution food and was forced to submit to haircuts once a month. The month arrived when I could see that the last of the hair I had entered with was being snipped off by Jewel, who had been a beautician up at the Cross, and palm reader part-time, before becoming the Blessed Virgin Mary.

They told me I was an exhibitionist. *Psycho-pathological*, they told each other, and even Jewel screeched at me when she had stopped being the Blessed Virgin Mary for a moment, and gone back to being Jewel from the Cross, *Your trouble, Lil, is you want to hog the whole show.*

Jewel knew a thing or two, and she became a friend behind these walls. She was young, and confided in me as in a mother, and I enjoyed watching her long eyes flicker over her thoughts as she put her story together. *I have been fucked by God, see*, she told me on the grass beside the wall. *They are scared because I am going to have God come out of me.* Jewel's strong crimped hair framed her plain face like a clinging animal, and her lips shook with the urgency of her tale. *They had to shut me up because I am going to be God's mum, see.* She smiled and simpered a simper like a tic. *It was that bitch of a mother of mine,* she explained further. *She wanted God to fuck her, too.*

As a student of life I recognised that life was going on behind our high walls, too. Father could stop me running wild but he would not stop me being alive and enjoying whatever was to be enjoyed.

The doctors did not trouble me much and Riser the head nurse was someone it was fun to imitate behind his back, the way he hit us over the head at mealtimes when we slobbered or would not eat, and the way his round buttocks stuck out when he became shrill at us. *You are a bloody moron,* he shouted at Esther, who was seeing if you could eat through your ear, *a bloody pea-brain, you are,* and I stuck out my bottom the way he was doing, and perched my hands on my hips as he did. Then rude May, who piddled wherever she happened to be, pointed at me and laughed with a mouthful of creamed corn so that she began to choke, and Riser had to yell, *Slap her on the bloody back,* and the new nurse belted May on the back until she stopped laughing and the creamed corn dribbled down the front of her dress. *You, Lil, no need to try your bloody smartness with me,* Riser threatened, and whacked the iron spoon into his palm. I looked as stupid and moon-faced as I could, the way I did for the doctors when they asked me questions.

Days were boring, full of basketmaking and walking up and down the same dull strips of overused grass. Everything here was undersized, overused, tired from so much madness and boredom. I watched the tops of trees over the high brick wall, but it was not the same as watching trees on the headland. But I was in the loony-bin for long enough to see one of those trees

flame orange like a tree of fire year after year, and fill
with parakeets that swung from branch to orange
branch, pecking their way all over this miraculous
burning tree.

Long Dark Nights

There were times when confusion overwhelmed me.
Frightening sobs tore themselves up from deep in my
chest where my heart was, and I could not see anything
but my life passing in anguish. On those days I rocked
from side to side with my pain. It tasted of salt and
shame, the loneliness that ate away at me, that cut like
a knife when I thought of Father, straddling the world
with his muscular legs. There was a space in my vision
of the world that Father filled and blocked like a great
rock at the mouth of a cave, and behind that rock,
locked in, I whimpered and shrieked for something I
longed for and would never have.

When these passions overtook me I was left alone,
even Jewel leaving plenty of space around me as she
walked up and down showing off her belly. That made
me all the more desperate, because the thing I longed
for, and seemed further and further from finding, had
something to do with the touch of another spirit
against my own. I shrieked louder and louder, locked
into my lonely self, but could not make anyone hear,
none of these faces here, creased with their own tur-
moil, or falsely serene from whatever consolation they
were inventing for themselves.

None of these faces could hear my cries for help,
and even when I summoned up the faces of others in
my mind, those who might have been able to come
close to me, they stayed at a distance, whispering and
pale like the shades of the dead. Mother nodded and
smiled her vague unlistening smile, fingering her pearls
and thinking about ferries, John's pain was even greater

than my own, and could not be transformed into consolation, and Alma was too sad to bear. The image of her hopeful plain face came to me in my tears, and I began to clutch at myself, to rip that unbearable image of sadness out of my mind's eye, until Riser would come over with an assistant and the vest, and threaten, and many times even the threat of the vest was less powerful than my pain. On those occasions I spent the rest of the day wailing and rocking, locked in the stiff grey canvas as I was locked in myself.

There were times when, locked in the canvas or locked for the afternoon in the room where the walls swallowed my voice, I could console myself by inventing works of great poetry. I amazed myself at such times by the way the words poured out of my mouth with such ease, and my mind created them so effortlessly it seemed they had always been there. *I am a great poet*, I would tell Riser when he came to see how I was getting on, and if I was feeling jubilant at my genius, I would let him in on the secret. *I am Shakespeare, Riser*, I would confide, and was not hurt when his hard laugh filled this small padded room, because I knew that it was the lot of genius to suffer.

Love and Marriage

I was growing used to expecting little from other people and their faces, full of themselves, and was becoming my own admirer. *Lil, you are not lovely, but I love you*, I told my hand, turning it over and over in front of me. *Anyone can be lovely, but you are rare.* In my boredom, in the hot droning days of summer, I decided I was enough in love to marry myself, and twisted a piece of silver paper from someone's cigarette around my finger, and I could turn my hand in front of me as I had seen girls do when they wanted their diamonds to sparkle, and admire the evidence of love.

When love was not enough, there was always fighting. Jewel watched and cheered me on and grunted along with me while Ruby and I strained against each other. Ruby was a big woman and I could take her on without being afraid of breaking something. *By Jove, Lil, by Jove*, she panted as we struggled together. *By Jove, but you are strong, Lil*. I felt the heat of her body next to mine, smelt her sweat, felt the slipperiness as my palm slid over her skin, holding her tightly. She sighed in my ear as I got my arms around her and squeezed, but when she sagged against me, moaning, and gave up, I had to push her away so we could start again, and pull and strain at each other's limbs until we were again locked together, breast to breast. Jewel panted with us, but would not join in, protecting her belly with her hands and becoming solemn. *But I have got God inside me, Lil, and cannot fight.*

Stone and Sky

As I had come to know the stars, all those nights out on the headland, I came to know sun and shadow in the loony-bin. I lay for hours in the interminable afternoons with my feet in the sun, the rest of me in the thick shade of the wall, and watched my feet turn brown. It amused me to smuggle a circle of orange peel the size of a sixpence out of the dining room and to give myself a white untanned circle on the front of each foot. *I am war wounded*, I practised saying, and here, where everyone muttered as they strolled and lay, I could say it as often as I liked. *I have been shot through the feet. I am a person wounded in war*. It gave me great satisfaction to think of myself that way, for indeed I had been shot through the feet, and could no longer move around, and had indeed been wounded in a war.

Lying like this gave me an opportunity to study the sky in a way it had never occurred to me to do before, and sometimes I became so lost in its blue, so filled with its space, that I forgot, and the shadow of the wall consumed my feet so that I lay stretched out ridiculously in deep shade, a mad woman with circles of orange peel on her feet. That blue entranced me if I stared long enough, and although there were days when I was impatient, and said, *Yes, yes, sky, I have seen plenty of you before*, the sky succeeded every time in drawing me up into its thoughtless blue, in which nothing could possibly matter for very long.

There were other things to examine, too, during endless afternoons full of cicadas. Sunlight became a friend that could always surprise me, and the stones and bricks of the wall were endlessly interesting in the way they held the light or filled with shadow. There were times when sunlight could lie in just the right way along the side of a square of stone in the wall, and penetrate that hard stone so that it became transparent, so anyone could see that this was a living thing, too, a family of crystals that could catch the light when they chose and make it break up the way a diamond could. *Lil, they will not let you out if they catch you talking to the blooming wall*, Jewel, who knew a thing or two, warned me when she was not being the Blessed Virgin Mary. But I had seen pictures of rows of people talking to a wall not unlike this one, serious men in hats and dark suits, and the sky that I had seen above that wall was of the same endlessly calming blue as this sky of ours, over our wall. *There is only one sky*, I reminded Jewel. *It is the only thing we need only one of*. I could see that Jewel was about to become the Blessed Virgin Mary and would probably spend the evening in the vest, because the Blessed Virgin Mary always became upset at the way her halo was kept from her, and even the mistress of God had to be restrained sometimes from forcing a spoon down her own throat.

But I wanted Jewel to share what I felt about that blue, this sunlight, this stone, and asked her, *Can you think of anything else, besides the sky, that we only need one of?* When she continued to blink and grimace in the way she did before becoming the Blessed Virgin Mary, I took her by the elbow and made her look at the stone. *Listen*, I told her. *They are speaking to us, do you hear?* But Jewel kicked at the wall so that crystals fell away, and was starting to grunt and pant with the stress of being the Blessed Virgin Mary. *It cannot be destroyed*, I told her, even though she was starting to shout, and become dangerously red in the face. *We can crush them, but they can never cease to be.* By this time they were coming across the grass with the vest and I picked up one or two crumbs of stone that lay on the ground and moved away with them in my hand, because there was nothing more I could do for anyone, be it Jewel or the Blessed Virgin Mary, if she did not want to be consoled by the endless life of things.

Feeding the Animals

When Father came to visit, or taunt me, in the loony-bin, I could only copy Edith, who was like plasticine and would stay in whatever arrangement you put her. I sat, or slumped, on my chair while Father's voice filled the small visitors' room with authority. It was easy to see how sane he was when he asked me loudly about the food and how often the sheets were changed, using only loud simple words as if I had lost my vocabulary as well as my mind.

I lost everything with Father and became a collection of cells held together in an envelope of skin, propped upright in a chair. During those visits I did my best to become stone, or sky, or anything that could go on living its own silent life when everyone thought it was dead. Father seemed to have vanquished me, but I knew I was biding my time. *I am biding my time*, I said to myself behind my impermeable envelope of skin, the same way I had consoled myself with the thought that *there is too much flesh for him now*, years before. I knew that I had a head start on Father, that I was young and strong with years of nourishment and walking, while he was old, or would be soon, and was weakened, under that brittle carapace of his, by all his underground passions.

Mother did not come to visit me in the loony-bin. *Your mother is a trifle indisposed*, Father boomed. I could see him believing his story as he invented it. *Your mother has been affected by the heat, and is gathering her strength*. I was not a satisfactory listener for his story, sitting so placidly on my chair, and I watched him invent more and more outlandish details. *Your mother has taken up epistemology*, Father said and waited for me to react. *Your mother is thinking of taking the veil. Your mother is becoming fluent in Swahili*. I continued to sit, so that Father finally hissed, *You are like a cow, Lilian, sitting fat-uddered on that chair*. While he glared I made up my own versions of Mother from what I had seen, and soothed myself while Father's voice brayed on, soothed myself remembering the gold on the edge of Mother's little notebook and the way her hair blew in wisps around her face, forgotten, if the ferry looked as if it might break its own record across the bay or if the right number of gulls was in the sky at the same moment.

My Other Visitor

My brother John had not grown up to have a twelve-piece brass band of his own. He had grown up to be a stranger who sifted the ruins of lives and houses and looked for things that might mean something. It was a job in which he could be silent, as he preferred, a lot of the time, and when he questioned the relatives or the owner of the burned house or the wrecked car, his silences and his closed indifferent face often led people to make confessions they did not intend. *They want me to care*, John had explained on one of his visits. *I have given it some thought, and I feel I am right*. His eyes were far away behind the thick lenses and the dark frames, and his smooth face expressed nothing. I had nothing to confess, but it was almost tempting to invent something to make his face listen. *They want me to care*, John said again, *so they will say anything, even the truth*. John was a loyal brother, although he could not care about things, and brought me a chocolate cake in a box once a month when he visited.

For a while I pretended to Jewel and the others that he was *my sweetheart*, and basked in their envy, but Esther, who was too clever for her own good, had asked me one day while I was busy eating, and not thinking of anything but the next mouthful, *What is his name, Lil, that cake man, John who?* and through a mouthful of potato I said *John Singer, of course*, before I realised. They all thumped me and pulled my hair until I nearly brought up my potato, and Riser had to bang some heads with a spoon.

John was a loyal brother. He sat with me for an hour or two once a month, and told me about fires and unlikely deaths. He cared about the truths of these obscure situations, and cared about playing his tuba with the Salvation Army, but that seemed to be all. At the end of his visit each time he touched my shoulder but did not kiss or embrace me. *Keep well, Lil*, he said, and walked away down the path, skirting Esther, who had decided he could be her beau, since he was my brother, and made rubbery kissing noises at him until he reached the gate. Those cakes filled their boxes, oozed cream, were sickening with so much icing and jam. All John's buried love surfaced in those gaudy cakes.

The First Goodbye

I had been primping myself behind the wash-house when they came to find me. As my hair dried in the sun I wound it around my finger and wondered if I could have ringlets. Without a mirror it is possible to be anyone and for the moment I was Ursula, with smooth brown ringlets and a smile that enchanted. I sat behind the shed on a box, with my ankles crossed as Mother had taught me, and waited for my prince. *There will be someone for you, one day*, Mother had told me over and over, because she was a kind woman and always hopeful of a miracle. Feeling my hair glossy around my finger in the sun, I had to let a tear or two slide for the way hope was unquenchable in some hearts, so I was crying, and thinking of Mother when they came to find me. They took me into the office where their white soles squeaked on the lino at every step, and squeaked me over to a chair. *You have a sit-down there*, they said, and fussed so that I knew something was up and began to cry again, and my smooth curls would not comfort me in this cold room that smelled of floor wax.

They tried to break it to me gently. I can see that now, but I sat with tears already drying on my face and did not understand, while they spoke to me of *angels* and *the higher service*. Their voices became more penetrating as I continued to be stupid, and rang in the small polished room until the sound beat in my ears like someone attacking me and I could not separate any of the words. *What? What?* I asked, and covered my ears with my hands, and forgot about my curls, but wished they would stop shouting at me about heaven and let me go back to the sun. I tried to stand, but they pushed me back into the chair and I knew better than to resist. *She is shocked, poor thing,* the new nurse said, but Riser shouted, *Bullshit, she is just stupid,* and shook my shoulder. *Lil,* he shouted into my face, so that I could see the way the wings of his nose moved when he spoke. *Lil, your mum is dead, see?* he shouted, and I understood at last, and would rather have gone on failing to understand. *Here, Lil,* the new nurse said, and gave me a handkerchief to blow my nose on, but I crushed it into a ball and put it in my mouth because I wanted to keep something in. There were words inside me for Mother, words that had waited for me to find the right time to say them to her, even just a word of goodbye, but I wished to keep them inside now. I had not said them to Mother when I saw her last, standing in her dressing-gown on the steps, anxious about the newspaper, and I would keep them forever unsaid. *Get out of that, Lil,* Riser yelled, and squirmed his fingers into my face until he had succeeded in pulling the handkerchief out, and the new nurse stood looking pale because she had not seen an *attempted self-destruction* before, and Riser showed her how to tie the tapes of the vest, although it was easy because I did not even think about resisting.

It was not for Mother that the tears flowed all day and fell on the grey canvas, but for the way everything passed and nothing was the way anyone had hoped. *There will be someone for you,* Mother had said, and had straightened the blue satin sash round my thick waist and told me, *You look very nice, Lilian,* and never believed when they told her I spent my time up a tree. Mother had stood feeling the gritty back of a threadbare stuffed donkey, and *watched the birdie* and giggled later, after the photographer had tried to kiss her in the darkroom, and had not thought that she would end up holding a stop-watch and wondering why her daughter was the way she was. *Mother*, I shouted, *Mother, it was not your fault!* I shouted until my voice cracked, trying to reach her, until Riser came and threatened me with the needle if I did not stop my *bloody bellyaching*.

When I was calmer I cried ordinary wet tears, quietly, with decorum, and they undid me from the vest. *My mother died recently*, I practised saying, with dignity, and told them in the ward, proudly, because such things did not happen often. *There has been a death in the family*, I said, and Jewel clasped her hands and shook her head, forgetting words as she often did, but May shrieked, *Who was it kicked the bucket, Lil dear?* and I heard myself say, *My father*, and could not stop it, or go back, so I still had the secret of Mother's death for myself. Ruby made me an armband from a black sock and looked solemn as she put it on for me, but the sock was tight and could not be forced any further up than my forearm and seemed wedged there forever. Ruby became red in the face and her mouth began to open and close until she was straining at the sock and yelling, *Get up there, you bloody cow of a bloody thing*, and everyone was laughing. Under cover of all the shrieking and crowing I could cry a few more tears for my dead mother, who would never know now if there was finally someone for her hopeless daughter, and whose scent of lavender water and camphor would fade from all her things and only come to life when I sat in the sun, smoothing a curl around my finger, remembering her.

The Cynosure of All Eyes

In the face of death we have only ourselves. I would have liked to spend a day or two staring into a mirror, discovering myself in the space behind my eyes. But there were no mirrors in this place. Loonies are not encouraged to admire themselves or even remind themselves who they are. Loonies are encouraged to look outside themselves. *Snap out of yourself*, Riser bellowed at anyone he saw daydreaming too peacefully over basketwork, and although we watched for our reflections in each other's eyes, not much of an image could be seen there. But in the absence of a mirror I discovered my silhouette and decided I could fall a little in love with that shape on the wall. My curves in silhouette had the best kind of substance and belonged together well. *Look*, I would shout when they locked us in too early at night. *Look at the sexpot!* I cried, capering naked, watching my shadow dance for me. Jewel was shocked, for the Blessed Virgin Mary was of course a lady and did not know what to do about such a lot of exposed flesh, but little Babs, who sat sucking her toes when allowed to, became excited, and leaped over the beds towards me making noises like a pup on a leash, and could not be persuaded to admire the shadow rather than the substance. *Oh, Lil, you think you are Easter*, said Dolly the German, who was as big as I was, but more square than round, and who had never quite got the hang of English. *Forever sliding yourself*, she said, *like Persissus*. I agreed with her flat face, like an Eskimo's, *Yes, Dolly, I think I am Christmas and Easter and my birthday all at once, and I am!* Dolly thought it was her we were all laughing at, and returned to the invisible knitting that kept her so busy, too busy to talk as a rule, and I was free to admire my silhouette some more, and saw that when I stuck out my behind and reached up towards the ceiling with one hand my shadow was not unlike that silver woman that had held up the lamp in Father's study. If I sucked in some of my belly I could believe I was young and slim and lovely, and had no interest in mirrors now, for they had never been as kind to me as my shadow was.

Rescue

I was pasty with loony-bin food by the time Aunt Kitty saw me, and fatter, naturally. Exercise was not encouraged here, and although I walked miles around the square of walled garden, pretending it was bush, it was not the same as my path along the headland. It was not even as interesting as Allambie Crescent. I fought it, but the soles of my feet became soft, the calluses peeled off in layers like a bad sunburn or bark at a certain time of year, and left my soles pink, soft, incapable of even a few steps over stones and twigs. Oh, I had fought. They had held me down, Riser and whatever other nurse was nearby, and forced my shoes onto my feet, but I had struggled and struggled and undone the laces as soon as they left me. But a few days in the vest taught me that they would always win and I tried in the end to be philosophical about my soles. *I will grow my own soles again one day*, I whispered in private to Jewel, *but just now I am baring my soles*. I laughed, because I was the only one to see the joke, and Jewel looked surprised with all the muscles of her face and said, *Goodness, Lil, I did not know you was religious. In that case you will be interested to know I have been fucked by God.*

Aunt Kitty did not ask to see my soles, but exclaimed at my unhealthy look, *Sugar, Lil, wicked sugar*, was the first thing she said when she saw me. Aunt Kitty herself was a person of very high colour that day, and her hands shook as she rearranged the clothes hanging from her thin shoulders, but she was a person of authority. Riser did not laugh, even when Aunt Kitty stumbled in the doorway, and when she turned to him and said in a dignified way, *Thank you, nurse*, Riser did not snicker as he did when I spoke, but nodded and left. Money had changed hands, I could see that. *Sugar, Lil, it shows in your face, they are poisoning you with sweet tea*, Aunt Kitty exclaimed. But she took my hands, even though she sounded so stern, and kissed me hard so that I could smell the moth-balls and the whisky. *You should not be here, Lil, consorting with lunatics.* I would have liked to tell Aunt Kitty that I had nothing against a lunatic or two. *I am not all that sane*, I would have said, *and anyway they are pleasant enough folk, most of them*. But I did not want to confuse Aunt Kitty, who had come to rescue me. I could see the zeal in her red cheeks. *You are not a child now*, Aunt Kitty said rather too loudly, so that I was afraid Riser would come and see how excited she was. We were not permitted to become excited without running the risk of the vest. *Albion has no right to lock you up*, she shouted, and I nodded and said, *Yes, yes, yes*, trying to stay placid myself and encourage calmness in her. Aunt Kitty's eyes became alarmingly small and full of cunning. *He is afraid of me*, she said. *He has always suspected that I would like to walk down George Street as naked as the day I was born.* It was hard to imagine twig-like Aunt Kitty naked, but the idea of George Street responding was an exciting one.

I will persuade him, Lil, she said, and for a moment in her red face full of cunning and dislike I saw Father's face. *Albion was always a bully*, Aunt Kitty said, and nodded as if she knew that I was seeing her brother in her face. *And for you, Lil, I will prick his little bubble.* Father faded from her face then and she looked haggard. *I am as dry as a pebble*, she complained, *and you have nothing here*. Her eyes were vague now and she began to gather her clothes around herself and stand up. *No, Aunt Kitty*, I tried. *Stay longer.* But Aunt Kitty was in a hurry now and her eyes slid past mine, looking for something other than her fat niece. *I am as dry as an old sock now*, she said, *and as parched for a drop as the backside of a chair.* Her laugh was like the cry of a bird and was enough to bring Riser to open the door. I watched her back leaving through the door, and felt swallowed up by my own despairing flesh, but she turned and over Riser's white shoulder called, *Albion will be routed, so do not worry, Lilian dear*.

Out of the Shell

When they came for me, to send me back into the other world, I cried to leave Jewel and Esther and Ruby. *I will miss you all*, I called, and waved, and was making something of this farewell, but Riser shouted, *Come off it, Lil, no good trying your bullshit now*, and gripped my elbow in the way he knew, so that I was outside the door before I could properly savour the sad pleasures of leaving.

I will not forget you, none of you, I screeched, but knew that it was not true even as I heard myself shape the words. Riser shook my arm so that I could feel the fat jiggle. *What is your game, Lil? No one is ever sad to leave a loony-bin, and here you are, blubbering*. I was afraid he would turn me around then and put me back in the ward with all those I was crying to leave, and I gulped down my tears, and he picked up the hem of my skirt and wiped at my face with it. I was afraid to leave now. I had forgotten what the other world was like out there, but I was afraid to stay, too, and had to be inserted clumsily into the waiting taxi limb by large limb. *Good on you, Lil*, Riser called and slammed the door at last, and my new life began in the back seat of a taxi that smelled of tobacco and other people's lives.

A Woman of Means

Aunt Kitty winked an unsteady wink at me and gave me a purse full of pounds: *Your father will support you*, she said. *There will be an allowance for you, for all your life*. I probably did not look surprised, because everything was too surprising out here beyond the walls, and surprise had exhausted itself in me. *Lilian*, Aunt Kitty shrilled, so that the taxi driver turned to stare, *you are a cool customer and no mistake!* I could feel her watching me, but I looked out of the window of the taxi, dazed by so much movement, and was too overwhelmed to wonder at anything.

Aunt Kitty took me up flights of stairs, past doors with visiting cards stuck to them crookedly with drawing-pins. At the top of the last flight of stairs there was the room she called mine, and it was an empty enough space to allow me in. I sat on the creaking bed and looked at the way the light fell on the bare white walls, and felt myself within my body, filling up some of this foreign space. *It is your room*, Aunt Kitty was shrilling. *Lilian, snap out of it and pay attention, you can live here now, do you understand?*

There was a window, and the sky was that calming blue, and other people's roofs could be seen there, and other people's windows, and other people's underwear drying on window sills. The streets below were full of women of the night, I had seen them as we arrived, and I could hear them all now, life going on raucously in the street below, where people bought and sold whatever they had, and boys from the country came to be corrupted.

Aunt Kitty could wait no longer for me to ask what had brought all this about, this room with its dry sounds, this purse full of pounds, and she shrieked into my face, so that I could not stop myself flinching: *I have blackmailed your rotten father!* She was excited almost beyond bearing. *My brother has been beaten!* A knocking began on the floor, as of a broomstick being hit against the ceiling below. Aunt Kitty began to whisper then, in a hiss that was uncomfortable to listen to. *I told him I would spread stories about his mad wife and daughter.* Aunt Kitty winked so that her whole face swallowed itself and re-formed. *I told him I would spread stories about his women and he gave in.* She took my hand and opened the fingers, and closed them around the purse. *It is an allowance, Lil, there will be more every month.* My hand closed around the purse, but it had been nearly ten years since I had had money in my hand, and it felt like nothing more significant than a small weight in my palm. Aunt Kitty shook me, but I could not respond, but could only sit feeling my body, the way it made the bed sag, the way it enclosed me in its powerful embrace. I could not move just yet, although I knew that when Aunt Kitty had gone I would be able to send my being out beyond my flesh into the empty space of this room, and begin to fill it. Finally, I knew, I would be able to take a place in this larger world beyond the walls, but just now I had mislaid all my words, and all the movements I could make, and was not used to having money in my hand, and a room all my own.

A New Life

In the beginning I was afraid of so much space and silence and afraid of the way I was free to come and go, or lie in my narrow bed all day if I chose. Choosing was not something that years in the loony-bin had given me much practice at. I sat in my small room, making the side of the bed sag, and stared for hours out the window at the blue and the roofs that lay out there. I sat stiffly, fully dressed as if for another journey, my shoes planted solidly in front of me as if I was about to stand up between two men in white coats and be taken somewhere. When the hollow rumblings of my stomach forced me out of the room and down into the street, I was afraid, and hardly breathed until I was back sitting on the side of the bed with a corned-beef sandwich in my hand.

A summer and a winter had to pass. Like a plant in a new pot I had to watch each season from the window of my room before I had a grip on my new life. My window calmed me at last, though, with the way it was steadily the same each day, and the roofs and chimneys stayed where they had been on that first day, and as time passed I was reassured. I took off my shoes and sprawled on a pillow on the floor then, and did not allow myself to be alarmed by the shops where I bought my food, but became bold. I dared at last to speak to the people behind the counters in the shops, and they were kind, and shouted at me in their faulty English as if I was deaf or moronic, but they smiled. I discovered good things to eat and drink, which I took back to my room like a squirrel, and sated myself, lying on the floor watching clouds sail past.

More Stories

Summer nights in my room were full of the yearning scents of jasmine and the keening of mosquitoes, and the shouts of other hot people abusing each other. On such nights the thought of another body next to mine was unbearable and I had no envy for all the couples in all the rooms, behind their walls, tangled hot and cross in sticky sheets.

On those nights I often left my room, excited as if going to meet a lover, perhaps even that tall man I felt must be waiting for me somewhere, and strolled down the hill. I walked through streets full of the sounds of lives that floated out so many open windows, down to my summer residence, the cool storm-water channel in the park, between the black trees.

The park on the bay was full of interest at nights, when every bush hid, or failed to hide, some urgent event or other. I enjoyed wandering until even my broad feet began to ache, watching so many individuals lusting, and crying, and sighing, and calling out profanities at the height of their passion. It was suggested that I might like to experience these thrills, but I refused all such hoarse offers, and if necessary William could be brought to warn off these hungry men, who could not stand having great poetry shouted at them, and would slink off in shame.

Down there, beside the water endlessly rippling its muscles, the night was enormous and the stars, those old friends, hung low and soft. The nights gradually grew darker and more quiet, as in all those small hot rooms around me men and women reached for light-switches and tried to sleep through their dreams. As I watched, one by one the yellow squares of window became black. There were always a few that burned on all night and into the dawn, and one that winked in code to me all night. I watched it, trying to interpret its message, but it winked on and on, its message for someone else.

The hollow clatter of metal shrouds against the masts of all those quiet boats was like music across the water, random, endless, soothing. Each boat had its own simple tune, which it played over and over all night with every variation, and if I listened hard, and left my body, and became only a listening spirit among the masts, I could follow each tune until it was overlaid by another, and I would follow that one then, until it in turn was overtaken, too. Like the lives of people, the music of the masts was something complicated and mysterious and composed of the clearest and most simple threads. I listened to one voice telling its story, then another, until I drifted away into the spaces between the stars, and left behind the body of the fat woman who lay among the debris of past storms, waiting for love.

At dawn the water shone grey like a blade. On such mornings I missed Rosecroft's old boat, and would have enjoyed sliding out across that metallic water, seeing the oars break the surface like puncturing skin. Down at the sea-wall I sat swinging my feet and watching the life of things resume. The rushes had all long since been cut from here, but the gulls screamed at the fish in just the way they must always have done.

Men with briefcases and dark suits strode off towards another day, with the taste of bacon still warm on their lips. I waved, and cheered at one man, who was almost running in his haste to get to some desk or other, and whose face was distorted by haste and anxiety, and already sweating even in this cool morning air. *Hip hip hooray*, I called, and the third time he realised it was for him, and looked around. *Yes*, I shouted, *I am cheering you*, but he put his head down and ran off down the path, showing that although he was dark and tall, he was not the hero I was waiting for.

Looking for Love

I was becoming intrepid now, and speaking to the new community of spirits I found myself among. I spent my days making small voyages of exploration. *It is better to travel hopefully*, I told the shoemaker who, like Father, felt he had the right to comment on my worn soles. I followed the tall dark men who walked slowly along these shabby streets, although they were looking for love in another form than that of a fat woman in a black coat. *Are you looking for love?* I asked them sometimes, and on this street, where love was the currency, the question did not surprise them. *No thanks, not tonight*, they said, or walked on pretending not to hear.

Here it was all tall buildings full of people with mysterious lives who came out at dusk to let their dogs relieve themselves in the gutter, and people who made me remember the mysterious mother and father of Joan, speaking fast in their mysterious language, and laughing their foreign kinds of laughter. I was shy at first, of so much life and bustle, and the way everyone shouted across the street at each other, and the way now and again one of them would stumble into the gutter and lie there snoring or groaning for a while. But soon I came to know these people, and began to join my life with theirs.

The men in sequins, and the women with men's hats on their heads, and cigars in their mouths, and the people of no sex at all with shaven heads, the people who yelled at the air in front of them, or suggested *good times* to anyone likely to listen: these people were my neighbours now, and were the kind of people I found I liked. *We are all looking for love*, I told them as we sat over our coffees, or stood on the street corner. My time in the loony-bin had made me serious, but these people knew there was not much to be gained by being too serious, *Yes, Lil, but some of us like to get paid for it*, Tommo shrieked, who made his living at night in the park, and spent his days exposing himself to anyone who was interested, and to many who were not.

A number of the girls had become my friends, I liked to think, and several of them straightened in their doorways and breathed out smoke in a smile when they saw me coming. When Zara suffered from a black eye, or Doreen's chin was bruised, or Shade looked sour, I did not linger to chat, because although they had not found love with their pimps, they had found something, and were doing their best to make the material at hand into a life.

On good days, when the sound of the traffic, and all those people looking for love, was like music, I stopped and passed the time of day with the girls. I liked to keep in touch with their lives, although I could not copy anything. *How are you going, Lil?* they all called, and introduced me to the new girls: *This is Marge, she is from Coffs Harbour,* they would say, and Zara would make a suggestive remark about bananas, and everyone would laugh. I was not exotic to them, except in the virginity I told them I had. *Are you really, Lil?* they asked, and touched me as if I was a holy relic. *You are having us on, Lil.* It amused me to shock them and hear their gasps: *I will show you my hymen if you like,* I threatened. *It is rare, a collector's item,* and Shade would explain to Marge from Coffs Harbour, who was sharp enough, but new to the city, that I was talking about my *cherry* and how it was still *unpopped*.

You, Lil, you have been around, they said, and I felt wise, a mature woman, for many of the girls were younger than I was, but I did not try to explain that they had already lived more life than I had. *Oh, I am too old to change now,* I cried when they wanted to pluck my eyebrows for me, or decorate my face with paints and powders and beauty spots out of a tin. I knew I was not too old for anything I wished, but knew I was no girl any longer, but a woman in her prime.

See, Lil here is looking for love, Zara would tell Marge, who did not know what to think of such an idea, but thought it was probably safe to laugh. We were all looking for love, and like the rest of the people in this part of the city, I was willing to try anything. *I can be anything I wish,* I told Zara. *I am the smooth white pages of a blank book.* Zara laughed her parrot laugh then, and wrinkled up her kohl-rimmed eyes at me, so she looked more than ever like a big ginger tomcat with fur on end from a fight. *Well, you are a nice thick read, anyway,* Zara shrilled, and we had to stop a few friends and tell them the joke, because, in the absence of love, a laugh was not bad to be going on with.

Brothers Look for Love, Too

My brother had grown into a tall dark man with a hat, but I knew he could not be the one I knew was waiting for me somewhere. He lived in some small house with a lawn and a driveway, somewhere or other, but there were plenty of evenings when I saw him walking up my tinsel street like a man who knew what he wanted. When I saw him there, his face turning green in the neon, I did not speak to him. Each time I saw him I turned my back, or slipped into a doorway, or simply became blind, because as well as being my brother, John was a man entitled to a life, and was looking for love, too.

So I turned into a doorway, and the bouncer there, a man who had lost his ears in some mishap, so his shaven bullet head was obscene, said *Hello, Lil, come for a stripper's job, eh?* and laughed for a long time, even stepping out into the street to find someone to share the joke with. I could not move on just yet, because John was prowling up the street, taking his time about choosing, and I had to bear this earless man's beery laugh, and try to maintain my dignity when he nudged me in my fat and shouted as if I was deaf or stupid, *I tell you what, Lil, if I was a female I would not sit on it and let it go mouldy*, and he laughed again in a desperate hooting way, and John finally passed, and I could leave.

I was an inquisitive person, though, and did not resist following John once, to see what kind of girl or boy he wanted, and was surprised when he chose Angelique, who was haughty and when on the job did her best to pretend to be French. I watched from a distance and saw how the corners of her mouth turned down disdainfully, and her eyes with the false lashes flickered up and down my brother's body, and spoke to his left lapel. They set off down the street together, and she on her high heels seemed to tower over him, and stalked ahead of him, not glancing back to check that he was following. My brother was not a small man, not stooped, not shabby, but in her tall elegant wake he seemed a little shambling man who would have holes in his socks. I waited, and later when she returned to her corner I saw how John was happy behind his glasses now, although only a sister would have been able to recognise it on his face.

Angelique, who when not on the job was Angela from Cobar, and whose love affair was with a pug with sinus problems, was not one of the girls I knew well or liked especially, for she was reserved with us all, and kept her smiles and enthusiasms for Pug. But she was of a kind heart, and when I saw her with Pug, feeding him morsels from her plate and smiling, full of love, I was pleased that John had chosen well, had chosen someone whose love had not all dried up.

Audiences

There was no headland to walk to here, and not even any Allambie Crescent to scandalise. No one much could be scandalised here, only a few innocents visiting from the suburbs or the country, waiting to be shocked, and rewarded to see the fat woman shouting hello to everyone on the streets.

When I caught sight of myself in shop windows I had to remind myself that I had been briefly beautiful. I knew that a photograph with a crease across it still recorded that moment, although I myself, now fat, stringy-haired, shining of face, puffy, refused cameras. The tourists and the visitors from the suburbs were sometimes intrigued by me and the William I shared with the street, and wanted to carry a part of me back to Toongabbie or Bulli. *Crazy as a two-bob watch*, they told each other, and tried to remember what I had said or recited to them, but if they had a photograph at all, it was of a fat woman in a black coat with both palms spread in front of her face.

I was not so old as not to imagine futures for myself, although when I did so I ran the risk of a whiff of the old poison returning. Would I always be a person people stared at, but left alone? Would I never find that spirit with whom I could join my own? I was willing to hope it was not too late. When I allowed myself to imagine being that close to another being, I drew back in fear, but I still yearned for love. My body yearned, too, my passionate hidden body that was ripe now under all the layers of clothes, ripe for ecstasy. I was full of hot blood, my flesh sprang out at me full of life, when I bathed, not yet marked by age. *I am a woman in her prime*, I told myself, but knew my prime would be over before too long. I tried to imagine love, but could do no more than gaze and dream into imagined futures, and wait for love to come to me.

The Dribbling Dart of Love

It was Lord Kitchener I fell in love with, one evening as I waited at the Quay for love to come along. I saw him immediately, swinging through the barrier in his dark business man's suit and his oxblood briefcase. He might have looked like any other man whose wife had polished his shoes that morning, and whose underwear was strung white and clean on some suburban washing-line once a week, but I knew who he was from his moustache, and the way the muscles of his calves thrust against his trouser legs as he stood waiting.

I moved closer to him through the press of commuters and watched what he was watching, the way the green side of the ferry swung in and smashed against the piers, and the way the long rope snaked out around a bollard. When I stood beside him, Lord Kitchener took a step away from me. Of course he was afraid, and did not know that this was love. I was fat and I shone with excited sweat. I was a woman people could see was not like most women, they could see at a glance from the layers of shabby clothes I wore, and the way I looked them in the face, and sometimes I spoke to them in ways that took them by surprise, and made them fearful. *Mad*, I saw them think as they watched me looking into their faces, *there is something wrong with her*.

I watched the way Lord Kitchener's moustache filled his face, and the way the hard muscles of his calves tensed as if he was about to spring across the water. I knew that this was the man destined for me, and destiny would have its own plans for the course of my love. I was full of happiness like warm egg, knowing that my tall dark man had come to me at last, and that even I would know love before it was too late.

I followed him onto the ferry, and felt him respond as I sat next to him. The finger of love was touching him, too, but he was a tease, and moved his thigh so that I had to move again, to touch it and feel the thrill up my side where it was so close to him. Although he looked away and did not speak, I knew him to be in love as I was. I knew, too, that he could not speak, because of the dark suit, the shining oxblood briefcase, the double knots on the laces of his shoes.

Side by side as if at a wedding we watched while the ferry drew out from the wharf, and I sat taking deep breaths from the proximity of my love. Was love always so easy?

In the centre of the harbour, in the last rays of the setting sun, our ferry was delayed by a liner being herded into dock. The white walls of the ship were hard to look at in the sun. Lord Kitchener shaded his eyes with a hand and stared up at where people in coloured clothes waved down, stared, took photographs. Next to me a woman pumped a little boy's arm up and down. *Wave, darling, wave.* He began to cry. Under my buttocks the ferry trembled as the engines were put into reverse to stop our drift across the water. Lord Kitchener stood, steadying himself against the movement with a hand on the railing. The gold band on his finger shot a ray of hot light into my eye.

The arrow of love had darted into my heart, and I did not need to follow Lord Kitchener as he got off the ferry at a suburban wharf, although I watched him striding away up the hill until the ferry moved on and hid him from sight. It did not worry me that he would unlock his own front door soon, and kiss some wife or other, and smell the perfume she had put on for his return. I sat on the ferry with the wind salty in my hair until the boat had emptied and filled, emptied and filled, many times in its course back and forth to the Quay. The sun set, the moon rose, stars could dimly be seen in the sky, and finally a big man in a singlet was brought to match my bulk and put me off the ferry at last. None of this was important, for I knew that the arrow of love had darted into my heart. It was not too late, and in its prime, my life would be made complete by a love of my own.

The Consummation of Love

I made discoveries, being in love, and found that love made me greedy for more. In the beginning proximity had been enough, but finally I began to hunger for a word from Lord Kitchener, or a sign. The greed of my love wished to be reflected and doubled: I hungered for a declaration from Lord Kitchener or at least loving banter.

I would fain die a dry death, I said, and smiled at him in his dark suit, which was adorned this morning with a tiny gleaming medallion of bird dropping. He had showed no surprise at seeing me on his wharf at this hour of the morning, when the dew was still damp on the pilings, but had given me a glance that made words unnecessary. My heart beat faster as I watched him.

A *dry death*, I said again, because he had not responded. The boy fishing off the wharf, his head shaven and purple from the ringworm and its cure, stared at me, and a drop of light slid down his line into the water. The harbour was sullen and glassy today. *Shall we try walking on it?* I asked, but I was beginning to think that Lord Kitchener was a trifle deaf.

What is love without the thrust and parry, the approach and retreat of the plumed male? Lord Kitchener sat, I sat beside him, he stood and strode away to another seat in the bow, I followed him again, and I had hardly reached his side before he was off again. I had never been one to worry about my own dignity, but could not prevent myself beginning to laugh as I followed my love from port to starboard, from bow to stern, upstairs and downstairs, and finally so much laughing forced me to do what Lord Kitchener's teasing could not, and I sat in the middle of the boat, near the hot throb of the engines, and laughed until there was a space around me on all the seats.

At the Quay I was lying in wait for him on the boat, and he did not see me as I took my place behind him. Around me all those experienced commuters took hold of something, and waited for the jolt as the side of the boat swung in and struck the pilings. Just in front of me, so close that one corner of the oxblood briefcase nudged my knee, so close that by pursing my lips I could make the hair on the back of his neck flutter—in front of me Lord Kitchener stood with his legs apart, holding nothing but the oxblood briefcase. When the boat met the wharf and everyone staggered, he staggered, too, and for a glorious moment I embraced him.

His back was pressed against my breast and that silver medallion on his shoulder brushed my cheek. My nostrils were full of the hot animal smell of his hair. I was almost able to join my hands in front of his chest, and for several endless seconds he remained in my embrace. *Ah!* I whispered into his ear. Even I had no words for such ecstasy.

I could not bear to leave him, and walked by his side up the streets of the city, smiling and proud to be breasting the pavement with my love beside me. Lord Kitchener was shy, and perhaps overwhelmed by my proximity, as I always was by his, and kept his head turned away so I could see only his pink ear, and a corner of that moustache. He walked so fast my fat bounced and I panted, having to keep up with him, so that I could not speak, but in any case I had nothing to say, there were no words big enough for my joy.

My love strode up the streets until he came to the heart of the city, the avenue of colonnades where the post office clock stopped everyone in their tracks once an hour with its booming. Near these colonnades Lord Kitchener turned aside, so quickly I almost lost him, and strode between the red marble columns of a bank where a man stood with his legs apart and a gun on his hip. Lord Kitchener nodded to this man with the gun as if they were old friends, and swung in between the marble columns with such familiarity that I realised my love must spend his days among the red marble, and that his oxblood briefcase must be full of columns of figures, of percentages, of rates of interest. I did not venture in past the man with the gun, because I knew Lord Kitchener was mine when he straddled the ferry with his strong legs, but would not be mine when he was a man in a bank. I sat on a bench in the shaft of sun that fell between the buildings, snuffing up the air in great gulps so that people stared and visibly wondered if the fat woman was having an attack. *I am not sick*, I called when I had enough breath to speak. *There is nothing wrong with me but love, and I am ready to die of that.*

Destinies

Love made me patient, and my patience was at last rewarded the day Kitchener chose to give me a sign. I had always known he loved me, because I knew we were destined, that this was the love I had always been looking for, and that he was the dark man that Jewel had seen in my hand, but when he gave me his sign, my fat trembled with joy.

His sign was unmistakable. I met him at the Quay, as I did on many mornings, and prepared to accompany him up the streets to his bank. He passed through the turnstile, swinging the oxblood briefcase, and passed me, as he always did, with only the most quiet of signals that he treasured my being there. But as he passed, a square of newsprint fluttered down from him, a square cut from the advertisement page, and it was a sign no one could have denied. I read it, and my knees turned to water under me, and the world became dark for a moment, because it had never been a necessary part of the story of my love for him to give me such a sign.

I held the newsprint between my fingers until it was limp from my heat. Then I panted up that hill, hating the snarling buses that morning because their noise made it hard for me to catch up to my love, who strode on in front of me, a gleaming dark head in the crowd. But at the bank I was near him, hearing myself wheeze from so much haste uphill, and he glanced around, and saw me. I held up his message, and nodded at him, might even have winked, and my smile was tender with triumph. He looked back as people crossed to and fro between us, and I knew that he saw how faithfully I had followed him, and that in my hand I held the

213

talisman he had left for me. Of course he did not smile back. He did not need to. The look he gave me was full of astonishment and joy, and it sealed our promise.

Across the street I nodded three times and winked. He knew that I understood. He spoke again to the man with the gun and disappeared inside.

When the two young policemen took my arms I denied everything. *Harassing members of the public*, one of them said importantly. *Causing affront and alarm*. I remained dignified. *I harass no members*, I protested, and a woman in lilac shantung turned and stared. My bag of books fell, my William dropped out, someone tittered at my huge black behind as I bent for it, a policeman shook my elbow, the scrap of paper flew out of my hand, nearly lost. *Now, now*, the policeman said. *Come along now*.

There had been other betrayals, but none as bad as this. The smell of hard-working blue serge and peaked caps full of hair was the smell of Lord Kitchener's cowardice. *There is some mistake here*, I cried, and they laughed as they stopped a taxi and pushed me in.

We had only gone a block when everything in front of my eyes cracked and wavered into tears. The tufts of the cabbie's hair, Queen Victoria standing black in the sun, girls in yellow dresses, all ran and shattered into prisms of wet light. With me in this taxi, whose smell of other people's lives was not enough to comfort me, was a broken machine that was beginning to wheeze and groan and make wrenched jerky cries of grief. *Steady on, love,* the cabbie kept saying. *Steady on. Easy on there, love*. Beside me a huge truck roared along as if trying to drown me out. We stopped at lights and my eyes cleared long enough to see a girl stare at me as she crossed the street with a long pink bun held up to her open mouth like a finger. Next time I opened my eyes I saw a bald man with a cello. It all seemed hopeless.

He stopped outside the white castle near the water. *No, no,* I tried to say. *Not here.* But groans and bleats were all that came out of my face as he opened my door. *Come on,* he said. *A bit of a sit-down.* When he held the door open, a soprano in pain suddenly began a scale. *Ah Ah Ah Ah Ah!* she sang up, and *Ah Ah Ah Ah Ah!* down again. When she began again on a higher note, it was in desperation. A violin wavered the same three shrill screams over and over, and from every window came the empty tinkle of pianos.

He took me down the stairs into the Gardens. At a bench under a tree he sat down and patted the seat beside him. *A bit of a sit-down,* he said again, and took a bottle in a brown paper bag out of his pocket. He swallowed deeply and his eyes filled with tears. *Tell me all about it,* he said. *It was a man in a bank,* I said, and when the cabbie began to laugh, showing long yellow teeth, I saw that he knew what I meant. *Who are you?* I asked, and licked my lips, which tasted bitterly of salt. He shook his head and pulled down the cuffs of his tight checked jacket. *I'm Frank to my friends,* he said. *Call me Frank.* Together we watched as a man with a sharp stick speared pieces of paper beside the path. *Blokes in banks are bad news,* Frank said. *Take it from me. I've known a few.*

It was many years since anyone had held my hand and rubbed comfortingly at it. It was even longer since anyone had held a handkerchief to my nose and said, *Now blow.* I blew. *Again,* he said, and I blew again. *Good girl. Now open your mouth and close your eyes.* The brandy was very cool in my mouth for an instant before it was very hot. I swallowed to get it out of my mouth and felt it searing down into my chest and I had to use the handkerchief again to wipe at the splutter around my mouth.

Close to us, on the edge of the lagoon, a huge black swan reared up on its legs and beat its wings towards us. I heard my voice cracked and adenoidal. *Bloody men.* The swan began to stretch its neck towards us as if about to go in for the kill and Frank stood up to make threatening gestures at it. *Can't help its nature,* he apologised. I wiped my fingers across the tears on my cheeks. *But you are a man,* I said. Frank considered this and took another long swallow that demonstrated an agile Adam's apple. *I am not that swan,* he said at last. *I am not any kind of swan. I am just a bloke,* he said.

We sat together on the bench while I watched the shadow of a flagpole inch across the grass towards me. From time to time, tears rolled down my cheeks as I thought about Lord Kitchener, but they were quiet tears and Frank did nothing more than pass me the bottle and wipe my wetness from where it had fallen on his sleeve.

Lord Kitchener's message had survived, had been snatched up and thrust into my pocket, and at last I felt able to take it out and read it again: *George will love you my place or yours.* The words were becoming worn and blurred but they remained my message from my love. I was willing to see now that I had been telling the wrong story. It was painful, but there remained a Lord Kitchener in my heart, who loved me tenderly and who would always be mine in my heart. I could crumple up this square of shabby newsprint then, and drop it, so that the man with the sharp stick would spear it on his next round.

The bottle was empty now and the shadow of the flagpole lay across my lap. Before it could reach up my chest it would be overwhelmed by the mass of shadow coming across the grass from the west, where the white building was silhouetted against a sky the colour of a bruise.

Frank had fallen asleep, the empty bottle slipping out of his hand and slithering to the grass. When I thought of Lord Kitchener, now probably holding the shuddering green post in the ferry on his way home, watching the wharf approach, I felt sad and calm. *I misunderstood*, I told the sky. *He is the wrong man*. I would have liked to find him, and tell him that I forgave him, but could not bear to see that moustache again, or those thrusting calves.

Frank spoke loudly: *Green doors*, and woke up. He glanced at me, felt for the bottle, and belched. We sat in silence watching the swan burrowing into its under-wing. *Royalty*, Frank said at last on a sigh, arriving at the end of some train of thought, and smiled dreamily at the lagoon where a cat's-paw of breeze shot across the water. *They are not better than the rest of us*.

Laughing and Love

Frank, or F.J. Stroud as I had known him before, liked sitting in a park with his bottle much better than driving his taxi. We sat together in the sun, and laughed at the way the pigeons knew it was lunchtime in the offices, and came down for pieces of bun. *Lil, you were always a good companion*, Frank told me, and I was glad that I had fallen in love with Lord Kitchener, for it had brought me back to Frank, and proved that no love is ever wasted.

Frank had a little room somewhere, as I did, but was *in arrears*, he said, and took a deep draught from the bottle. *I have a little*, I suggested, but Frank shouted, *I have never wanted your little, Lil, and will not now*. People stared as we lolled on the grass, and there were days when we lolled all day, watching the people frown and pour into the offices in the mornings, frown and eat their sandwiches at lunchtime, frown and then hurry home.

Like me, Frank was a man in his prime, but visibly slipping now, sped on by his bottle. *We are all getting on, Lil*, Frank sighed and swigged. *We are none of us young any more*, and although I wanted to cry, *But,*

217

Frank, I am only just starting! I knew he was right, and that the great love of my life, Lord Kitchener, had swept past like a tide and left me different, not full of hope and imagined futures. There was a grey hair or two in my hair now, I saw with sadness, and when I caught a glimpse of myself in shop windows I saw there were the beginnings of lines around my eyes and mouth that made me look like a fat parody of Mother as she had sat over her stop-watch.

Love seemed a thing of the past, and youth was finished, but life remained to be explored, and I was not cast down. *I will spend my maturity enjoying life,* I announced to Frank. *I have spent too long locked up and alone, one way and another. I will spend my life now being part of things.* Exhilarated, I was determined to love long, and with gusto.

A Friend Gone

You are as fat as ever, Aunt Kitty told me, *but have a better colour.* She lay on the hospital bed in a very shrunken way, her cheeks fallen in and yellow now, her knees drawn up as if she was cold or afraid. *I am full of oysters, Aunt Kitty,* I said. *They are supposed to make you feel lustful.* I thought this might make her laugh, and she needed to, lying so tiny beneath the hospital covers, her eyes grown huge with what was happening to her. Aunt Kitty laughed so that the woman in the next bed turned her face in spite of the tubes in her nose and stared at us. *You have a lot of lust yet,* Aunt Kitty said, *but be careful of bad oysters.* Her laugh had come and gone in a moment and left her face more frightened.

Aunt Kitty, you have been my only friend, I said, and took her cold hand in both of mine, and kissed it, feeling the skin cool like a lizard's against my lips, because she was dying. *Oh, Lil,* she said, *you are the*

218

person I would have liked to be. Aunt Kitty plucked at the bedclothes as if it mattered. I would have liked to scoop her up from this cold bed and pop her into one of my pockets and take her somewhere warm. *But we have foxed Albion*, she said, and managed a wink, and although I knew Albion would never be beaten, I nodded and winked back. *You did everything*, I said, to comfort her, but the truth was I knew only that she had set me free, and was dying now. I sat there while she slept, her hand light in mine, and felt the woman with the faceful of tubes watching as warm tears ran down my cheeks and tickled, hanging from my chin, until they fell.

The serenity of the corpse was most delightful. In life Aunt Kitty had never appeared so rested and so placid. Over her serene corpse, Father and I watched each other and a cousin from somewhere, who was a stranger to me but who had hoped to be remembered in Aunt Kitty's will, snuffled into a hankie. Father was full of himself as he stood in his uniform and squared his shoulders. He was full of his own glory and was serene about his fat daughter standing mulishly by his sister's corpse. He did not speak to me.

It had come as a surprise at first to see Father looking military, but soon it appeared inevitable. I had not seen him with his gun, but knew that there must be one, somewhere in his study at Rosecroft, and did not need to see him do it, to know how he must posture and stride before the mirror, admiring himself in khaki.

Over Aunt Kitty's corpse he did not speak, but later, when she had been slid into the flames, and we wandered in the gardens, wondering just what had happened, he came up to me. Unlike that snivelling cousin, who was still hopeful, I knew that Aunt Kitty had left her all to me. There was not much, but it was enough that I need never need Father again. When in his sick khaki he approached me through the flowers, I stood my ground and tried not to be afraid. He looked at my face, glowing from so many oysters and so much freedom, and took me by surprise, jabbing my belly where my breakfast sat keeping me warm. *Lilian*, he said as if reminding me who I was. *Lilian, you are an example of the degeneracy of the white races.* I must have stood blinking in my surprise and Father hissed, so that the creeping cousin stared, *You are sterile and degenerate, and as corrupt as a snake.* Father should have grown his moustache back, but never had, and his long upper lip moved in a strange way when he spoke, as if carrying on a conversation of its own. I could not help laughing, and saw Father congest, and ran to water at the knees in sudden fear. He thickened, his khaki collar appeared too tight, and his eyes filled his face. I thought he might wrestle me to the ground there among the tidy flowers, or hit my glowing face until it broke apart under his hand. He did none of these things, but seemed to remind himself of who he was, thrust his shoulders back so that the khaki over his chest became as taut as a well-made bed. He turned away.

John wandered among those neat flowers, too, my brother who would always be a stranger I would love, because we had given each other what we could, even when that was little enough. *You were good to me when I was in the loony-bin*, I told John among the flowers that were meant to take the sting out of death, and could taste the cream and the cake that were the proof of my brother's love. *It was nothing much, Lil*, John said, and we stood searching each other's faces for something, but we had little enough to offer each other, and had never had much in the way of words.

Lest We Forget

Over the seas they began killing each other again, and here people put fat in tins and sent it to besieged

Britain, and there was no longer anyone on the streets who was yellow-skinned, or who spoke their English differently. They had all been taken off somewhere or were in hiding for the duration, or pretending to be deaf and dumb.

There is a war on, everyone reminded each other, as if we might forget. *And we must all do our bit*. In the shops and tearooms, signs told us that *Loose Lips Sink Ships*, but I did not think a little William would hurt anyone.

I had no fat for Britain, needing all of mine for myself, but I did my best for the war effort. For those women in trams, managing so many knitting needles at once and being deft about turning the heel of some khaki sock, I had words of encouragement and free recitations. *I would normally be charging a shilling*, I told whoever was within hearing, *but I am doing this for nothing, out of patriotism*. The women said nothing, but I noticed they knitted faster when I recited, and felt that I could be proud of doing my bit.

It seemed to be all women these days. I wondered where they had been all my life, these women who could drive trams and buses, and be policemen and bank-tellers. Their faces looked stern under their peaked caps, as though they wanted to make it clear that they were not enjoying this, but I heard them humming as they wound the great wheels of the buses, and laughing in uniformed groups, and I did not believe they were not having a good time. I knew they were only pretending not to care.

Kings and Queens

There was a war on, and everyone was wondering if it would ever end, or if life would always be like this, and an ugly blushing girl was being crowned Munitions Queen. She reminded me of myself, except that I would have never been so diligent and produced so many bombs and bullets. She stood on a box, under a banner with a huge number written on it, and wore a dark red sash like a terrible wound across her chest. It was not hard to imagine that this would be the only thing that would ever happen to her.

She blushed and ducked her head, and gulls wheeled overhead, waiting for the eating to start, and the great dark trees of the Domain swallowed the sunlight into their leaves. A man in a boater shouted into a microphone and everyone cheered. The Munitions Queen was pushed from behind until she was standing in front of the microphone which was too tall for her, and she made a sound like a dog barking that was amplified so that pigeons fluttered up off the grass in fear.

That Munitions Queen was a squat girl, as red in the face as her sash, and was trying to swallow her head into her chest, so that her pale neck was exposed to the axe. I watched, because I saw myself there, and because I, too, can be cruel, and enjoy a joke. *I am honoured*, I heard as she began to read her speech from notes that fluttered in the sun, but she could not go on until she had taken her glasses from her pocket, and put them on so that they glittered in the sun like her tiara. She was *honoured*, and *touched*, and *only doing her little bit*, and no one tried very hard to look solemn, but nudged each other when her voice shook with patriotism on the words *my King and my country*, and a pretty girl who should have been Queen, if such things were awarded on golden good looks, laughed behind her slim brown hand when the Munitions Queen leaned forward so far into her notes that her tiara slipped and had to be retrieved.

If I had not been cruel I would have left and walked down to the blue water's edge, perhaps even cleansed myself with a quick dip to wash away the terrible frailty of people, but I was cruel, too, and stayed. I stayed there on the edge of the munitions workers' picnic and laughed with everyone else while that ugly girl with a hairy face and thick red cheeks like meat, like mine, was married to the Munitions King. Her red sash could hardly contain her chest. How often had any man held her hand? She was looking for love, too, it was easy to see. The Munitions King was a handsome boy with a big chest, and muscles that filled his shirt. If he had not been cross-eyed he would have been standing at attention somewhere, or dead with a rifle in his hand. But he had been saved for this moment, when he kissed his Queen and had to catch her as she stumbled, somehow, and nearly fell of the platform. *I pronounce you man and wife*, someone boomed, a drum banged, and a bagpipe began to shriek in pain. The Munitions Queen tried to hide her face against the large chest of her King, but was not allowed any such comfort. She had to take a glass of champagne in one hand and a knife in the other, to cut the cake, and then her wedding was over. The platform was empty, the red sash was rucked around her waist, the wind was suddenly chill, and goose bumps rose on everyone's arms.

Water has proved the smartest grave, and I considered that clean death when I left the picnic behind at last and went down to the harbour. Water would be a purifying death, though a difficult one for a strong swimmer like myself. Everyone is tragic, and I am less tragic than many, but I would have been willing to breathe water, and die in panic. It would have eased the pain in my chest, where sadness lived, to have taken everyone's sadness to myself and drowned it. That blue water would prove the smartest grave, and I would not object to my flesh being nibbled by small inquisitive fish, and my bones being rolled along the sand by the tides.

I cried for the Munitions Queen and everyone else, but there was no need. The Munitions Queen would be as old as I was, one day, and by then her day of glory would have become a story, part of her history. *The time I was crowned Munitions Queen*, she would say until it was a pleasure and not a pain, and with each telling she would enjoy it more, and feel more as if she, too, had had a life. *That cross-eyed fellow, Bob, he was my King*, she would explain, and almost remember how to blush. *And I was sweet on him, of course*, and no one listening would know that so much of Bob, so close and all at once, had made her desperate with anguish. No one would know anything but the story she chose to tell, and she would be proud, in the end.

Impossible Freedom

Now, when the streets were full of men in khaki, when everyone knew how to load a gun, and Father in his uniform should have been vindicated at last, and given a platoon to lead, it was too late for him. *It was his heart*, they told me, and I laughed, because I knew about that, and knew that it could not have been his heart that killed him. *She is deranged, poor thing*, one of the nurses said to another. *The grief has unhinged her*, and I laughed louder.

I had allowed myself to dream of Father's death at times, had stared up at the loony-bin sky, or at the square of it framed in the window of my little room, and had felt myself expand and rejoice at the thought of his death. At such times life had become so large, so infinitely full of possibilities, that I had become dizzy. I would stand and walk a few paces to recover myself, and the earth would tilt away from under my feet.

Now they told me he was dead, had dropped down suddenly clutching his chest, while talking to another man in khaki, and at the moment all I could do was laugh in a high-pitched way that did not belong to me, and be thought callous by the people at the hospital. They had arrived too late to be able to do anything for Father, but had still brought him to this building that knew what to do with death in a way that Rosecroft did not. And now that he was dead I knew that when I stopped laughing I would be overwhelmed by a cold vastness that was beginning to surround me. With Father gone, the world lacked edges, and went on grey for ever into the distance. There seemed no reason to do or not do anything, with Father lying cold on that hospital bed. *You would like to pay your last respects*, the people in white told me, and locked me in alone with Father's corpse. I had dreamed of this and had on occasion rehearsed the speech that I would make to him. *You are a vile and degenerate man*, I would begin. I had stirred myself into a frenzy more than once.

But now I stood over the body of what they told me was Father, and I recognised the long upper lip, and the mouth that even in death was unforgiving, and I was consumed with unwilling grief, and felt the world was a barren place, full of nothing but the angry hard sobs that were wrenching themselves up, from somewhere even deeper than my heart, from somewhere secret where my being had its source.

All My Family

There were men in khaki everywhere, and for a long time I saw Father on every street corner, standing erect in his uniform, or stepping out into the road to hail a taxi. Once or twice I surprised myself, breaking into the beginning of a thick run, feeling my mouth shape the word *Father* before I realised that the khaki back belonged to some red-cheeked patriotic country lad, or some wooden man *doing his bit* but determined not to enjoy it.

John had some job that was *top-secret*, he said coyly, and *of vital national importance*, and he flinched when I shrieked, *Oh, you are a spy, you mean*. He surprised me. *Lil, do not taunt me*, he said. *We only have each other now and you should not taunt me*. I was silenced by surprise. John's top-secret job was transformed him into someone I did not recognise, as he had been transformed several times before in our lives, when the brother I thought I knew turned out to be someone else altogether. *I forget that Father is gone*. I told John in explanation, and he nodded behind his glasses. He said, *I am making the most of it, and have wished him dead for years*. I had never been so brave, for all my bombast and noise, and even now I was tied to Father in a way I could not change. *He hated me*, I said, but John laughed his sudden hard laugh. *He did not hate you*, John said, wiser than me after so long. *He just thought you did not matter*. He saw that I was upset then, and took off his glasses in the old way, and began to breathe on them, and polish them on his handker-chief. *It is all right, Lil*, he said finally, and looked at me without his glasses, so I knew he could not see me. *None of us matter, Lil, but life is none the worse for that*. I could not agree, although I saw what he meant, seeing the world from a top-secret job where the way he did not seem to care would be valuable. But I could not pretend not to care and everyone would keep on mattering to me. *I would be no good as a spy*, I told him. *Luckily I do not have to be one. I have bigger fish to fry*. I did not know what I meant, but like all those others I wanted John to care, or at least wonder. *And I am doing my bit for the war effort, too*.

Bombast

Then one day there was cheering in the streets, for more Japanese had been killed than anyone could

226

count, and they were still slowly dying. The streets were full of khaki, but people's faces were not pinched now, but glad with victory, and glad with the larger victory of having survived. I could not believe that death could come in such quantity, and turned away from the pictures of that final victory that paper-boys thrust at me. *I am sickened*, I told them. *I am safe in my age, but you could die that death.* The paper-boy stared and opened his mouth so as not to miss a word. *Do not forget*, I told him, and meant myself, and all the possibilities that I represented, and also meant the deaths he wanted to sell me. Mother would have loved them, but I did not. *If you forget, it will happen to you*, I said, but he had recovered now, and laughed in my face with his cold green eyes, and was sure nothing could ever happen to him.

It angered me, and roused me to inspired speech. I did not bother with a box, in the Domain, but stood on a tree root that stuck up a convenient height. *The vermin will not perish*, I shouted. *The vermin will flourish on our corpses. Michelangelo will be gone and Shakespeare will be gone and the cockroaches will breed in our eyeballs.* I was making myself sick, and drawing a crowd. I heard hecklers and laughter, but I ignored them, for it was necessary to share my vision of apocalypse, it was choking me like hands around my throat. *We are fragile*, I shouted, *we are as fragile as an eggshell*, and by now no one could hear my voice, grown shrill with conviction, because my public was too busy laughing at this huge woman who was claiming to be fragile. *You will be sorry*, I called, climbing down off my root. *You will be sorry, but it will be too late.* I chose a man close to me who was showing me his meaty tongue as he laughed: *You will pray for a quick death then*, I told him, my skin still crawling from the terrible pictures I had seen. *You will envy the dead and cry for mercy and there will be none*, I told him, and saw his face close down, for my words had killed his laughter and his tongue had disappeared. He would laugh again, but not at the thought of the final horror.

Life's Journeys

Father's death made me weightless and I was discovering new ways of journeying through my life. *It is better to travel*, I would remind myself, when my room began to close in around me, and Frank was nowhere to be found. *No one enjoying life can afford not to journey*, I told the people beside me in the bus. But on a bus or tram, everyone can pretend not to hear a large woman talking nonsense. In a bus or tram they can always get off, if the large woman should sit next to them and begin telling them the story of her life, or some other fanciful tale, or reciting Shakespeare at them. There was pleasure in the size of that audience, but its quality was inferior, and I discovered soon that there was a taxi purring on every corner, waiting to take anyone anywhere, with a small and attentive audience inside, of one or two people who could not get out at the next stop, and who might be going anywhere at all.

It was the work of a moment to open the door and step in. There were folk who did not understand the importance of making a journey every day. *Get bloody out of it, Lil*, some of them shouted, and clamoured until some policeman or other arrived and looked solemn. Many of them threatened, but their shouts and feints were empty, because I was stronger than almost any of them. Men got out of their taxis and pulled at my arm, but their bulk was from too much beer and bluster, while mine was from years of practice, and the strength of a simple life.

Once I was in that front seat, settled in all my massiveness beside them, the wise ones decided it was easier to take me somewhere, and tell me we had arrived. I did not much care if they drove only a block or two before they told me we had arrived, because the arriving was not the important thing.

There were those, too, whom I met this way and recognised as fellow-souls. There was a young man, who although so young looked as if he might be nursing a history of some sad past, a young man with a sad cross face who seemed pleased to be joined in the front seat of his car. *Hop in, Lil*, he said, although I had already done so, and he drove until he decided that I had arrived, and went on his way looking less cross.

They could become objectionable. One man, whose brilliantined hair was combed back so fiercely that his forehead looked scraped and angry, congested and stood over me looking nasty, but silent. His moustache was like Father's had once been, heavy and dark, hiding his mouth. Like Father, this man gave nothing away. I was used to a lot of shouting, liked it for the chance it gave me to shout back, and this man's silence frightened me. In the face of that silence I stopped being a woman of independent means and fighting spirit, and became that weakest of beings, a mere daughter.

I sat on the front seat of his taxi and in silence this man seized my ear and began to twist it until I could not move fast enough to get out of his taxi, but once he had hold of my ear he did not seem to want to stop twisting it, until he had me doubled over, trying to twist my whole body with my poor ear, and I was reduced at last to tears and shrieks as I had not even let out in the worst of the old days with Mother's belt against my skin. This loathsome man remained silent, and when at last he let me go, and I could straighten up and look into his face, he was as expressionless as a mask. He stared at me as if I was something that was not worth spending an expression on, serene in his nastiness. My ear burned in my head, I panted, I ran at the nose, and I had to watch this cold man get into his taxi and prepare to drive off and leave me defeated and destroyed.

But although this man was like Father, he was not Father, and I could find it in me to fight back. I wrenched open the passenger door and with the pain of my ear filling my head I jerked that door backwards with all my considerable strength. The hinges held, but something creaked in a strained way, and I felt that a few more heaves would snap that door straight off its hinges, and then this man with his plastered hair and fat moustache would finally have to pay attention, and be touched by the chaotic hand of emotion.

Of course, long before those obstinate hinges could snap, strong policemen's arms were holding me, and plenty of people were shouting. I liked the feel of those strong arms around me, longed to be held even tighter, and struggled so that a second policeman had to be brought along, and finally I stood with the arms of two powerful young men around me, and that was a kind of love, and consoled me for the chill that had entered my heart in the face of this silent contemptuous man. I stopped struggling then, and laughed at the way the door hung, bruised like my ear, and how that brilliantined man's mouth was opening and closing at last under his moustache and making loud sounds of grief and fury. This was his property, and property called forth feeling.

Taken Away Again

I loved the feel of the policemen's arms around me, and knew now that I was past the point where any man's arms would cling to me, except to stop me doing something people disapproved of. I loved it, and struggled against those four young arms, and felt myself writhing against them, as my life had never let me writhe against any man in passion.

But when they brought up a grey van, and thrust me into it, their hands unsympathetic on my bottom as they shoved me up the metal steps, I did not enjoy it any more, and the glee drained out of me like water from a sock. There was a metal bench in this van, that I crouched on, and a shutter that let only enough light in to see how dark it was, and how small. I could not move my bulk in this space. My arms were trapped by my coat, caught up under me, my legs were cramped by the metal bench opposite, my head was crushed by the metal roof, and I could hear frightened gasping, the breathing of someone close to panic, and knew it was myself locked again in the kind of space that was as suffocating as a nasty death.

I was much older, now, though, and had learnt a few things. I did not let myself be suffocated, and I would not let the poisonous air of panic engulf me. *It is all right, I will be all right*, I repeated to myself, but the van jerked and roared, the air hummed in my ears, my stomach heaved, and when we stopped with a jolt and I was flung sideways and scrabbled against smooth metal without being able to find a way to get upright again, I grew hot and mad as if with the old fears.

The door opened, though, before fear seized me, and when I saw sky, and sunlight on a corner of building, I was calmed and remembered who I was, and that I was someone enjoying life and its experiences, not someone who could succumb to the first sweat of fear. *Who do you think you are?* I asked the policemen, no longer warm embracers, as they came towards me. *Young men, who do you think I am, some lifeless criminal or other?* But their young faces were closed now under their caps and they did not speak, did not look at my face, only at my fat wrists as they seized them and hurried me into the building and jammed me against a counter like a counter in a shop, but there was nothing to buy here except a fat policeman with a greasy yellow face like a pocked cheese, and I did not wish to buy him. *There is nothing I want here*, I said in my grandest manner. *There has been an error made, and I will leave now.* But the policemen beside me gripped my arms above the elbow, in the flesh that hurt, they knew how to hurt as well as hug, these men safe in their serge, and I could not move, only feel my book bag slip out of my hand. I felt crooked and twisted in my coat, felt the hair slipping into my eyes, felt chaos might not be far away. The man like a cheese pushed his cap back on his head and scratched his scalp so that dandruff floated down and thrust his big yellow face at me. *There is nothing you want here, eh*, he said, mimicking the way I spoke, and mincing in a way I never did. *Nothing you want, eh, well, we want something, dearie, we want a few of your particulars.* He leered at me across the counter and I drew back at the contempt and lechery in his face, and my instinct was to clutch at my particulars and not let him have them.

But we all grew weary of standing at this counter, and I was sick of the way the policemen's thumbs were pressing into the flesh of my arms, and the way the counter was hurting the flesh of my chest. I gave them my particulars and held my head up, and tried not to feel belittled, crammed against this counter with the policeman breathing hard over each laboured letter, licking his pencil so that his tongue became purple. They wanted to know when I was born, and I let the words ring out proudly across the counter, and the cheese policeman thought, and leered some more, and used his fingers to count, and finally said, *Well, Lil, I would not have said you was in your first youth, but here you are a woman in your forties, you are old enough to know better.* His finger ran down the form again and he said: *Height*, but I had had enough of answering and being sneered at, and did not answer. I nearly fell as the policemen ran me backwards against the wall and straightened me forcibly against it. I stood proudly then, thinking of the executions of brave men against such walls, but when they had measured me they bundled me forward to the counter again and stood holding me crookedly. The cheese policeman, more pocked-looking than ever now his tongue was purple, made a great show then of leaning over the counter to look me up and down and said, *Well, Harry, what kind of build is it would you say, I would say build stout, eh*. They all laughed, and I wanted to shrink in shame, and I was beginning to loathe these men, who were not just doing their job now, but taunting me and loving it, full of hatred for me, and what had I done to deserve all this?

Come on, dearie, the purple tongue said, *come and we'll take your picture, something for us to remember your lovely face by, and will you autograph it for us?* The policemen on my arms sniggered, for this man had stripes on his sleeves, and his jokes had to be sniggered at, and they pushed me against another piece of wall and took my picture. How cross and fearful I must have looked, how despairing, how loathing of these men! I wanted to cover my face with my hands, but the policemen stood beyond the reach of the lens, holding my arms out stiffly like pieces of wood, so my naked face was laid bare to the black eye of the lens and a little of my soul was stolen from me.

When the camera had clicked and my fear was caught for ever in it, the policemen let me go for a moment, as if we had all gathered here just for the moment in which the camera had caught its truth. It was only a moment, but it was long enough for me to recapture a morsel of myself and my dignity in being who I was, a substantial woman of character. This woman, who they had tried to mock, still had life in her. I turned my back on the camera and the men, bent over, and pulled up my old black skirt, and there was silence behind me as these men confronted the fact of my large bottom in its large cotton underwear. *If you care to leer and mock, let me give you something to leer and mock at*, I shouted, but when I was forcibly straightened up, and my skirt pulled back down over my bottom, there was no leering and no mockery on their faces any more. They had a serious look. I had wiped the laughter off their faces, and taken back the centre of the stage of my own life.

I went quietly with them to the cell where they locked me in with a blanket and a smelly dunny, but I was serene now, having silenced them and proved my power. There was a window in the cell, high up, and I calmed myself watching the blue until it faded into mauve and pink, and finally it was black and my neck was sore from staring up for so long, remembering heaven.

Their Honour

In the morning they took me to the court, and I was scornful of the way everyone whispered in the corridors, and the way they bobbed their heads as if under the axe when they entered. Up above us all, the magistrate was a tiny man dwarfed by his huge bench, another counter, but there was even less I wanted to buy here. The air was full of the murmurings of the damned, outside and at the back of the court where we all waited. We were crimes pressed together on a hard bench, in a murmuring that was all around us, although no one could be seen talking.

Names were called out in nasty flat voices and people went sheepishly or swaggeringly to the front to confess that they were that person. I watched and grew anxious, for those flat voices, and the flat grey light, and the hunched figures standing in the dock were making it hard for me to remember that I was Lilian

234

Una Singer: no one cared, here no one knew my name, and the machinery of this court would roll on over any event or person, I felt, and I began to feel myself disappearing.

I hung on, though, repeating my name to myself, and reminding myself that out there in the real world there were people who knew me, even one or two who might be thought to care for me a little. I hung on, thinking of Frank and Zara, and the man from whom I bought my oysters, with an accent like a foreign language. I hung on, numb from the bench, and at last I heard my name called out in that flat nasty voice: *Lilian Una Singer*. I stood up so quickly, and so awkwardly after sitting for so long, that people began to stare, and I called out in a voice I refused to allow to be reedy: *I am she, I am Lilian Una Singer, and proud of it.* Everyone stared and even the tiny magistrate peered down from beyond his counter: everyone stared, and acknowledged my large existence, and I was restored. Some policewoman of an age to match my own, and with large plain cheeks like mine, bustled me down into the dock, with no gentleness in her hard hands as she pushed at me.

Words began to bounce around in front of me, and I clung to the edge of the dock and tried not to be confused. I awaited my moment, for I had decided that I owed myself a moment in all this gabbled ritual. *Stands accused of offensive behaviour to wit the opening and closing and slamming of car doors on the 15th day of June 1946 apprehended and arrested by Inspector Lush and Constable Sparkman and brought before this court.* All this was gabbled like a spell being cast, but I was a bigger witch than any of them and would not be outshone by their puny magic. I felt my magic threatened, though, felt myself ignored and made tiny again by uncaring men who did not know or care that I was Lilian, and had a soul. There seemed no point at which I could interrupt this spell, so I gathered my courage, which was leaking out of me into this grey room, and cut across it all: *I will not be spoken of like this*, I called out in a dignified way, and was gratified by the silence that fell around me, although I did not know what to do with it. *You are all travesties*, I called, rather wildly now, the words coming at random, *and offensive behaviour is wind in company, and I have never been guilty of wind in company*. There was a tittering around me, then, and a mumbling of more animation than before, and I took heart, and felt myself expanding, and held the dock strongly, staring up at the pin-head of the magistrate behind his bench.

I was preparing more words, enjoying this feeling of having an audience, and turning all this theatre onto myself, but the policewoman with meaty cheeks was opening the gate of the dock and pulling me out, and piping words were coming from the tiny head up there, and a gavel banged on the bench, and all at once I was out of the court, deprived of my audience, being hustled with no gentleness back down the hallway of the murmuring souls, and back into the world where faces were made of wood, and did not hear no matter what you said to them.

He has given you hard, a policeman said to me as he propelled me into a van. *Your big fat mouth has got you two weeks of hard*. I thought I must be losing my grip because his words made no sense to me, although I understood each one, and they were not the strange words of the smiling man who sold me oysters, but there was no time to ask him what he meant, or to ask anyone anything, because they were pushing at my bottom again, and I was sprawling again on the metal bench of the dark van, familiar now, and smelling of the piss of someone else's fear, greater even than mine.

Hard

I found out what *hard* was in the laundry of the jail, among steam that made me melt, and the hissing and churning of great vats. When I first entered, pushed by a warder with hard hands, I was bewildered by this huge echoing space full of cream-painted machinery and gleaming stainless steel. Above the din of the machines the voices of the women were as shrill as sea-birds, and their cackles, when one of them shouted something they found amusing, frightened me. I was confused by the chaos of such volumes of water, such a roaring and hissing of gas under the vats, such powerful blasts of soap and the smell of starch.

The warder shouted something at me and I shouted back, *What? I beg your pardon?* but she turned and left behind a clanking of locked doors, and I stood alone among the steam until a muscular woman in the coarse green prison clothing poked me in the stomach with a hard forefinger and pushed a broom into my limp hand. I saw her mouth move, and heard a vague roar of words, but could not understand. *What? I shouted again. I beg your pardon? What?* The muscular woman stared at me with contempt, as if I was an imbecile given into her care, and she grabbed the broom in my hand and shook it, so hard my teeth rattled together. She shouted again, and I could not understand, but she had vanished now behind something that spurted and bubbled dangerously, and I stood with the broom, confused, until I caught a glimpse of her among cream pipes, and she made violent gestures at me, so I tried to oblige and began to sweep.

It was hard here, I was beginning to see, and I had to learn very quickly how to do things I had never done. All the other women I could see seemed to know how to do everything: how to fold sheets in pairs, walking gravely into each other and exchanging their corners, how to sweep, and how to scrub floors. I could see women doing all these things. I could resist feeling foolish in most situations, but was reduced to feeling contemptible when I realised my life had been privileged.

Here, Miss Fancy-Pants, the muscular woman said, suddenly at my side again, snatching the broom from me as I was fumbling with it and making the mess on the floor worse. *Here, see what kind of a botch you can make of a bit of scrubbing.* She pushed me down on my knees like a cow and thrust a scrubbing-brush into my hand, and I began blindly to scrub, baffled by so much shouting and hostility. The women in green all knew each other and shouted familiarly, slapped each other, touched each other's faces, pushed back the hair on each other's cheeks gone lank with steam. They called and laughed and I could not follow what they said, as if I had suddenly become foreign, or truly mad at last.

I was dizzy from being on hands and knees for so long, and was becoming anxious about the amount of water I had spread on the floor around me, when a siren pealed out suddenly. The muscular woman was nudging me with the toe of her shoe, and, red in the face and wrinkled with rage, she pointed at the wet and soapy floor I was kneeling on with my knees and skirt sodden. She mouthed in fury at me and all I could do was stare open-mouthed back at her, close to tears at all this rage, and at my own confusion and incompetence. With a great hiss and clank, the machinery around us suddenly closed down and in the blessed silence the muscular woman, cords standing out on her neck with the force of her shouting, roared at me. *You, Miss High-and-Mighty, how dare you, how bloody dare you, you will clean up this disgusting mess or get no bloody dinner, Miss bloody Smart Aleck.* I tried to say *But how?* but she had turned away and my voice was lost in my throat, came out nothing more than a croak. I was left kneeling in my puddle of dirty water, and had not felt such despair for years, and such an emptiness, having someone shout so harshly at me for no sin I could see. I knelt like a sick cow, my head bowed in my bewilderment, and heard all the laughing women clatter out of the room towards their dinners, and when I heard the laughter fading down the hallway I recovered myself enough to feel angry, and stand up, a person again, Lilian Una Singer, not an animal.

I found my way to the dining room by following the smell along the gloomy corridor and all my anger and bewilderment evaporated in the gigantic hunger I suddenly suffered. But at the door of the huge barn full of long tables, the muscular woman stopped me with a strong palm in my chest. *Well, Miss Prissy, have you cleaned up that mess you made?* and another woman in green yelled through a mouthful of cabbage: *Course she fucken hasn't, she's a fucken bludger, Lois.* Lois spun me around then and pushed me out of the warm room where everyone was filling themselves with warmth and chat, and pushed me back along the corridor to the laundry. There Lois saw my sad suds, and pushed me so hard I fell against a machine with a cry of pain that was not all physical. *Scum!* Lois shouted. *Wipe up that bloody slops or there'll be no bloody dinner, and I bloody mean it.*

I was numb now with the outrage and hurt of it, and used my ingenuity. There were no rags, no sponges, none of the things I had ever seen women wiping at floors with, so I took off my coarse green shirt and used that, kneeling in my singlet wiping up the suds, wringing them out clumsily back into the bucket, until the floor was damp but no longer awash. I was trembling now with hunger and unhappiness, and could not wring enough moisture out of the shirt in the end, but put it back on, seeing no alternative, and trusted to body heat to do its job in time, and dry me.

Back in the dining room, I was allowed in now and went to where the food was. There was no meat left, and only pieces of cabbage, and the carrots no one wanted, and sodden potatoes from the bottom of the pot. But I ate without caring, cramming it in, and the women left me alone until I had eaten. Then Lois came over and fingered my wet shirt, and made loud sounds of disgust. *She used her bloody shirt, she is a filthy little miss, eh?* The women glanced over at me, sitting hunched up wet and dirty at the table, but they did not care, and looked away again and took up their conversations. Lois hissed at me with the muscles moving in her jaw: *You will learn, Miss Smarty-Pants, and we will see who will have the last bloody laugh, my lady.* My cabbage rose in my throat to choke me, such dislike was in this woman's face, and I was without resource.

Later, four of us were locked together into a cell with bunks, and on that first night, confused and tired after that day of hard labour, I hoped I could restore myself by entering into conversation with these women. *I am Lilian*, I said by way of introduction, for I could not tell if these three women had been scrubbing or folding with me, I found they all looked too much alike in their green garments. *I am Lilian*, I said, and smiled, and tried not to succumb to the soul-stealing effects of the walls of an institution, and indifferent faces. The three women looked towards me as I stood under the bare bulb: we all looked ugly under that light, and when they turned and looked at me without smiling or speaking I wondered if it was my ugliness they found loathsome. *Yes*, one of them nodded at last, and then they went back to talking among themselves in a way I was not invited to join, and I stood in the glare of the bulb and wondered if I existed at all, or if I were invisible.

I tried to remind myself that newcomers are never made welcome in small societies. It was hard to ache in every joint and to long for a bit of a laugh or to share a bit of a story, and to have women beside me who were as unreceptive as any wall. I lay on my tiny bunk, which sagged dangerously under me, and which was so narrow I could not turn over. I lay with the light raining down on me and felt tears sting under my lids and run warm down my cheeks. How many years it was since I had cried, I did not know, but it was years since I had been reduced, as I had been on this day, to being invisible.

There was not a soul here, had not been a soul since I had been thrust into the van, who knew or cared who I was. I was invisible, and how much difference could there be between being invisible and being dead?

I wept silently, and heard the brutal women in green laughing, not at me, I hoped, and whispering urgently. All I could hear from my bunk was *pss pss pss*, like a small dangerous fire.

Currying Favour

I could not seem to please the women here. There were women in tight uniforms that made their busts like small edifices, and there were others in shapeless green garments, but I could not make an impression on any of them.

But I was not an imbecile, and learned quickly. I learned where the sponges were kept, and how to sweep the lint and dirt neatly into a pile and get it into the dustpan. But even when, after a day or two, I had mastered these puny skills, the women still treated me as if I was reprehensible. My voice began to shrink and disappear. I heard it sometimes in the dining room, I heard myself piping to the hard-faced women who doled out the food: *Hello*, I heard myself, *How are you?* I heard myself speak to the woman next in line, with her smeared tin tray: *Looks good*, I would say, *I am hungry, too*. But they never answered, except with a look of contempt, and after Lois yelled at me one day, *Stop your bloody sucking-up, Singer, it will not work here, none of your rich bitch tricks will wash here*, I stopped trying to raise a smile or a word from anyone. The woman next to me in line, perhaps seeing that I was on the point of tears, took the trouble to say, *You lot, you are the fly-by-nights, see, and us regulars cannot be bothered with you*. Then she moved away, just another woman in green, but I thought about what she had said, and saw how bitter it must feel for women who were condemned to fold sheets for years, to have someone like myself, prissy of accent and incompetent with a broom, coming in and leaving again in two weeks. I tried to tell myself that I, too, might be guilty of the same unkindness if I could see freedom being flaunted before me, as they could when they looked at me. And freedom was a relative thing, I saw: I was as free as a bird in their eyes, for what was two weeks, even two weeks of hard, in a sentence of years?

I understood, but it did not reduce the pain or the frightening emptiness, the feeling that my grasp was loosening with each lonely day that passed. I was slipping away from myself, and in the morning when the siren woke us up, I lay for a moment and reminded myself: I am Lilian Una Singer, student of life, and this is an experience. But the hours of being invisible and unheard wore away my certainty as the day passed, and by bedtime I was fearful, exhausted, fighting the panic of being no one at all.

It reminded me, of course, of that other place where I had lost myself. But I did my best not to remember that, because I felt myself close to slipping back into the grey canvas room where no being could prosper. Each morning I reminded myself of my name, and sometimes brought a little William to bear on the situation, my most faithful companion, always waiting in my memory for the hours of greatest need. To the warder with her stick hanging from her belt, who counted us into the dining room at breakfast, I said each morning, *What day is it today?* and when she told me, I comforted myself for the first hard hours with the thought that another day had passed, and that eventually all fourteen of them would have worn away, and I would be allowed to leave.

In the World

By the time the day of my release arrived I was wearied into lethargy by so much ignoring. I stood at another counter while they ticked my belongings off on a list and returned them to me, and when I stood again in my own clothes, some of my being and voice returned, although my voice sounded scratchy and strange to me now, the voice of someone who had been declared missing, and was not sure if she could find her way back.

Ah! What a greeting the street was, with Frank waving his bottle at me from beyond a tram, and the din and richness, the clamour and bustle, the colour and exuberance, all the life! How I loved it, coming out of a hell of silence! I almost knelt on the pavement and kissed it, for I saw now that this was my home, I belonged here. I was recognised, I had a part to play here, in the life of the streets. I swore I would never allow myself to be withdrawn again, but live always among these people, and be seen and heard, noticed and remembered. *Frank, Frank*, I blubbered, and hugged him so tightly I heard him grunt. *Frank, I almost died in there, oh, Frank, tell me who I am.* And Frank, that true friend, hugged me back and cried in my ear, *Why, Lil, what did they do to you, you are Lil Singer, of course, larger than life, and the person who matters to us all.*

Poets Abound

My life resumed, but on a more public level now, and always on the move. *Mobility is the key*, I told people in confidence as I stepped into their taxis. Inside I was queenly, waving from the wrist to those we passed, who sometimes stared, sometimes did not notice. Today my driver was a sad Slav of some kind with three deep creases in the back of his neck and a gold ring on his little finger. I chose to ride in the back, with a woman in lilac shantung. I had seen this woman before, her shantung was familiar, and so was the lacy hankie she held up now in front of her face. The driver did not argue with me when he saw that the woman in lilac did not intend to cause a fuss. *You are Lil Singer*, she said, informing me, and I could see and smell that she had had a drop or two.

We drove up William Street, past a Rolls-Royce as pink as a licked lolly, up the hill towards the Cross. We were borne along in the taxi on a gush of power, the springs bounced under me, sun glittered off the bonnet, and it was easy to see today why we all went on living, *Yes, I am Lil Singer*, I said, *and will give you a short recitation*. The woman in lilac shantung gazed and smiled from behind her hankie and looked more familiar to me as the moments passed, and seemed to enjoy the recitation, beginning a little light applause between her gloved hands when I had finished. The driver, that lugubrious man, turned and showed me two gold teeth in a wild Slav smile, and then in some thick phlegmy language, flecks of which landed on the seat back between us, began to declaim. It went on for a long time, until cars behind us were blaring. It was easy to see why he had left his country. Exile would be the only place for such snarled language. *I am a poet*, he told me thickly before driving on, and although I did not believe him, I admired his attitude, and was pleased that my example had inspired him into a flight of invention.

An Encounter with Silent Dignity

Others failed to show the right attitude, and revealed themselves without knowing that they did so. The man in the back seat of another afternoon taxi was one of those who say nothing rather than say anything foolish. He stared, of course, at the sweating woman with all the chins, who had jumped in at the lights, but could think of nothing to say that might not have made him look foolish, and sat instead with a foolish look of expectancy on his face, in bogus calm. A man of character would have spoken to me, but this man, in his neat jacket and short fur of hair, was no man of character.

The taxi-driver was a man of character, and did not sit in bogus calm, or any other sort. He shouted and pushed at my shoulder, until the lights changed and he was forced to drive on, but continued slapping at my leg until all around us cars were honking at his erratic course from lane to lane. *Keep your eyes on the road*, I told him, and turned to the bogus man in the back seat, who was staring out of his window as if Market Street was interesting. *This man is driving badly*, I told him, and he was forced to glance at me. *Yes*, he agreed, and smiled a wan smile. *Where are you off to?* I asked, for it would be important for him if he could rise to this occasion. If he could manage that, and not solidify in bogus calm, his life might change. But he did not answer, looking mysterious and shaking his head at me. He did not realise that something was happening that he would always remember, that he would be mentioning this incident to people fifteen years from now. *What did she say?* they would ask. But, unchanged, he would have to shake his head and smile mysteriously, and say *I don't remember*, as if concealing something.

Timidity is no good to anyone, I told him now, perhaps a little louder than I intended, perhaps a little annoyed with his smugness, for he retreated into his corner of the cab and might have jumped out to get away, except that he was too timid for that, too, *You are a success*, I said, and he looked successful, with his smooth clothes, and sitting in the back seat of the taxi, not watching the meter. *But you are hollow*. A muscle in his jaw moved when I said that, and I hoped he would speak to me at last, but he wound down his window instead and waved at a policeman on a corner. *I am disappointed in you*, I told him as I opened my door and got out, ignoring the driver, who was still shouting, and now trying to hold me. *And you a husband*. For I had seen the gold band on his finger, and guessed that he would be too ashamed to tell his wife about all this. But when the sting of his failure had left him, after the years had passed, and I was famous and dead, he would be proud of having a story to tell about me then. His life had been made richer by that small story, and he would never know when he told the story of *How Lil Singer jumped into my taxi* that the story was against him.

And why should the policeman care? He pretended not to be able to hear the man with the gold band, and waited ponderously until the traffic cleared, and then ponderously crossed the road, and listened with a head bent to the cab window, ponderously unbuttoning his pocket to get at his notebook, and by that time I was watching from a block away, from the prominence of Central, and could see what an obstruction this stopped taxi was, and how the policeman would have to order the driver to move along.

246

The Arm of the Law

Policemen became my friends, now that I knew how far I could go without running the risk of *hard*, and I became familiar with the different kinds of policeman that the city produced. My preference was always for the young blushing ones, buttoning up their lips under the caps that seemed a little too large for them. They were good at cajoling, and it was easy to imagine them at home with their children, when they cajoled me out of a taxi or someone's car that had stopped too long at the lights. They were not usually too cross with me. *Come along now, Lil*, some fresh-cheeked young policeman would coax me, as if I was three, like the chubby child he had left at home that morning. When I was three I would have enjoyed a little of that, but now I felt it was too late, and I could not start again, with a sensible and cheery policeman for a father, who knew how to deal with women in taxis. *But it is too late now, young man*, I told him, *too late*, and I watched him push back his blue serge to inspect his watch. *Too late for what?* he said, curious, even though being curious was against the rules of being a policeman. *I would have liked cajoling, and to be taken up by strong arms*, I told him. *I longed for it.* His chin was beginning to flush purple now, and he took a step closer to me, dislodging a scrap of paper from under his shoe like a diversionary tactic. *I said come along*, he said, trying to be strict but fair, but it was too late for being strict but fair, too.

Those policemen went home, too, with their story of Lil, to tell their wives. I loved the knowledge that these muscular men would be taking me home, into the warm kitchen where their wives stood mashing potatoes and the baby gaped and gestured. *I saw Lil Singer today*, he might say. His wife would stop her mashing and wait with the saucepan in her hand for her husband to join her small life with my big one, by telling his story. *She was causing an obstruction*, my policeman would say, and kick at the lino in his inadequacy, for there are born story-tellers, but policemen and their formulas are not among their number. *She said some stuff at me.* His wife would go back to her potatoes and turn pink, the way he liked, with the exertion of mashing. *What did she say, exactly?* she might ask, but it would be unreasonable to expect him to remember, and the baby might have her own ideas, and a better flair for a story than her father.

Fame

I was beginning to be a public figure and was enjoying it, the way people nudged each other and pointed. My story was beginning to have a part in the stories of others, and I was becoming a small part of history.

I was at my best on a slow tram, or a bus lurching down George Street. Everyone greeted me, and I greeted them all as I hauled my weight on board. *Morning, everyone*, I called, and they looked, even the ones who did not know me, and who were playing the game of not noticing anything. Women in lilac frocks, freshly powdered after tea and scones at David Jones, were fascinated by my moustache of sweat.

The air is free, I told the conductor who came with her wide-jawed leather pouch and stood in front of me while the tram rang its bell, but this was a stony-faced one who looked as if she had woken up with a headache. *Did you wake up on the wrong side of the bed?* I asked as nicely as I knew how, to cheer her up, but she tightened the skin on her face another notch and thrust her grey palm at me. *Fares, please*, she said, and tried to stare me down, but no one could. *Fares, please*, she said again, and her voice was becoming shrill and nasty. I watched her lips, where the lipstick had worn into the grooves, and the saliva was collecting in one corner. She was becoming excited, and jabbed her seamed palm towards me, but stopped short of touching me. *I will not wear out the seat*, I told her, *and will breathe only the air I am entitled to, and will provide a free recitation for your pleasure.* I had to raise my voice over her squarks, and began a little William, but saw her lips pucker into fury, and she twitched the bell-rope so that the tram stopped there in George Street, outside the marble bank. I made myself comfortable and spread my large knees apart under my coat, and listened to all the different sounds this furious woman could make. She snapped closed the leather pouch as if to lock me inside, and threatened, and pointed, and even stamped her foot once, so some cigarette butts jumped and the dust flew. *We will not budge, not until you have paid*, this woman shouted. *I know who you are, Lil bloody Singer, and I am telling you I am not impressed.* She was on the point of becoming eloquent and I sat, listening and smiling a little, to encourage, and to bedevil her further. *They told me about you, up at the depot*, she hissed, becoming proud now, and coming so close I could feel her hot angry breath on my face. *I told them you would never get away with your tricks with me and by Jesus I meant it.* She flushed, hearing herself blaspheme in her pride and rage, and had to begin shouting again, to cover the moment where she had taken the Lord's name in vain, and in uniform, too, when she was devout and made sure she went to Mass for her immortal soul's sake, and would never have said such a thing if the fat devil easing her knees apart had not provoked her past bearing. The driver had come up behind her by now, too, and saw that this was a woman's fuss, full of shrillness, and was preparing to play the tower of strength, and calm all that emotion with his man's steadiness and sense. *Now now now*, he said, and stood hitching up his pants and looking magisterial. *What's the fuss here, Flo?* Flushed Flo pointed her trembling finger at me and I nodded and smiled, getting ready to enjoy a long dispute. I knew that it would end with a small crowd, and a blushing policeman the centre of attention as he tried to lever me off the seat. I would not resist, but I would not help either, and in the end he would be forced to hug me hard, plant his feet solidly on the floor of the tram, and heave so that through his blue serge I would feel his breath coming heavily, and perhaps even his heart beating. For a few moments I would be enveloped in his strong young arms and smell his sweat, and see from the closest possible range how the down grew on his earlobe.

I was looking forward to all this, and the morning promised well, but a blushing woman with a raffia shopping basket came forward. *Please*, she said, *please!* Flo stopped for a moment in the stream of her outrage to stare. The woman burnt brick-red under an ugly smocked bonnet like a tea-cosy. Everyone was staring, and she had the appearance of a woman not used to much attention. Her upper lip began to perspire, but she was driven by something urgent, and said, in a voice made unsteady by so many people staring: *I will pay, I am in a very great hurry, I must catch my ferry, I will pay the fare.* This was the easy part, and then she had to turn to me, her eyes grown small and red with urgency and embarrassment: *Will you let me pay, Lil? Because I must catch my ferry.* She looked to me like a good woman, and I could see spinach at the bottom of the raffia basket, and could imagine her pride in making the tea-cosy hat. She was a brave woman, too, and it has always been my policy to reward any kind of courage. *Thank you so much*, I said in my most impressive way. *I should be charmed.*

After she had fumbled and found the change, and poor Flo had had to take it, and swallow her rage and righteousness, ripping the ticket off and thrusting it at the woman, the tram began to jerk along George Street again. The woman with the tea-cosy did not know what to do. She would have to tell the story of her courage to the family later, over dinner, to the husband chewing his way through her leg of lamb, the children squashing their potatoes. How would she tell such a story? Would they believe her? She stood swaying with the tram, holding the rail, still blushing as if a fire raged inside her. She was waiting it out, until this terribly public event would be over, and in the sea breeze on the way to Manly she could slowly swallow her public flame, and arrange the story so that she would feel it could be believed. Her children would listen with potato in their open mouths, and would be struck by the way their mother's face became the colour of a flower as she told her story, and would have to be reminded to swallow their dinner. *It is rude to stare*, their father would tell them.

You are familiar with me, I told the woman as she waited for the cool air of her ferry, *but who are you?* I seized her wrist above the raffia bag, to make her sit down beside me, because I wanted to participate in the story she would tell about the two of us. Now that she was beside me, and we were nothing more alarming than two middle-aged ladies on a tram seat, she became calmer. *I am Agnes Armstrong*, she told me, and smiled, because close up she could see that I would not bite her, or embarrass her any more. *And what else?* I asked, and she peeked in to consult the spinach, then said, *Well, I am a wife, and a mother of two*. But I was still not satisfied. *What else are you?* I asked, but she was standing up now, the Quay in sight, smiling and glad that this was nearly over. That gave her courage, and she laughed recklessly and lifted her chin like a young beauty, and cried, *Oh, what else I am would take a year to tell!* and I had made her beautiful for that moment. She was off the tram then, springing away for her ferry, but I could see that her face still had the echo of that smile and

251

would see her home, and be with her while she told her remarkable story.

Love at Last

There was a morning when Frank startled me by leaping up crookedly so he nearly fell, waving the bottle by its neck, yelling, *Hey Johnny, Johnny! Got your sister here! Worth a few bob to you?* He was preparing to chase my brother through the jammed cars, but I caught the edge of his coat in time. In my grip, the hem tore loose in a long ribbon and one shoulder seam cracked open like an egg. *Me coat!* Frank shrieked so that two secretaries in shocking pink looked, shocked, and snickered. *Me coat!* Frank continued to wail, and my brother, his face pink from its morning shave, and hidden behind his glasses, vanished among the bobbing heads along the pavement without seeing anything.

It was too late now for Frank. It had never been the right time, but now under our bush, or down in my storm-water channel, or on the beach by the park, we could offer each other the touch of our skins by night. A hand in one's own can be a great comfort, and the feel of a warm chest pressed against one's own. *If I loved women, Lil, it would be you I loved*, Frank told me, who was now beyond love of anyone, boy or man or woman. But we lay in our blanket on the beach, and watched those friendly stars, which had been my companions for so many years. Frank's hand was soft in mine, and warm, and we exchanged the small messages of our blood through the skin. When we embraced and my face was lost in the leathery skin of his neck and the cold strings of his hair, our bodies lay tightly together. There were times when we seemed one flesh, separated only by the accident of bodies. In the dark his voice in my ear was moist and intimate and when his lips found my cheek, and pressed it for a moment, I melted in my body and floated away into the night sky, into the spaces between those smiling stars. *I am passionate, too*, I whispered into his hair, and felt his arms tighten around me: *I am passionate, too*, I admitted at last, *and this is more than I ever hoped for*. Frank kissed me again on that spot on my cheek, and with a sigh feel asleep in my arms, and until dawn I held him, and felt his life against mine, beating and flickering together in love.

History

History is not the past, but the present made flesh. I saw more, as I became older, fatter, more easily tired. *Look*, I told myself, moving up William Street, and when I looked around I saw the window of an abandoned brothel, that was broken in the shape of a map of Australia. *Look*, I said later when I had forgotten, and was looking only at my feet, shuffling along a path in the Gardens: *Look*, I reminded myself, and surprised a woman who happened to be passing. When I looked up I could watch a paper bag full of wind that was chasing a cloud across the sky. *Listen*, I told myself, and heard the waves against the harbour-wall, a gull being peevish, the white tapping stick of a blind man against the stones. *Listen*, I told myself, *this is history*.

It was important that others should see what I, from my increasing age and slowness, was able to see. Passing women, blind men, gulls, would give ear only to speeches, not to a few words they could dismiss as an old woman muttering to herself. I took myself, then, down to the Domain again, that place of speeches under the indifferent trees, and found myself a box to stand on among the wild-eyed Reds. The Domain of a Sunday was the place where the history and meaning of the world was being resolved, and I knew that I had

253

a contribution to make. History belonged to me, even more than it belonged to the passionate young men leaning forward on their boxes and ladders in the way they knew Lenin did. But although history was mine, I stood on my soap-box waiting for words, and this time none came. Pugnacious men had gathered, and tourists arm-in-arm, but everyone became bored in the end, because the fat woman had nothing to say after all, but could only stand there and keep making a beginning. *Look*, she kept saying, or, *Listen*, and they all wandered off at last and left me with a small audience of those yellow-eyed sceptical gulls, and a bulky man readying himself to speak. *I am history, and so are you*, I yelled finally, so that the gulls took fright and wheeled into the air, and the bulky man's words were released from him, and he began to shout. *The running dogs of imperialism*, he was shouting, so hard I felt a fleck of his spit land on my cheek. *Jackals and capitalist lackeys on the body of the proletariat*. I did not know what he was talking about, or why he was so angry, but watched how the muscles around his mouth forced the words out like bullets, and how his eyes saw nothing but his own visions. I forgot mine, for the moment, and stepped down off my box, because I recognised that this angry man, with his mouthful of rhetoric, was Rick. I had last seen him in a morning coat of perfect fit, becoming Ursula's husband and bearing her off on his arm to a future of roses and smiles. Now he had become this angry man in a shabby brown suit, and was almost bald, so that I had to look again, to make sure.

He was not surprised when I told him who I was, but glanced at me briefly and said *Yes yes* as if it did not matter that Lil, who had been invited to be a bridesmaid at his wedding, but had relieved everyone by declining, was here now in front of him. Rick's eyes had always been green and distant, but now they flicked from side to side as he spoke, as if he was reading the grass. *The international ground swell is mobilising, Lil,* he told me urgently. *We will be the spearhead of history.* He grasped my forearm like a prophet. *It is destiny, Lil, we will all be men of destiny.* I could see it would have made no difference whose arm he grasped. *But I am my own destiny,* I told him loudly, for I could not be trumped, even after so many years, by Rick with his cold bottle-glass eyes. *I have always been my own destiny, and loved my inventions of myself.* Rick nodded, but he was not listening. He smoothed the baldness of his head, an untidy worn patch of grey scalp, and said: *Lil, I will be receiving a sum tomorrow.* His hand touched my arm again. *It is just a temporary embarrassment.* The words ran out of his mouth too easily: *Small pecuniary difficulties of a strictly temporary nature,* he said, and smiled a smile of strong stained teeth that was meant to convince me. *I am not convinced,* I told him. I could not stop myself speaking loudly to him, although I had no reason to think he was deaf. *I am not convinced by you,* I shouted, and saw him flinch and look at me again, using his eyes this time, and he was beginning to turn away so I could see his sad stooping shoulders and the thin cloth over them, flecked with dandruff, and he was any other pitiable old crank. *People have been kind to me,* I said, and stopped him, and emptied my purse into his dirty palm. He took on flesh again then and his shoulders became manly. *Tomorrow, Lil,* he repeated, and was still calling out, *I never forget a loan, Lil,* as I walked away from him in sadness and satisfaction.

Old Friends

Life and its plots had made me able to believe anything of what could unfold, and when I met Jewel again I was not surprised. *I know what I know, Lil,* Jewel said mysteriously, and winked. *It said in my hand I would get out and become God's mum, and here I am, out.*

Like all of us, Jewel was much older now, and had grown wiser, in her own way. At first, when a woman had gestured and called to me from across the road, I had not recognised her, because her face was painted a streaky black, in which her eyes were bloodshot and wild. She was old enough now to have grown into her face, and it was pleasant to have her sit me down beside her at the edge of the fountain and take my hand in hers. *Lil, you have not changed one bit,* she exclaimed. *Except now, look, it says you have found love, like I always said you would.* I laughed my big laugh then, that knew how to make a lot of noise, from making people stare in the streets.

Jewel said, *What do you regret, Lil? Tell me, and take my mind off my troubles, because they are after me again, Lil.* She crushed her palms together as if to press a new destiny onto the lines there. There was nothing much I could do to help her, but I could tell her what I regretted, and pass a little time.

She nodded seriously as I spoke, as if taking notes. I regretted almost nothing. There was a leather-bound copy of William that Father had given me long ago, before he knew that William was not just words. I regretted that, and it must have bubbled heavily, like a desperate drowning person, as he dropped it over the stern of the boat, but it had already been too late, I had already learned enough to keep me going. There were a few people I regretted not hitting. They might have thanked me for it in the end. I regretted not having said *yes* to F.J. Stroud, all those years ago. And of course I regretted the islands in the sun, the jungles, the gibber deserts, Niagara Falls, sleds drawn by reindeer, the feel of a whale lifting my boat into the air under me. Naturally I regretted all that.

Jewel had begun to leak tears as I waxed enthusiastic on all that I regretted. *By Jeeze, Lil*, she moaned, *I wish I was you, and regretted what you do.* Not many people have ever been moved to envy me, and I was silent with surprise. *Those who tell you they regret nothing are lying,* I said at last, *or lacking in imagination.* I wished someone was there to write it down, because this seemed wise enough to be worth a little immortality. And Jewel would not remember, and was hardly listening. *I have got me fate in me hands,* she said. *But they are after me, and want to stop me fate.* Jewel's face was starting to run with her tears. The black was coming off on her fingers and the tears were making pale streaks down her cheeks. *They are after me and will not let me be God's mum,* she said, and wiped sadly at her black fingers on the thigh of her dress. *Do you think they will recognise me and take me away?* she asked. What could I say? *No,* I said. *No.*

Glory Boxes

Frank had stopped driving his taxi some time before. I think there was an accident, police, a great deal of meaningless noise. Now his room had arreared so far that he had been dislodged from it, and lived in the storm-water channel in the park. We found that the storm-water channel was as good a place for two as for one. *This is the life, Lil,* Frank said, and leaned back against the curve of the concrete. *I could live here real well.*

Frank was a tidy man, house-proud in our storm-water channel. *Everything in its place and a place for everything,* he said, and propped the bottle upright between two bricks. *Things go missing, Lil, if you are not neat,* he said, and kept a hand on the neck of that bottle, even though propped between its bricks it could not go missing anywhere.

My room at the Cross was becoming smaller, meaner, stuffier, each time I went back to it, and Aunt Kitty's money was shrinking week by week. In any case, there is no wallpaper like stars, and no bed as soft as the sound of a sea breeze in leaves. *Come on, Lil*, Frank urged, *I will even have a go at carrying you over the threshold*. And at last, with my book bag full of the few things I treasured, I joined Frank in the great room of the park. *There is plenty of wood for fires, come the winter*, Frank said. *The abos did okay, and so will we*.

I loved my life with Frank. I had never set up house with anyone before, and loved the feeling of coming home at the end of the day to the place Frank and I shared. Frank had tried to carry me over the threshold, and we had clawed and grasped at each other, panting noisily and gasping, until we fell together on the grass. Frank had wheezed noisily for a few minutes and then said, *You cannot say I did not try, Lil, but you are a bride and a half, and I am only half a husband*.

I enjoyed the way Frank rolled us into our newspapers for the night, and loved to wake up when the birds were being insistent in the trees overhead and the sun was sending yellow fingers along the wet grass. Frank snored on beside me and I heard the city wake slowly, and the birds take second place as hurrying men in suits and women in high heels began to clatter along the paths to the city, and everyone got ready to die another day away. When Frank woke up, gradually, nodding off again before he got up and tidied his newspapers into a pile under a stone, we had the pleasure of sharing our dreams. I had not often woken up in the company of others, and shared dreams while they were fresh, except in the loony-bin, and no one wants to share their dreams in a loony-bin. Most there do not know that there is a difference between a dream and a life.

The sleep of the chaste is full of dreams. Mine were of burning towers and seas sweeping in over strange lands, lapping at trees and castle walls. *I do not admire chastity*, I told Frank, nodding off again over his bottle. *I do not admire chastity, although I am a virgin.* He woke from his stupor at that word and suddenly thrust his jacket sleeve up and flexed his skinny arm at me. *We will soon put that right*, he cried, and strained to make muscle appear, so that veins engorged along his arm and he began to cough. *I like my dreams*, I told him, and helped him pull his sleeve back down. *Deflowered, I might miss out on dreams.*

Our bliss was not conjugal, but chaste, but I did not envy anyone, and told the people on the buses, *I am a contented woman, and wish for nothing*, and they stared at me, and none could say the same for themselves.

A Life in a Bag

Jewel joined Frank and me in our storm-water channel when she came across us there. *Jeeze but you have got yourselves a good spot*, she admired, but would not drink out of the bottle that Frank waved at her. *I am expecting*, she said primly. *I do not drink while expecting.* Jewel had been expecting God's baby for as long as I had known her, but now she was certainly expecting something from the bulge under her dress. *Jeeze, I like it here*, Jewel said with satisfaction, and became part of our household, bringing with her a dowry of her belly and a plastic bag full of stolen baby bootees. *This is my life*, Frank told her with pride, and held up his gunny-sack, which held all that he owned. Jewel stared with her mouth open, breathing audibly in the way she did when she concentrated, then crowed suddenly. *And this is mine!* patting her gigantic stomach. *Ah, but Jewel, can you wear your life?* Frank asked, winking at me and pulling his boots out of his bag. *Or shave with it?* He held up his razor, for Frank was still fastidious about his face, and shaved after a fashion from time to time up at the hostel. Jewel frowned in silence, but finally thought of her answer. *Your life will not be able to talk back to you,* she cried, *but mine will, and will be famous!* Frank winked at me again but had no answer for Jewel, because it was true that his life would never grow up to be anything very much now.

All Happy Families

It is a funny kind of family, Frank said, but seemed to enjoy it. In the nights we built fires from wood frayed by the tides, and invented a few hard names for the stars. Like the others of long ago, we who sat on this dark beach had been slowly transported, by the nature of our lives and the choices we had made, to the stern lip of another land. The privilege of the first ones has always been to impose names of their own invention on the new world. *Hebdomedary*, Frank would say after a long silence. *How about that, Lil? Or concupiscence.* When the flames reached in and singed the wood it spat salt embers that pulsed on the sand before dying.

Those autumn nights were the times when we told the stories of our lives, either the ones we had or the ones we would rather have had. Jewel and I watched by cool starlight and hot flames as the tears slimed down Frank's cheeks. *The wife,* he'd say and look for the bottle leaning against his leg. *Me little girl,* he'd say, and the cork would make a hollow mocking sound. Those who spent their days smiling and worrying at each other, and their nights behind walls and windows, would claim that Frank had never had a wife or a daughter and had never wanted anything but the loving boy he had never quite had. But we listened and threw another stick onto the flames, and later I held him as he shuddered and hiccupped under the dew.

Across the water, as black as the inside of an ear, the yellow lights of those in the old country winked feebly at us. When our memories or inventions failed us we watched the yellow semaphore. *Snug as a bug in a rug*, Jewel said. She could just as easily have meant the three of us by the fire, or those secure in their houses and beds around the bay.

Mother and Young

Jewel was close to her time now, she thought, and had stopped being sick every morning, and moved slowly, like a cart. *No hospital*, she always said. *I will not have no hospital where they lock you up*. On those occasions when I tried to reason with her—*But, Jewel, if there are complications;* whatever *complications* were, I knew them only from *Gone With the Wind*— her eyes began to roll and her breath came faster. If I persisted—*Jewel, we must be realistic*, I would say, wondering at myself for the words—she would run down to the beach and sit among the rubbish, threatening to drown herself, baby and all. *Won't catch me locked up again*, she said, and hissed, *Incineration, that's what it is*. Her face as she sat among the rotting oranges was anxious but determined, her chin very pointed. *It is mine*, she said, shielding the lump under her dress. *Mine*. When I tried to come closer, saying something that was meant to soothe, she stood up, stumbling on rubbish, and waded out heavily into the water until she was standing up to her thighs in it, and I turned back. *It is mine*, she tried to explain more calmly later, *and they are all jealous because it is me that will have God's baby*. She stared down at her belly and made round gestures with her hands. *It is mine, see?* was finally all she was able to say.

No Humbug in a Baby's Bottom

Some women have babies and others have stories. I would have liked to have both. Nothing in my experience equipped me to be a midwife, but as a student of life I knew it was never too late to learn, and I wanted to add all experiences to my store. It was necessary to prepare for Jewel to become God's mum, because her bulge was getting bigger by the day. She still insisted that God would not be born in any hospital, but would emerge into the world on our beach, among the orange peels and lost sandals, where the storm-water channel deposited its gifts. I could not imagine this, but life had astonished me before now, so I did what I could to prepare myself.

I read books, spending days in the library, and the librarians looked twice when they saw what kinds of book Lil Singer was asking for. *I am a student of life*, I told them with dignity, Jewel's secret safe with me, and they were silenced, these young librarians who knew nothing except how to whisper. The books had not been quite as specific as an earnest student of life could have wished, but I learned what I could from them, and then went out into the streets, where I had always learned so much, and looked for some practical experience.

When a baby dribbled at me invitingly, up at the Cross, I decided it was time to begin to learn. *I would like to hold it*, I told the man, barring his path. The passage of years had not made me any less monumental, and this was a small man. *I am on my way home*, he said, but I only moved closer. I saw his fear in his eyes. He was afraid that I would rip the baby from his arms and gallop down the street with it, or squeeze its round head like an orange. *She needs changing, you see*, he tried once more, a male animal defending its young, but I was already reaching for the thick padded bottom and the swaddling chest. This father was graceful in defeat. *Here, get a hold of her like this*, he said, and in a moment I had a baby in my arms for the first time. *She is Dianne*, the father said, and blushed with pride in spite of everything. *She is our first.*

The baby pouted up at me like a tease, grinned gummily, frowned. Her hand waved up and down at my face, a finger brushed into my laughing mouth, and she laughed a small wicked laugh. *Aaaah*, she crowed, and I crowed back, *Aaaaah!* A man in woman's clothes stopped and looked with a hand up to his mouth; two ladies of the night waved across the street at me and called, *Pretty as a picture, Lil!* I asked, *Were you at the birth?* and this man, who would never parade his baby down the street again, blushed fiercely as he said, *Yes.* I held Dianne high in the air, my thumbs hooked in her tiny armpits, and said, *I need to know*. This father, whose pride in his daughter was more powerful than any fear, said suddenly, *She popped out just like a pea out of a pod*, and nodded around at the small crowd that had gathered. *Lil Singer*, I heard voices whisper at each other. *With a baby.*

This was a father not used to crowds, it was easy to see, but he nodded at the man in frills, and at the lady of the night on his left, whose black eye was at the yellow stage. *Just popped out like she'd been doing it all her life*, he said, and everyone laughed, even the policeman who had decided to stand on the edge of the crowd and *keep an eye on things*. I knew that little Dianne would grow up listening to the telling and retelling of the story of the day she was dandled by Lil Singer, and might tell it herself at last.

What Is Needed

I was anxious, but Jewel was serene, knowing she was prepared to become the mother of God. *I got all the necessary*, she said haughtily when Frank had had a bottle or two, or began to screech that she was loony, thinking she could have a baby on our beach. *Look*, Jewel said, and held up her plastic bag of bootees. *I am ready, see?* But Frank sprayed spittle in his derision. *It's nappies you need, Jewel*, he cried. *Use your loaf, Jewel, think of all that shit!* His laugh made Jewel cup her belly with her hands, *Nappies for its bum, nappies for its bummy bum bum*, Frank sang lustily. Only his cough stopped his song going on until dawn.

Frank was scandalised, too, that Jewel was not preparing a name for her baby. *Got to think of a few names*, Frank said. *It's just a thing till it's got a name*. Jewel looked frightened, as she always did when called upon to act. *What will I do, Lil?* she appealed, and although I did not feel strongly about names, I disagreed with Frank. *For years you were only F.J. Stroud to me*, I reminded him, and he smiled so that I could see how grooved and stained his teeth were from the years of smoke and drink. *Yes, Lil*, he said, and Jewel watched as if to surprise a secret. *Those were the days, eh?* Jewel continued to stare, but what lay between Frank, or F.J. Stroud, and me, was opaque to anyone but us. But something in the way we smiled at our memories made silent Jewel speak: *Was youse two sweethearts, then, was that it?* and our Jewel was preparing to become sentimental over sweethearts of long ago.

Leaving the Nest

No one came for Jewel, but she left in any case. She had become much more silent as the nights in the storm-water channel became colder, and her belly became an unmanageable size, and things began to fall apart. *We are gunna go north, Lil*, she said at last one morning, her eyes crazed now with the idea of the north and how it would be warm there, and mangoes falling off the trees. *They will not find us up there, to lock me up.* She could not stop herself glancing over her shoulder, and jumping at small sounds. *I will change my name,* Jewel said cunningly. *Then we will be right.* She winked at me and nodded. *I have got it all worked out, see.* Frank woke up with a snort and a fart and waved the bottle at her. *What do you mean,* he shouted, *change your name?* Jewel looked sly and pursed her lips, but could not resist telling us, *I will call myself Ruby,* she said. *Get it?* She began to wink at me as if she intended never to stop. *We will be right as rain,* she said, and picked up her plastic bag of bootees and left for the north. *Bye-bye, Lil,* she called from the fence where Frank and I stood watching and waving as she laboured away up the street. When she had disappeared Frank burped and put his arm around me so suddenly that he knocked the wind out of me, and said, *Well, Lil, it is just me and you now, like a pair of old farts,* and we both laughed so loudly the birds flew up in fear out of the trees.

The Last Loss

Frank took good care of me in our home by the water, tucking my feet into the newspapers at night, combing my thin old hair for me by the hour as we sat like a pair of baboons in the grass, grooming each other in peaceful silence. He took good care of me, but he was a sick man. He was yellow in the morning, yellow and trembling until he had sucked long enough at the bottle in the brown paper bag.

We are gunna die, Lil, Frank told me one dank night when the tankers mooed to each other like full udders in the fog. *And you will be the lucky one, Frank, and go first,* I said, and we both let slide some cool tears, thinking of how lonely I was going to be without Frank. *You will go first, and quickly, Frank, but I feel my death will come at me slowly*, I told him, but I did not try to resist, because if my death wanted to come at me slowly, that would be what happened.

Frank was planning his death, one step ahead of its arrival, and lay shivering and coughing by our fire with a few last tales to keep him warm. He was once a wealthy man, he said, and had written a will, he said, and left his estate in its entirety to me, he said. Another bottle, and he would claim to be the lost scion of the podgy House of Windsor.

I thought of my own death while Frank fended off his. Every third thought, on such cold nights, was my grave. There were noises in my head, too, rushing and roaring noises from time to time, and a feeling of birds massing behind my eyes, getting ready to fly somewhere. I would have liked to go like that, on the sand, with Frank making noises in his sleep beside me. Stars had never frightened me, even the black spaces between them had never frightened me. But Frank went first, as we had guessed. It was not in my arms, as we would both have wished, but on some street somewhere, staggering into the gutter with a last cough, or in some cold hospital bed with the screen drawn around him, because they had picked him off the street only to give him a bed to die in, or on some stretcher with the wailing of the ambulance filling his last moments. I had held his sick old hand, and embraced his thin old body, and watched him walk up into the city, and when at last it had been clear that he would never return, I wept long tears, but regretted nothing, because Frank and I had given all there was to give, and no love had ever been more true than ours had been.

Love Stories

I missed Frank more than I could say, and had to find some echo of the love we had shared. At the movies I found plenty of men with moustaches that I could pay money to and fall in love with. I loved their strong white teeth, and the way they caught heroines in moments of crisis, and kissed them. I squirmed in my seat then, and wondered if it would ever have been possible for me. At such times, in the sweet hot darkness, with the couples around me holding hands, and others up in the back stalls giggling and being noisy with peanut shells, I remembered all my beaux and let my eyes fill with easy movie tears. I was lonely now. There was no Rick to hit me, no John to conspire with, no Ursula to woo. There were no more sandy young men handing me leaves up in a tree, and no more hungry geniuses who were willing to cry for me. When I remembered that F.J. Stroud had even been willing to confront Father for my sake, the tears began to flow so noisily that the couple in front turned to stare. Having seen what there was to be seen, they turned back and giggled into each other's necks in a way I envied. *This is my experience of being alone*, I told myself, and tried to believe that I would be rewarded in the end, like all those swimming-eyed luminously tearful heroines I resembled so little.

When the movie was over, and all the couples had wandered out, dazed from so much darkness and each other, I remained for them all to stare at on their way up the aisle. I sat, filling my seat, with my book bag beside me trying to be a companion. When even the lonely men in gabardine coats, and one or two ladies with blue hair, had all left, I still sat on, watching the purple plush curtains and waiting.

I could not have said what I was waiting for, but when the manager came and told me, *The show is over*, and asked me to leave, my grief turned to anger and I would not move. I clung to the arms of my seat, and the short fat man who was the manager went away. He came back, of course, with the pimply young projectionist, and gestured curtly at him, so that I saw

I was about to be approached from both sides, and would not be able to resist their combined strength. I laughed in my cunning then, and got down on the floor, between the cast-iron legs of the seats, bolted to the floor, and the manager ordered the projectionist in after me. *Get her by the short and curlies*, he shouted. *Get her on out of there.* My feet were braced on one row of seat-legs, my grip was firm on another. The young man crawled towards me, on his stomach in the dust and spilled sweets like myself, his young face bursting with mortified blood. *Go on, lad*, we heard. He crawled closer, so that I could smell milk on his breath and see how his nostrils flared at the dust. *What is your name?* I asked, and I saw his mouth shape the word *Terry* before he realised what he was doing and bit the word off. *You were born to be hanged, Terry*, I said pleasantly enough, *I can see it from your eyebrows*. When his red face lunged at my hand and his teeth came close to breaking the skin I found it necessary to back away between the seats, standing up and throwing a milkshake container at the manager as a farewell gesture.

Out on the street I could not see any men with moustaches and strong white teeth, who would take me in their arms and be mine forever. Cars were embracing and men picked their noses while they waited for the lights to change. Chrome glared in the sun and made my eyes water all over again. The lights changed suddenly, a mother snatched back a child, an ice-cream cone flew out of a small fist and lay melting between the cars. There are moments when the cranky tears of a hot day sound like a machine seizing for lack of oil.

It is my season to be alone, I told myself as the afternoon sun poured over my back. *It is my time in the wilderness. I will be content with that, even if I cannot be happy.*

How Many Birthdays Left?

It was a race now between my death and my decay. Few people knew the exact date of my birth, and few cared, but I did, and I did not want either death or decay before I had done everything I could. *I want a birthday frock*, I told the woman in the St. Vincent de Paul shop. *I want to look very pretty, a birthday girl.* The woman was full of aplomb and smiled a gold-toothed smile, fuller of Jewish charm than dowdy Catholic piety. *Certainly, madame*, she said, and came out from behind the sad cartons of cracked boots, holding a tape measure like someone in a salon. It could have been that in her old country, where charm and gold teeth were more common than here, she had often held tape measures around large women, and done it with the same aplomb she did now. *And how old are you, if it is not indiscreet?* the woman asked as she embraced me with the tape, but I wanted to play ladies and keep my secret: *Oh, terribly old*, I said secretively. *And I am going to have a birthday in King Street.*

I had never worn blue nylon frills before and could not recognise myself in the small mirror. *Is this me?* I asked, watching squares of myself in blue nylon as the woman moved the mirror up and down for me. *Yes*, she smiled, so that her gold glittered, *it is you, and you are Lil Singer, I think*. I was always pleased to be recognised, and was feeling a little hysterical from the blue nylon. *My life is almost gone*, I told this sympathetic woman, who had the air of one who had been surprised too many times to be surprised ever again, *but I think it has been worthwhile*. I laughed at the cracked boots, so that a woman in flowered cotton, who had peeked in at the door, left again quickly, and my laugh turned to crying, because I would have liked another life, or even the same one over again.

There were many guests at my party, though most of them in their folly and simplicity of mind did not realise they were watching a celebration. King Street stood and stared as I paced slowly in front of a tram that rang and rang its bell like a birthday chorus. When the driver leaned out of his cabin and yelled, I waved at him like the Queen, feeling the blue frill shiver in the breeze, and called *Thank you, thank you,* because I knew that, under the words he was shouting, he was doing his best to wish me a happy birthday. At the top of King Street I stood aside and waved as the tram twirled around the corner into Macquarie Street, and I had to sit for a little while in the gutter to catch my breath. *It is the excitement of my birthday,* I explained to the policeman who appeared beside me. *When you are old, you will know what I mean.* I nodded closely into his young face, where the blood roared with youth beneath the skin. *It is tiring, being old,* I told him, *even though I have never cultivated the burden of memory.*

He left me at last, with backward glances, and although I did not want to walk any more, I levered myself up off the pavement at last and began to walk back towards the park. I longed for the cool grass against my back, and forced one foot after the other against a great weight pressing me backwards. When I fell in the middle of that crowded lunchtime pavement I felt my broad feet slide out from under me, and felt the unfriendly clutch of gravity. Everyone stared but no one stopped. I must have been a frightening sight, and it was years since anyone but myself had seen my white thighs, and I saw the glare of them stun the strangers as they stared and stared from beyond the circle of shock that enclosed me. My eye-shade had slipped over one eye, down over my nose, its elastic folding an ear over onto itself so the roar of the traffic, and a bus snarling up the hill beside me in the gutter, were sounds inside my own head, hurting, trying to get out. I laughed and laughed, feeling my fat shake, and could not stop laughing, because my legs, stuck out in front of me in a big foolish way, would not move to bear my weight again. I struggled, and sat on warm bitumen and settled the eye-shade over my head again and again, and my laugh was louder as my fear was greater. I laughed until I heard it sound like a roar of fright, trying to pretend to everyone and to myself that it was just old Lil making a monkey of herself and having a fool-around with her eye-shade.

I seemed stuck for ever to this patch of grey foot-path. *This is not the spot where I wish to die*, I thought, *not this bit of my native place*, and I wondered if I had shouted it, the way the dark suits were staring. Everything was staring eyes and a hopeless sweat of never being able to rise again, like a cow gone down finally, but this was no sweet pasture, and the hot grit was vile under my palms. I began to realise that I had to ask for help, but did not know how, because I had not asked anyone for help for too long, and I was having a problem with my words. They were not organising themselves in my mouth as they had always done, but were coming out in a kind of mooing. The faces stared and moved on, someone tittered, and there was no young red-faced policeman now when I needed one, only faces that did their best not to see me, busy men striding so quickly they were on me before they saw, and had to side-step with a skip so as not to lose the pace of their day. One could not step sideways in time, his life was moving so quickly, but had to step over my purple hand as it propped me up, and met my eyes and was frightened. I held up a hand, and could not stop the noises coming out of my face, and it was all the best I could do to ask for help, and I was trying through the thick blubber of my lips to say, *Just get me on my feet and I will be right as rain*. But it was not words that were coming out of my face, and my hand continued to wave out towards those white faces and they moved away like lights at night, and others took their place, but no one could break the circle around me to touch my hand and bring me back to my body.

Until at last the woman in lilac shantung was kneeling beside me, and her handbag of lizard-skin was lying in the grit. The woman took my hand and knelt so violently I heard stitches crack, and supported me with an arm around my shoulder, and I could smell her perfume. I watched very closely as the pearls gleamed against the skin of her neck, which was no younger than mine, but had not been exposed to so many cold nights on a beach. The woman in lilac shantung was wearing lilac gloves, but as she knelt beside me, becoming dirty, she tore off those gloves and smoothed the hair back from my face with a soft pampered hand. *Lil dear, you will be all right in a moment, rest for a moment*. I was not surprised that she knew who I was, but I was pleased, and lay back against her arm knowing again that fame of a kind must have come to me, for a stranger in lilac to be calling me so familiarly by name. But when she looked up, still kneeling beside me, and spoke appealingly to one of the suits, making her voice helpless and charming, so that the suit stopped, and promised, and moved off on his errand of mercy, I recognised that charm, that tilt of the ageing throat, with the pearls slipping against the skin. I recognised that the woman in lilac shantung was Ursula, and I was silenced by surprise.

In the ambulance I could see her knees and was touched by the way the skin was grey with pavement dirt, and how each knee was capped by the large round hole in each stocking. On the skirt of the lilac shantung were marks and smudges now that looked permanent, like those on my own, humbler clothes. In the smell of starched sheets and antiseptic I was calmer now, and fingered the lilac shantung, and would have liked to smooth the skin of the knees, but did not dare. I whispered, and although the words did not quite come out the way they were intended, Ursula understood, and brushed at the marks, and wet a finger with spit to see if they would be removed that way. *No, it does not matter, Lil*, she said. *It is time I gave up pretending.* There were many questions we could have asked each other, because the girls we had been when we last saw each other had long been lost in the elderly women we had become, but Ursula had been watching me grow old and famous. She would have read about me in the papers, would have cut out the pieces, perhaps, to show Rick when he was still her husband, and not the bride of Trotsky. And I was too weary now for any questions, and the movement of the ambulance through the streets of my city was making it too hard for me to shape words or even thoughts.

All My Sisters

I continued to resist and smile, and tried to pretend I could return to my life in the park, until the Sisters smiled and took away my book bag. *We will keep it safe for you*, they said, and they were right, I had no need of books now, or anything else. All that I was to know, I knew. They were kind and pale-skinned, all those nuns, and I came to enjoy the fragrance of starched cotton and old incense.

In the beginning they all looked the same to me, their faces all smooth and dry, like the clean sole of a foot, under their veils. It surprised me, how weak I had become, and how it became less of a luxury, and more of a necessity, to have one or another of those pale women brush my hair for me, or button my clothes. *Here we go, Lil*, they murmured and smiled. In the beginning I said, *Thank you, Sister, thank you, Sister*, until I was sick of it, but when I learnt their outlandish names I felt easier, and realised that Sister Annunciata could be made to giggle under her veil so her flat black front shook, that Sister Evangelina of Montefiori could answer me quote for quote from William, no matter what I tried her on, and that Sister Federica with the moustache was too pious, or sad, to be any fun, but spooned the porridge into the mouths of those who could not manage, and crossed herself instead of laughing.

Even nuns grow huge under their habits, and Sister Isola could have balanced my weight on the other end of a see-saw, and would have tried if there had been one handy, in spite of being a serious woman at times, with large brown eyes full of innocent intelligence, and took seriously her responsibility towards all these nuns and helpless old people.

Sometimes the kiddies visited us, and would be red in the face from their charitable deed. *Merry Christmas and God bless you*, some blond innocent would say, and try to smile as she handed me a cube of bath salts or a bookmark. God was still nobody I knew, but I knew about kindness, and watched the heat in her cheeks as she did her best to provide me with *a few minutes' chat*, as they had all been told to. I decided that she needed a little of my wisdom, and told her. *Do not worry about getting old gracefully, girlie, be foolish and loud if you feel like it*. I saw her beginning to look alarmed, but I had more to say: *Dignity and respect are humbug, remember that, girlie*. This blond girl was still smiling a fixed smile at me but she was inching away and her eyes were darting past me, enviously watching her classmates, who were happy shouting at deaf Bess, or looking at the hand-crocheted handkerchief that Doris's daughter had made for her. My poor red girl, who was so clean and scrubbed and optimistic she could only have been class captain, was at last rescued by Sister Isola. She brushed her off towards tremulous Annie, who had missed out on a visitor, and roared in her big fat way, which I liked because it was the same big fat way that I roared: *Lil, do not bully the poor child with your wisdom*. She winked from her big brown eye, so that we both had to laugh our big fat laughs, and everyone stopped for a moment and stared, even deaf Bess and the girl who was becoming hoarse, trying to *have a little chat* with her.

You should be ashamed, Lil, Sister Isola said later, and I was, because I could remember being young and blushing, although I had never had the consolation of being class captain. But I could also remember how you remembered things, at that age, and hoped she might remember what I had said. *Everyone should be warned off humbug*, I told the room, when Sister Isola had gone. *Humbug is bad for one's immortal soul*. Deaf Bess, sitting by the window, nodded and smiled at me, nodded and smiled, and Doris said loudly, *Three rows of triple chain and a scallop of interlocked filigree stitch*, and smoothed and smoothed the hankie, shredded with age and too many tears, on her knee.

Visits

They told us carefully what would be happening. We had all been led or wheeled into the big dining room and Sister Isola had spoken with great clarity above the burblings and poppings, the crackling noises of old uncontrolled farts, the snores from the ones who were too far gone to be awake even for this, and above the occasional shouts of deaf Bess, who thought she was whispering. Sister Isola explained very carefully about the saintly visitor we would be receiving, the great honour, the blessedness of being so close to someone so holy. *It is the Pope*, I thought, and felt a ticking pulse of the old excitement and devilry in my veins. *I will go down in the books as the one who made the Pope listen*. I was already preparing what I would like to tell him, and jiggling from one buttock to the other on the hard seat, and rehearsing a few good phrases, because now that my time was nearly up, I wanted more than ever to be remembered in the books.

It was a disappointment to realise at last that Sister Isola, solemn today in her fat, was talking simply about another holy woman, one who washed lepers in Calcutta and did not flinch from the starving. I was disappointed, but even in this, my old age and great weakness, I was able to accommodate myself to the vagaries of life, and began to prepare another kind of thing to say. I was not so sure, though, of being brave with someone who had seen suffering on a large scale. I would have been more sure of myself with a man who had spent his life in cloisters full of red robes.

Sister Isola understood me like myself: *Now*, she said, *I am fond of you, and do not wish you to be exposed to the temptation of sin.* She smiled her wicked nun's smile at me, which made her eyes disappear into her cheeks the same way mine did, and there was a wink, so fleeting no one could have held her responsible for it. *We have planned something you will enjoy, Lil. And you are a good girl, and will understand.*

When they dressed me in my woollies, and took me to the front door on the day of the visit, I did not object. They had been praying and cleaning mightily for weeks now, and deaf Bess had been given a new frock, because of so many breakfasts on the other, and quivering Annie had been propped up in the wicker chair with the cushions carefully arranged. While I was waiting, sitting on the doorstep watching the gate, I could hear the crowing and clucking as the nuns encouraged the evacuation of all the old bowels. The nuns had explained that the morning cup of tea would be brought *afterwards*, in case there should be any accidents, and Sister Annunciata was brushing the thin hair of all the bed cases, and trying to straighten their wobbly old necks on the pillows. There was such a mewing and murmuring, such a bustle of starch and bombazine, such unaccustomed flowers in vases, and such a glare of polish and shine that I was pleased to be leaving, and stood up impatiently, and shouted *Taxi! Taxi!* until it drew up at the gate.

Taxis had begun to smell differently since I had last been in one, and everyone seemed to drive much faster and more recklessly. For the first few miles I sat back against the plastic and panted, and prepared to stick my head out the window like a dog, and be sick. At last I remembered I was not a dog, and said in a loud though reedy voice, *Slower, driver, slower, or you will part me from my breakfast*. He drove more slowly after that, and I began to enjoy my day, and made him stop so I could join him on the front seat, and loved it all.

It is not everyone who has a chance for a last look, but I did. I saw the white castle by the water, where Frank had offered solace when it was needed. I cried a little, for Frank who had gone in pain, probably, but quickly. This man who drove was not Frank, but was old enough to be sympathetic, and did not mind stopping for a while, and let me cry for Frank. *Call me George, Lil*, he said, and I was not sure I fancied his freedom with my name, but he was the guide for my last journey, so I shook his hand and called him George. *George*, I asked, *am I famous?* George laughed a phlegmy smokers' laugh and cried, *By George, I'll say you are, Lil, if that is the kind of fame you are after*. I did not know what kind of fame I was after, but I was pleased. *Any kind will do, George*, I said, and dried my last tear.

George took me past the station, where I had caught the trains, and buses, when I had still travelled to the country, and he made a slow stately tour of the university. I would have liked to get out, and weep a little over the quadrangles, the bell tower where F.J. Stroud had cried his slimy tears, and would have liked to make myself dizzy once more in that steep lecture hall. But my old swollen legs would not support me that far now. And I was intimidated by the young girls striding in their pants, and boys with long hair and beads around their foreheads. None of these people copied their notes from one page to another, I could tell, and none wore pink sashes or had glory boxes, though I thought they probably schemed and sighed just as everyone always had.

And Duncan? I wondered, watching a serious pair of men in tweed—the men in tweed would never change, and would always take themselves seriously, but would be forgotten—where was Duncan, and what had become of Joan? I lay back against the sweating plastic seat, watching the men in tweed pretending they were the great minds of their generation, and could imagine Joan leathery, a famous horsewoman, out there with the men when it was time to muster, shouting with the best of them, red in the face and as foul of mouth as the rest. I could imagine Duncan on the other side of the dusty mob, proud of his leathery wife, could see them later in the kitchen with the corned beef between them. I could imagine them sitting there together belching, easy companions and mates after so many years.

But it was also easy to imagine Joan tired of the isolation, the absence of cheap Chow feeds and men to shock, and the Country Women's Association no fun to scandalise, but just dull the way they all left you alone and sneered at your scones. I could imagine the row with Duncan, the flight back to the city, to a life of alimony and gin perhaps, or great art in a smell of turps, or renunciation and good works. Joan was someone it was easy to write many histories for. Duncan was even easier. He would have grown drier and sandier with each year, would have lost his hair, would always have a pale forehead while the rest of his face was as brown as the earth, from the felt hat he would wear year after year. It would be dark with old sweat around the band, and holes would eventually

278

wear through on the folds, but it would have to go to his grave with him.

The story of all our lives is the story forward to death, although each of us might hope to be the exception. I have lived, and have seen more dawns than most people, and more different expressions on the faces of ordinary men and women in the street. I have seen much, but would not claim to have seen everything. I would not mind another century or two, to see some more. Perhaps in my second century I could choose to be lovely, slim, delectable as a peach, the jewel of some man's heart.

My life now is in its time of long shadows over the grass, the sad look of faraway hills slipping into dimness, a blue so melting as to be one with the sky. I fill myself now, and look with pity on those hollow men in their suits, those hollow women in their classic navy and white. They have not made themselves up from their presents and their pasts, but have let others do it for them—while I, large and plain, frightening to them and sometimes to myself, have taken the past and the present into myself. My flesh will become still one day soon, cold within a few hours, disgusting in a week, clean white bones eventually, or a handful of ash. But my name will live, in the different kinds of smiles on the faces of people remembering me, and that is enough immortality for me.

Death will come to us all, might come as we wash our hands before dinner, or walk fast to catch a bus to take us somewhere there was no need to go. There have been as many deaths in the world as there have been lives, and although on the slippery seat of the taxi I might shed some tears for Frank and Duncan and Ursula, and their private deaths, and for my own, fast approaching, in the eyes of history all that is invisible. *Drive on*, I told George, and he heard the tears in my voice and turned to stare, but I was impatient with the curiosity of the living now, and waved my hands at him until he looked away. *Drive on, George*, I cried at him. *I am ready for whatever comes next.*